THE UNCOMMONERS

THE CROOKED SIXPENCE

THE UNCOMMONERS

THE CROOKED SIXPENCE

JENNIFER BELL

CORGI BOOKS

CORGI BOOKS

UK | USA | Canada | Ireland | Australia
India | New Zealand | South Africa

Corgi Books is part of the Penguin Random House group of companies
whose addresses can be found at global.penguinrandomhouse.com.

www.penguin.co.uk
www.puffin.co.uk
www.ladybird.co.uk

Penguin
Random House
UK

First published 2016

014

Set in ITC New Baskerville 11/16pt

Printed and bound in Great Britain by Clays Ltd, Elcograf S.p.A.

A CIP catalogue record for this book is available from the British Library.

ISBN: 978–0–552–57250–7

All correspondence to:
Corgi Books
Penguin Random House Children's
80 Strand, London WC2R 0RL

MIX
Paper from
responsible sources
FSC® C018179

Penguin Random House is committed to a
sustainable future for our business, our readers
and our planet. This book is made from Forest
Stewardship Council® certified paper.

For Mum and Beth,
the heroines of my story.

Chapter One

Ivy rocked forward as the ambulance turned a corner. Everything inside rattled.

'OK then,' the paramedic said, looking up from his clipboard. He was a bald man with faded tattoos all the way up his forearms. 'What's your full name?'

'Ivy Elizabeth Sparrow,' she fired off, tapping her yellow wellingtons on the floor. It was so stuffy; she needed fresh air. She looked over the paramedic's shoulder and wondered if she could ask him to open one of those blacked-out windows. She could see her frizzy brown curls bobbing in the glass, even more out of control than usual.

The paramedic made a note with his biro and turned towards the rear of the vehicle. 'What about you?'

At the other end of the bench, leaning forward, legs apart, sat a boy in a grey hoodie bearing the band logo of The Ripz. His wiry blond hair had fallen in front of his eyes but Ivy knew he was glaring at her.

'It's Seb,' the boy replied drily. 'I'm her brother.'

The paramedic smiled as he jotted down the name. Ivy tried to push Seb out of her mind. This was all his fault.

She leaned over to the stretcher and took Granma Sylvie's hand. It felt softer than usual. There were Velcro straps across her granma's chest, a brace supporting her neck and a misted oxygen mask covering her nose and mouth. Ivy had never seen her look so fragile before.

'And how old are you both?' the paramedic continued.

'Eleven,' Ivy replied, shuffling ever so slightly closer to Granma Sylvie.

'I'm sixteen,' Seb said in a deep voice.

Ivy frowned and glanced sideways at him. He had only turned fourteen last month.

'OK, good.' The paramedic's face softened. 'Now, I understand that you're both very concerned at the moment – but trust me, the best thing you can do to help your gran is to stay calm. When we get to the hospital, we'll take her into casualty so the doctor can have a good look at her, and then she may need an operation, so she'll be in for a while.'

Ivy grimaced. She knew of only one other occasion when Granma Sylvie had stayed overnight in hospital – everyone knew about *that* – but it had happened before Ivy's parents were even born. 'Do you know what's wrong?' she asked.

The paramedic frowned. 'I think she may have broken her hip, and possibly her wrist as well, but we won't know till we see an X-ray.'

While he scribbled down some notes, Ivy stroked Granma Sylvie's hand and wondered if she'd suffered broken bones *that* time as well. Probably. She'd had a car crash during a freak snowstorm and had been unconscious for days; when she woke up, she couldn't remember what had happened during the accident, or anything before it. The police only knew her name because she was wearing a necklace with SYLVIE engraved on it. Retrograde amnesia, Ivy's mum called it. Ivy knew the exact date of the crash because the family discussed it so often: 5 January 1969. Twelfth Night.

'Before we get to the hospital,' the paramedic said, 'I need to confirm what happened.' He checked his watch. 'I make it eight thirty a.m., so the fall must have happened at about seven forty-five? And you said that your gran slipped in the kitchen while you were both in the other room . . . ?'

Ivy imagined Granma Sylvie losing her balance and tumbling onto her back, legs in the air like an upturned beetle. If only she'd been there to help.

Seb swallowed. 'She was baking mince pies. We heard her shouting.'

Over our shouting, Ivy remembered. She shot her brother a look of regret. They had been arguing about the stupid new Ripz poster he'd got for Christmas – Ivy had accidentally knocked her orange juice over it; if he hadn't been ranting at her, they might have got to Granma Sylvie sooner.

The paramedic flipped his paper round. 'OK, that'll do. Are you able to get hold of your mum and dad?'

Ivy sighed. *If only*. More than anything, she wished her parents were there now.

'I've texted them but there's been no reply,' Seb said. 'I'll try calling when we get to the hospital. Mum's working, but we might catch her before she starts her shift.'

Ivy had said goodbye to her mum yesterday morning. If she was there now, she would have clapped her hands together and taken charge of this whole mess in an instant. Ivy and Seb had done nothing except ring the ambulance.

'Our dad's in Paris,' Ivy added in a quiet voice. 'He's working too.'

Their dad was a consultant for the famous Victoria & Albert Museum in London, which meant that he was an expert in everything old, and people from around the world were always asking for his advice.

The paramedic raised his eyebrows. 'So that's why you're staying with your gran?'

'Mum and Dad were with us over Christmas,' Ivy explained, feeling the need to defend them. 'They just had to go back to work early.'

It had never really bothered her – them staying in London and leaving her and Seb six hours away in Bletchy Scrubb with their granma – but then this kind of emergency had never happened at the same time before.

The paramedic put down his clipboard and turned to Granma Sylvie, who, despite the neck brace, made an effort to smile. Ivy doubted she could even hear what was being said with that thing on; she hadn't corrected the paramedic about Seb's age.

'OK then, Mrs Sparrow, I'm just going to check how you're doing.' He untucked Granma Sylvie's blanket and rolled it away until her arm was exposed. There was a thin cotton sling around it, secured behind her neck. Delicately he loosened the knot and slid the material out from underneath. Granma Sylvie winced.

As the sling was taken away, Ivy caught her breath. Her granma's entire arm was purple and bloated like a giant aubergine.

The paramedic took the damaged wrist carefully between his fingers. 'Hmm, looks like that swelling is getting worse. It must be sore.' He studied it from every angle. Ivy caught a flash of gold on her granma's skin. 'I don't see any clasp on your bracelet. I think we might need to cut it off to make you feel more comfortable, Mrs Sparrow. Is that OK?'

Ivy's chest tightened; she imagined Granma Sylvie's was probably doing the same. That solid gold bangle was one of the few items that remained of her granma's life before her amnesia. She had been wearing it at the time of the accident and Ivy couldn't remember her ever taking it off. The bracelet was special to her, everyone knew that.

Granma Sylvie squeezed her eyes closed. Ivy heard a rasping, 'Do it.'

The paramedic found a pair of small silver pliers. Ivy shivered as two soft *snickts* pierced the air and the two halves of the bangle fell away.

'Ivy, my bag . . .' Granma Sylvie lifted her other hand, pointing shakily.

Ivy reached down for the handbag and held it open. Very carefully, the paramedic placed both pieces of the bangle inside.

'Will you look after it for me?' Granma Sylvie asked.

Ivy nodded, forcing a smile, and opened the bag to check that the bracelet was safely in the inside pocket.

'Be careful,' the paramedic warned, 'the ends are sharp.'

Ivy made sure not to touch it as she zipped up the pocket.

'Here,' Seb grunted, picking something up off the floor. 'You just dropped this.' He handed Ivy a black-and-white photo, the size of a postcard. Ivy had seen it many times before because Granma Sylvie always kept it in her handbag. It was the only photo of her from *before*. The police had found it in the glove box of her car after the crash. 'Weird,' Seb said, raising his eyebrows. 'I haven't seen that since I was little.'

We used to look at it all the time, Ivy thought. But she didn't say anything.

'Granma still doesn't know who the other woman is, does she?'

Ivy shook her head. The photo showed a woman standing beside Granma Sylvie. She was slight, with sharp dark eyes and unruly hair poking out from under a round black hat. She wore a thick tartan dress and studded cowboy boots. Granma Sylvie was dressed in washed denim dungarees with what looked like satin ballet shoes on her feet.

'What were they *wearing*?' Seb asked. 'It's like really bad fancy dress.'

Ivy shrugged. 'Who's to say it wasn't the fashion?' She didn't really think it could have been; she just didn't want to agree with her brother.

'Keep that safe,' croaked a voice. Ivy turned.

Granma Sylvie was waving her good arm in their direction.

'Sorry.' Ivy hastily tucked the photo back into the handbag and fastened it up.

Seb slid away from her before she had to push him.

Chapter Two

'Dad?' Ivy squinted. The split-screen image on Seb's phone was distorted and moved in slow motion. She nudged Seb in the ribs. 'I told you video call was a stupid idea. Why didn't we just ring them?'

Seb grumbled something about reception and repositioned the phone higher on his knee. 'If you owned a phone, like most people, you'd know it's easier to three-way call using video chat. But you don't. Because you're weird.'

Ivy rolled her eyes. *Whatever.*

'Mum? *Dad?* Can you see us now?' The video flickered. Ivy shifted in her seat. Around her, the A&E department of Bletchy Scrubb Hospital was teeming with people: doctors in white coats with stethoscopes draped round their necks; solemn-faced relatives; nurses carrying clipboards; and hobbling patients clutching swollen limbs. Ivy ran her eyes over the linoleum floor and glossy white walls. There wasn't a trace of tinsel or glitter anywhere. Three days after Boxing

Day, and Christmas had been forgotten about, just like that. Granma Sylvie would hate it.

'*Ivy? Are you there?*'

'Dad!' *Finally.* The image sharpened and Ivy grimaced. Her dad was far too close to the camera, his pale freckled face taking over most of the left of the screen. On the right, Ivy's mum could be seen sitting at a table in her staff canteen. She was wearing a pale blue nurse's tunic with a silver fob-watch hanging from the top pocket.

Her mum tucked a stray wisp of brown hair behind her ears and leaned closer, frowning. 'You're back now, but you keep going all fuzzy.'

'I'm on the train to Paris,' Ivy's dad called. 'My reception's bad. Can everyone see me?'

'We can see both of you now,' Ivy said. 'Did you understand what I just explained about Granma?'

Her dad frowned. 'Yes, just about. I can't believe it. Is she all right? Are you two all right?'

Ivy shrugged. 'We're OK.'

'Seb,' their mum said sternly, 'are you looking after your sister?'

Seb was slouched in the hospital chair beside Ivy, his scuffed white trainers resting on a plastic coffee table with the phone wedged between his knees. His headphones snaked into his lap.

'Yes,' he muttered. 'Don't worry.'

Ivy thought for a moment. 'Seb lied about his

10

age; he told them he was sixteen.'

Seb's eyes turned to slits as he looked at her. 'If you're sixteen, you can be on your own. It's the law.'

Ivy pulled a face at him.

'It doesn't matter about that now,' their dad said. 'As long as you stay together. How's Granma?'

Ivy gazed over at the blue cotton curtain fluttering a few metres behind Seb's shoulder. It concealed a small room where Granma Sylvie was lying on her stretcher. Ivy paused before answering, trying not to get upset again. 'She's asleep right now. We're in A and E but the doctor said she's going for an X-ray later. What do you think we should do?'

Her dad hesitated. Ivy could hear the rattle of the train in the background.

'There's only one option, really,' their mum said, pursing her lips. 'You both return to Granma's house and sit tight till we get there. Even if I leave now, it'll be a good few hours before I get to Bletchy Scrubb.'

Their dad started nodding. 'Agreed. Seb, you can pay for the bus back to Granma's house out of that money I gave you yesterday.'

Ivy's heart lifted. 'So you're coming back? Both of you?'

Her mum swept a hand across her forehead. 'Of course we are. You've done a great job so far, but don't worry. We'll sort everything out when we get there.'

'I might not arrive till late this evening, but I'll be there,' Ivy's dad told her. 'You'll be OK, won't you? Make sure you have something to eat – look after each other.' He paused and lowered his voice. 'Or at least *try* to.'

Ivy glanced at Seb, who was flicking through the track-list on his iPod, only half concentrating on the screen. 'I'll try.'

After their dad had waved goodbye, their mum blew a kiss and hung up. Seb put his phone away and his headphones in his ears without saying another word. Ivy sank back in her chair, her thick blue duffel coat creasing up around her. She wished her mum and dad were with her now; this place was horrible.

She crossed her arms and stared out aimlessly across the waiting room. A man in a grey trench coat was coming through the main doors. He was wearing pointed black shoes and a wide-brimmed hat that hid his face. Ivy watched as he slipped between the staff and patients around the reception desk and then flitted past a pair of security guards. He was heading towards them; towards the cubicles where people were taken from the ambulances.

The longer Ivy watched the man, the more certain she felt that he didn't want anyone else to notice him. He kept looking from side to side, timing his movements to coincide with those of everyone around him. As

he drew closer, Ivy spied two gnarled yellow append-
ages poking out of his coat sleeves. She recoiled as she
realized what they were.

His hands!

The skin across both palms was covered in pustules
and shrivelled, so that his fingers looked like diseased,
rotting twigs.

Ivy lowered her face as he went past. She wondered
what had happened to him. Maybe he had been in some
terrible chemical accident. Certainly it was nothing
normal – she'd never seen anything like it, not even
in movies. When she raised her eyes, he was standing
at the end of a long line of cubicles – the row that
Granma Sylvie was in. He peeked behind the nearest
curtain, waited a moment, then turned and tried the
next one. Ivy watched him repeat the process again and
again. He seemed to be looking for something.

Or someone, Ivy thought. She froze as she realized that
he was heading in Granma Sylvie's direction.

Seb was nodding his head to a beat, air drumming
in his lap.

Ivy sprang out of her seat, thumping him on the
shoulder. 'Seb!'

He shrugged her off and pulled one headphone
away from his ear. 'Ivy, what's—?'

'There's this man . . .' She turned. He was three
curtains away. 'Quick!'

She hurdled over Seb's legs and dashed along the row of chairs, her wellies squeaking on the lino.

Seb sauntered after her, fixing her with a stare. '*What is wrong with you?*'

Her heartbeat quickening, Ivy ripped open the curtain to Granma Sylvie's cubicle. 'Granma, are you . . . ? Oh.'

Her granma looked peaceful, her eyes closed and her hands placed delicately across her stomach – exactly as she had been when Ivy saw her last.

Ivy looked back along the corridor, searching for the man in grey. It was empty; but the man couldn't possibly have had time to disappear. She'd looked away for barely a second.

Seb tramped up to her shoulder. 'This better be good.'

'You don't understand,' she whispered. 'There was this strange man here. I thought he was going to do something to Granma.'

'*What?*' Seb's jaw tightened. 'Why can't you be normal? Like, for once . . . ?'

It was just starting to rain when they reached Granma Sylvie's house, almost an hour's bus ride later. Droplets drummed against Ivy's hood and tumbled through the frizzy hair that stuck out beneath it. She looked up at the familiar higgledy-piggledy outline of the house, with its clay chimney and crumbling plaster walls. It used to be a farmhouse, or so Ivy's dad had told her, which explained why it was in the middle of nowhere.

'You're paranoid,' Seb said, striding past her. 'You know that, right? All the books you read have, like, twisted your mind or something.'

Ivy marched after him. 'I'm *not* making this up,' she insisted. 'There was a man in there with gross hands, and as we were leaving A and E, I heard a nurse say that Granma's notes had gone missing. What if it was the man who took them?'

Seb sighed. 'Ivy, that guy – whoever he was – was obviously just a patient or something. Like, a burns victim. Maybe he was crazy like you. Whatever, anyway – I just want to get inside and eat.'

Ivy yanked angrily on the strap of Granma Sylvie's handbag as she swept past Seb towards the front door. If books had 'twisted her mind', then playing the drums had made her brother deaf to reason. He never listened to her. Ever.

'Ivy . . .' All of a sudden Seb's voice sounded odd.

'*What?*' she snapped, turning back to him. He was holding a shaky finger out towards the house. Ivy followed it and almost tripped over. She didn't under-stand how she could have missed it . . .

The front door was ajar. The frame was splintered, and there were deep scratch marks around the lock.

Seb lowered his finger to his side as if he wasn't sure

whether to stay or run. Finally he whispered, 'Police.' He got out his phone and tapped the screen. Ivy could see it from where she was standing. The words *No Service* flashed as he tried to make the call. *Perfect.*

'What do we do?' she asked.

Seb tiptoed over the gravel towards the house and peered in through the front windows. 'The curtains are drawn,' he hissed. 'I'll have to go in and use the landline.'

Ivy nodded. *Right. Good idea.* 'What about me?'

Seb looked back at the door. 'We'll go in together; you stay behind me.'

As Ivy set foot over the threshold, her skin prickled. There was a slow scratching noise coming from inside, like thick wallpaper being ripped off a wall.

Her eyes flitted into the shadows of the hallway. She just about recognized Granma Sylvie's antique writing desk – the one with the curling legs and tea-stained top – toppled over on the floor. The drawers were all missing and a pile of thick cream writing paper had been strewn across the carpet.

Seb removed a walking stick from an upturned umbrella stand and raised it above his head. As Ivy followed him, her mind raced. That scratching noise was definitely getting louder the further they went into the house. She wondered what could be making it. She waited as Seb paused to open the kitchen door.

'Ready?' He reached for the doorknob with a trembling hand.

Ivy nodded. As the door opened and the air from the kitchen slipped out, she caught a strong whiff of damp dog. *Strange.* The kitchen never smelled of anything other than baking.

The lights were already on, even though Ivy was certain she'd turned them off before they got into the ambulance. Her heart raced as she inched forward. To her left, the kitchen cupboards were minus their doors. Fragments of wood, exploded food cans and torn packets lay scattered across the worktops, and smashed crockery filled the sink. A dirty patch on the wall was the only evidence of where the fridge used to stand. It now lay belly-up on the kitchen tiles, its contents pooling out like vomit.

Ivy took a few steps forward, crunching over spilled breakfast cereal and vegetables. Her gaze fell upon a set of muddy animal tracks trailing across the kitchen floor.

Seb's voice was faint. 'Over there . . .'

Ivy drew her eyes away from the prints and followed his hovering finger . . . Right across the opposite wall three words had appeared:

WE CAN SEE

Each of the letters was the size of a dinner plate and appeared to have been scratched into the pastel wallpaper, which now revealed the blood-red of the previous decor.

The implement inflicting this damage, she saw, was a feather – large, glossy and black.

As it continued to write, it hovered in the air like a wasp; then, after scoring two further words into the wall, it disappeared with an indignant puff. In its place, a tiny silver coin materialized, dropping to the floor with a *ping*.

With a gasp, Ivy read the words in all their bloody glory:

WE CAN SEE YOU NOW

Chapter Three

Seb paced up and down the kitchen floor, carving a path through the smashed glass and food tins with his trainers. He was holding what remained of Granma Sylvie's only telephone. The receiver was broken and the cord had been ripped out of the base.

Ivy steadied herself against the back of a chair. Her skin was prickling with shock. 'You saw it flying too – right? What was it?'

'I don't know.' Seb's face was stony. He rubbed his hands down the back of his jeans. Ivy could see sweat forming on his brow. 'What does *We can see you now* even mean?' He gestured around the room. 'And the break-in doesn't make any sense. I've checked the other rooms downstairs but it doesn't look like anything's been stolen. Whoever was here, they've just trashed the place.'

Ivy scanned the room again, picking out what remained of her granma's unique furniture, old books and favourite photos. Her throat swelled. Most of what Granma Sylvie had collected over the years was irreplaceable. Ivy couldn't understand what someone would gain from destroying it. It didn't make sense.

As Seb put the phone down on the kitchen table, she studied the animal tracks again. She splayed out her fingers. The prints were at least four times the size of her hand. Whatever animal had been here, it was much bigger than a domestic pet.

'There's no way to call the police from here now,' Seb said. 'We'll have to cycle towards Bletchy Scrubb till we get mobile signal and then try Mum and Dad.'

Ivy nodded in agreement as the wall behind her crackled. She rotated slowly till she was facing it again. 'Are you seeing that?' she asked.

Seb swallowed.

The *We can see you now* was disappearing shred by shred, as if the wallpaper was repairing itself like living skin.

Seb dragged his hands down his face, pulling his cheeks as if trying to wake himself up. 'Why is this getting worse?'

Ivy clenched her fists. The only way to stop herself from freaking out was to try to understand what was going on. There must be some logic to it. She re-ran the last ten minutes from the beginning. Granma Sylvie's front door . . . the scratching . . . the fridge . . . the animal tracks . . . the feather . . . the coin.

The coin.

Ivy searched the kitchen tiles and spotted it in a puddle of tomato soup.

'Careful,' Seb warned as she bent to retrieve it.

Ivy's fingers floated above the coin for a moment before she picked it up and wiped it off. It was about the size of a one pence piece, except silver and bent slightly in the middle, so that it hugged the curve of her palm. After a split-second she discovered something else. The coin was *warm*; like it had been left out in the sun.

'Anything?' Seb asked, stepping closer.

Ivy tossed the coin into her opposite hand to discover that the temperature wasn't the only odd thing about it. It was as if the coin was tickling her, leaving behind a strange – but not unpleasant – tingle on her skin. Squinting, she held it up to the light. The metal was worn in places but she could still make out words written around the outside. 'It says: *Blackclaw, Ragwort, Wolfsbane* and *Dirge.*' She looked up. 'What do you think they mean?'

Seb jerked his head back. 'How do I know? Maybe it's one of Granma's old antiques. She sold coins in her shop, didn't she?'

Ivy thought back to the little leaded windows of Granma Sylvie's antique shop in Bletchy Scrubb – she'd run it with Granpa Ernest right up until his death. 'Yeah,' she agreed. 'But they weren't like this.'

Seb's shoulders stiffened. 'What do you mean?'

The coin was still warm, which was weird enough, but now Ivy felt another sensation, something she couldn't quite identify. It was like the difference between holding a stuffed toy cat and a real cat. It was the feeling of holding . . . life.

'I mean . . .'

Something brushed at the edge of her hearing – *a voice*? She hesitated. No, she must be imagining it.

'What I mean,' she said again, 'is that Granma's coins didn't exactly appear out of thin air. And this one *did*.'

Just then a clatter sounded from somewhere at the front of the house.

Seb's head shot round. 'What was that?'

Before Ivy could answer, the noise came again, followed by the rumble of voices.

They were not alone.

Chapter Four

Ivy's skin turned to ice. 'What if that's them – the people who did this?'

Seb hurried towards the back door. 'Let's not wait to find out.' He leaped over the remains of a china vase and shot through the patio doors into the garden. Ivy pushed the silver coin into her coat pocket and scrambled after him.

The rain sounded like a snare drum as it hit the flagstones. Ivy tried to keep her balance as she followed Seb round the corner and into the alley between the house and a neighbouring field. She wiped her eyes clumsily, completely forgetting that she had a hood.

'Ivy, watch it!' Seb called.

She ground to a stop, arms flailing. Beside the toe of her wellington boot was a large brown hessian sack, the soil spilling out of it. *Granma Sylvie's potatoes.* Ivy winced. She'd grown them in that sack for ever. 'Sorry,' she whispered.

Carefully she hopped over it and inched towards Seb, who was crouching down next to the garage at the front of the house. The rain chimed off its corrugated-iron roof, masking the sound of her footsteps. She tucked herself behind a section of dense yew hedge and angled her head till she could see. Her jaw dropped.

What the—?

In Granma Sylvie's drive stood a funeral coach, complete with four black horses. It was long and rectangular, with glass sides and a strip of ornate carving along the top. Every inch had been lacquered with ebony gloss which matched the head-feathers of the horses. Ivy had seen something like it only once before, on the way to school. Her mum had slowed to let it pass. *That* coach had been carrying a coffin. This one was empty.

No . . . wait.

Ivy squinted. It wasn't empty. Inside she could see a boy. His image was made fuzzy by the rain, but he had dark hair and cinnamon-brown skin. He was sitting with his knees up and his hands clasped around them, his head bent so Ivy couldn't see his face.

'Seb!' she hissed, but his gaze was fixed elsewhere: on Granma Sylvie's doorstep. Ivy turned to see what was going on.

Standing beneath the porch were two men in matching black uniforms: a balding, red-faced fellow with a huge belly and, beside him, a tall lean figure with slicked-back hair, chalky skin and dark glasses. Both men wore ankle-length cloaks, gloves with gleaming silver studs across the knuckles and hats shaped like a pirate's tricorne.

'Shall I use this now, sir?' the red-faced man asked. 'Try to flush out anyone who might still be here?' In his hand was a large conch shell – one of the spiky, salt-encrusted ones you found on rocky beaches. When the other man didn't reply, he said, 'Officer Smokehart, sir?'

The tall man turned towards him slowly, his chin raised. 'Lower the shell,' he said. His voice sent chills shooting down the back of Ivy's neck. It sounded like a knife – vicious and cold. 'If there's anyone inside, we don't want to give them time to escape. They might reveal something useful under questioning.'

Ivy shivered. There was something about Officer Smokehart that wasn't quite natural. Maybe it was the way he was standing: straight-backed and still, like a robot.

'Just imagine, Constable,' he breathed, steepling his thin fingers, 'what answers might lie behind this door; what dark revelations we might find festering in the shadows. For over forty years we've lived without knowing the truth of what happened that night.'

'Twelfth Night,' the constable said, a little uncertainly,

setting the conch down on the ground.

Smokehart gritted his teeth. 'Yes, of course *Twelfth Night*. It is the greatest unexplained mystery of the modern era. The entire Wrench family – a mother, father daughter and three brothers – disappear on one fateful night. We don't know why they vanished, or how. We don't even know what role they played during the Great Battle . . . until now.' His thin lips curled into a smile. 'The quartermasters will have no choice but to promote me for this, mark my words.'

The constable gulped and stood to attention. He looked at the broken lock. 'Looks like we're not the first ones here, though, sir.'

Officer Smokehart peered down through his dark glasses. Ivy wondered why he was wearing them – it wasn't as if it was sunny.

'She has many enemies,' he said, considering. 'It's possible that one of them has got to her before us. Arm yourself.'

The constable nodded quickly, swept back his cloak and pulled out . . .

Ivy squinted. Surely she was seeing this wrong. The rain was distorting her vision; it must be. White plastic. Long handle. Rounded head of bristles.

No, it was a *toilet brush*. As Smokehart drew an identical one from the loop on his belt, Ivy noticed

something else. The bristles
were moving slightly. If
she concentrated hard
enough through the
drumming of the
rain, she could hear
them crackling. And
what was that jumping
from the end . . . *sparks*?

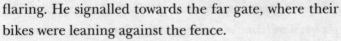

Ivy's legs started to
tremble.

From his crouched
position, Seb waved at
her furiously, his nostrils
flaring. He signalled towards the far gate, where their
bikes were leaning against the fence.

Ivy nodded down the road towards Bletchy Scrubb.
That's where they needed to go.

'Don't think we should spend long here, sir,' the
constable commented, pushing open the front door.
'We've got that young tea-leaf in the carriage – needs to
be taken back to Lundinor for processing.'

Smokehart raised pencil-thin eyebrows above his
dark glasses. 'Not long? Constable, if this really is where
Sylvie Wrench has been hiding for forty years, then
we will stay *as long as is necessary* to uncover whatever
evidence may be inside.' Holding his toilet brush aloft,

he marched over the threshold into the hallway beyond. The constable followed.

The name *Sylvie Wrench* was ringing in Ivy's ears as she saw Seb getting to his feet. *Sylvie . . .*

She walked slowly, as if in a dream.

Granma . . .

'Ivy,' Seb mouthed. 'Bikes.'

She snapped back to reality and followed Seb across the gravel to collect her bike. Her wet hands trembled as she tugged her hood back and fumbled with the strap of her helmet. *Sylvie Wrench . . . Twelfth Night . . .* Her head was spinning. She got onto her bike and put her foot on the pedal.

And then a voice like thunder filled the air: '*This is Officer Smokehart of the First Cohort of Lundinor Underguard! You are breaking GUT law. Remain where you are, by command of the Four Quartermasters of Lundinor!*'

Chapter Five

Ivy shrieked, 'Seb, go!' She slung Granma Sylvie's bag across her back before kicking away from the ground. Up ahead, Seb's wheels squealed as he shot onto the tarmac and skidded round a corner.

Ivy flashed a look over her shoulder, pedalling frantically. Officer Smokehart was in Granma Sylvie's porch, holding the conch shell to his lips. The constable had already climbed aboard the black coach.

Rising up off the saddle, Ivy pushed down on the pedals as hard as she could. What sounded like a hailstorm started up behind her, drawing closer.

The horses . . . !

The coach was on the road.

'Stay close to me,' Seb shouted. 'This way!' He turned off the road, darting through a small gap in the hedgerow and heading into a field. 'They're too big to come after us,' he yelled. 'They'll have to go the long way round.'

Ivy could see what he was planning. Ahead of them, the road curved round the edge of the field. Seb was cycling straight across the grass towards an open gate on the opposite side. If they were lucky, they'd get there before the coach.

Ivy hurtled after him. Her bike squeaked and groaned over the bumpy ground. Glancing back, she could see the top of the coach above the hedgerow – it was gaining on them now. The constable was craning forward, flicking a whip through the air, while the horses' head-feathers tossed around madly.

'They're catching up!' Ivy warned. She didn't know how much longer she and Seb could stay in front.

'Go faster,' he yelled at her, his cheeks bright red, his legs a blur. 'We have to make it!'

Ivy surged forward into the battering rain. Seb was only metres away from the gate.

'Ivy!' he shouted, crossing the road.

She looked back at the coach, which was nearly upon them. She caught a glimpse of the dark-haired boy inside, pushing against the glass, steadying himself against the jolts.

Smokehart's voice filled the air again. '*STOP WHERE YOU ARE!*'

Ivy faltered as she reached the road. The horses were metres away. She stared helplessly at Seb. His eyes were wide. She screamed his name, and then . . .

The carriage was between them.

A splintering, creaking noise split the air. The constable howled. Ivy was thrown head first off her bike; her helmet took the worst of the impact as she thudded into the hard earth beside the road. Granma Sylvie's bag crunched painfully against her ribs and cold mud splashed onto her cheeks.

When she opened her eyes, she saw a face: angled cheekbones, dark-chocolate eyes, skin like polished teak.

It was the boy from the coach.

'You all right?' he asked. The rain had soaked his long, straggly hair and was running down onto his shoulders.

'Uh . . .' Ivy murmured. Her brain felt like it was made of marshmallow. She struggled with the strap of her helmet and eventually tugged it off. 'What happened?'

'Underguards,' the boy grunted. 'Must have been too interested in chasing you to notice the ice on the road.'

Ivy raised a shaky hand to her temple. *Underguards . . . ?*

'They've overturned in the next field,' the boy continued. 'Looks like your friend saw it just in time.'

Friend? The fog in Ivy's head started to clear. Her neck prickled as she remembered: *Seb.* Carefully she lifted herself up. Her bike was lying some five metres away, the wheels trilling as they spun. A familiar figure was staggering across the grass.

'Ivy!' Seb called breathlessly. 'Are you OK?'

She tried to get to her feet. The boy helped her up. His skinny figure, slim-fitting jeans, black leather jacket and red high-top basketball shoes reminded her of the lead singer in The Ripz. 'Easy,' he said. 'You're gonna feel like you've just had a sack of flour dumped on your head, but just try to breathe. Everything moving?'

Slowly, systematically, she wiggled her fingers and toes and tilted her head from side to side. She suspected there were probably a few cuts and grazes hiding beneath her coat but she wouldn't need an ambulance. 'I think so. Seb?' She focused on him as he approached. His gaze was fixed on the stranger in front of him.

'Who are you?' Seb asked. Now that they were next to each other, Ivy could see they were probably of a similar age. 'Are you one of them?'

The boy arched an eyebrow. 'One of the Ugs? Hell no. I'd rather be a ghoul.' His eyes went nervously to a spot by Ivy's feet. 'I've had my fair share of running from them, though – if you two want to get away, you don't have much time.'

Ivy glanced down, wondering what he was looking at. Standing in the grass by her feet was a small leather suitcase with brass latches. A brown paper tag was tied around the handle. *Strange* . . . Ivy hadn't glimpsed it in the field earlier.

She bent over and gripped the handle. 'How did this get—?' The question caught in her mouth as a wave of tingly heat spread through her fingers. She gave a short gasp: the suitcase felt so much like a hot potato, she struggled not to drop it. She'd had this sensation before, when she held the silver coin. The only difference was that touching the suitcase felt more intense.

The boy stiffened and threw a gloved hand towards the case. 'That's mine.'

Ivy held it out to him. 'All right, I was just—'

Just then, she heard the rattle of a harness in the road.

'The underguards,' the boy hissed. There's no time . . .' He snatched the case, unfastened the latches, opened it on the grass and dropped onto his knees beside it. 'Are you coming?'

Ivy's head was spinning. 'Coming where?'

Seb dug his fingers into her shoulder. 'Ivy, we need to do something – now!'

Too late.

The rapid fire of hoofbeats sounded on the other side of the hedgerow. A wild neigh followed the clatter of something loud and heavy, and then Officer Smokehart came tearing along towards them. He moved impossibly fast, his arms pumping as his black cloak mushroomed up behind him. Ivy noticed with a jolt that his face and neck were no longer smooth and pale; they were covered with tiny scarlet dots, like drops of blood. In his outstretched hand he waved his toilet brush, the bristles alive with blue sparks.

'Go – *now*!' The boy yanked on Ivy's arm, hauling her to the ground.

She felt wet grass under her hands as something pushed down on the back of her head. She saw the brown suede lining of the suitcase expanding before a cold feeling slipped down her spine and she was swallowed by darkness.

Chapter Six

Daylight disappeared, along with the fresh smells of grass and wet mud. Ivy gave a dusty cough and reached forward blindly into the shadows. Soft carpet cushioned her hands, sending waves of heat through her body. Her skin felt ticklish. It was the same sensation as before.

'Seb?' she cried. 'Seb! Are you there?'

There was no response. She took a couple of deep breaths but her heart was pounding, her whole body shaking. She smelled old leather and boot polish. She had no idea what that meant. She tried crawling forward. Wherever she was, there had to be a way out.

After a few paces Ivy heard a click, and a sliver of light materialized far in the distance. Her eyes watered with relief as she scuttled towards it. It quickly grew to the size of a letter box, shedding just enough light for her surroundings to become clear. She gasped as she saw the brown suede lining of the suitcase.

Wait – was she *inside* it?

Was she *inside a suitcase*?

She hurried towards the rectangle of light, and when it was big enough, clambered out onto a cold stone surface. Looking back, she saw an identical suitcase to the one she'd picked up in that field – the same fastenings, battered leather and brown paper tag – standing on the floor.

She glanced down at her legs and started. They were *tiny* – the size of rolling pins – but getting bigger. Her bones creaked and her trousers bubbled as if blisters were forming under her skin. In seconds, everything had returned to its normal size.

Trying hard not to panic, she got shakily to her feet and looked around. She was in a huge sandy cave about the same size as her school sports hall. The high ceiling was fitted with two glass discs that oozed butter-yellow light out over the floor, which was packed with the widest assortment of luggage Ivy had ever seen: stacks of suitcases, toppling pillars of hatboxes, piles of handbags and turrets of metal trunks. It was like some sort of cloakroom fortress. She spotted a single opening in the cave wall which appeared to lead off into a dark tunnel.

'Seb . . .' she whispered. She needed to find out where he was. She turned back to the suitcase. The lining seemed to disappear into darkness like some sort of optical illusion. She checked the tag on the handle: *Lundinor* was written on it in black ink.

Lundinor . . . Officer Smokehart had said something about that. The dark-haired boy had called him an *underguard*. She wondered what it all meant.

Just then, the suitcase began to shake. Ivy retreated from it as it rattled across the stone. The dark lining exploded with blond hair and grey sweatshirt.

'Gonna throw up,' Seb spluttered as he fell out of the case and onto the floor. His arms, legs and torso rippled back to normal size as if made of plasticine.

'Seb! Are you all right?' Ivy was filled with relief as she stooped to help him up. His hands felt clammy and cold.

'I really need to—' Before he'd finished his sentence, he was vomiting.

Ivy dodged out of its path just in time. An expensive-looking leopard-skin briefcase was the unfortunate victim. She covered her nose and ushered Seb into a corner of the cave.

'Looks like bag travel doesn't exactly agree with your friend,' a voice remarked, close by.

Ivy spun round. The dark-haired boy was standing behind her, dusting down his knees.

'He's not my *friend*,' she corrected in a tight voice. 'He's my brother. And of course he doesn't enjoy *bag travel*.' She said the phrase like it was a medical term.

The boy smirked as he closed his suitcase. His dark hair fell across his angular face. 'You two use rugs or vacuums, I suppose? You sound posh enough.'

'*Posh?*' Ivy shook her head. 'Rugs or – *what?*'

Behind her, Seb's retching noises stopped. She heard his heavy footsteps staggering over.

'Air are ree?!' He swallowed hard, teeth clamped together, and pointed a shaky finger at the suitcase.

'Good question,' Ivy said, resting her hands on her hips. 'Where *are* we?'

The boy scratched his head. 'What do you mean *where are we*? Arrivals chamber. Lundinor.'

Lundinor. There it was again . . .

Seb took a large gulp. 'Lun-di-huh?' He cleared his throat. 'Does anyone want to explain how we just crawled through a suitcase to get here?'

The boy narrowed his eyes and assessed Ivy and Seb very carefully, as if taking notes. Then he reached into his leather jacket and pulled out a comb. It was dark brown, made of plastic. 'What's this?' he asked, studying their reactions closely. 'And what's it used for?'

Seb and Ivy exchanged an uncertain glance before Ivy fumbled for an answer, more out of politeness than anything else. 'It's a . . . comb?' she said slowly. 'You untangle your hair with it?'

The boy went very still for a moment, then sucked in a huge breath and dragged a hand along his jaw. 'No.' He shook his head. 'You can't be. You shouldn't even be—'

All of a sudden the tinny voice of a shopping-centre tannoy filled the cave.

'*Traffic build-up in tunnel thirty-four D. Underguards are on site.*'

Ivy searched for where it was coming from and spotted a conch shell hanging from the ceiling, just like the one Officer Smokehart had used. Somewhere outside the cave she heard the crunch of footsteps.

The boy looked around. 'Don't just stand there,' he hissed. 'Hide!'

Seb threw himself behind a large sun-bleached portmanteau. Ivy looked around desperately, but before she'd had time to pick anything, the boy seized her arm and pulled her behind a set of matching tweed trunks.

And not a moment too soon.

Lumbering through the cave opening came a hulking man in the same black uniform as Officer Smokehart – *an underguard.* He had a thick grey moustache and huge wiry eyebrows, beneath which his small black eyes hid like flies.

Ivy's heart pounded as she watched him plod into the centre of the cave and sniff. She shot a glance over at the pool of vomit. Seb was hiding a metre away from it, directly opposite her. She could see his scuffed trainers poking out from behind the portmanteau.

Wait . . . I can see him.

Ivy jerked forward, but the dark-haired boy hooked his arm around her chest to keep her still. He twisted round, making sure she could see his face, and gestured for her to be quiet. His eyes looked hollow with fear.

Ivy peered back out. She couldn't whisper over to Seb – the underguard would certainly hear her. She just had to hope that the man didn't spot him.

'Ha-hum.' The underguard tapped his polished boots on the floor. 'OK, go ahead,' he instructed, as if speaking into a walkie-talkie.

On his command, a short brown feather popped into the air. It floated in front of him and then tipped up-right, zipping to and fro as it wrote a message. The man focused on the words intently, nodding as he read.

Ivy thought back to the feather in Granma Sylvie's house and shivered. She squinted.

NOTICE TO ARREST

SUSPECT ONE: FEMALE, 4' 10". PALE GREEN EYES, BROWN HAIR. AGE AND NAME UNKNOWN. LAST SEEN WEARING DARK BLUE COAT AND YELLOW RUBBER BOOTS. POSSIBLY DANGEROUS.
SUSPECT TWO: MALE, 5' 9". GREEN EYES, BLOND HAIR. AGE AND NAME UNKNOWN. LAST SEEN WEARING GREY HOODED

SWEATSHIRT, WHITE TRAINERS AND JEANS.
POSSIBLY DANGEROUS.
SUSPECT THREE: VALIAN KAYE. MALE, 5' 7".
DARK HAIR. 15 YRS OLD. LAST SEEN WEARING
LEATHER JACKET, DARK TROUSERS AND
FINGERLESS GLOVES. EXTREME ATTITUDE
PROBLEM. KNOWN THIEF.

REPORT ALL SIGHTINGS TO OFFICER
SMOKEHART.

The underguard's eyes widened as he read the last line. The feather twirled, gave a puff and vanished.

Ivy's body went rigid. Suspects one and two were unmistakably her and Seb. The underguards were hunting for them, but she didn't understand why. She thought back to what Smokehart had said on Granma Sylvie's doorstep. *Sylvie Wrench . . . Twelfth Night . . . disappeared . . .*

She wished she could discuss it with Seb. His trainers had now disappeared behind the portmanteau – *thank goodness* – but now she saw his face reflected in a pair of shiny briefcase locks. His cheeks were bulging, his lips pinched together.

No!

Seb threw up onto the floor with a sound like a plug-hole being unblocked.

41

The underguard jumped as the sound reverberated around the cave. He immediately turned in Seb's direction.

'Who's there?' He growled.

Ivy tried to dart forward, but the boy's arm prevented her. She felt his other hand clamp over her mouth.

'Well, well, well . . .' The underguard stepped forward, grabbing Seb by the top of his hoodie. 'What do we have here?'

Seb tried to break free as he was dragged out from behind the portmanteau. 'Get off me!' His face was greenish and sweaty. 'What's your problem?'

The man shoved him out into the middle of the cave and took a good look at him. Ivy could almost see him checking off the description of Suspect Two. His eyes narrowed. 'My problem, son, is *you*.' He slid a tiny object out from under his long cloak. Ivy saw a flash of silver between his fingers.

'A *paperclip*?' Seb exclaimed. 'What are you gonna do with that?'

The underguard smiled wickedly and shook the paperclip twice. It unfolded till it was straight, and then lengthened. In a streak of silver it leaped out of the underguard's hand and onto one of Seb's wrists.

'Hey!' Seb's hands snapped together, and then the paperclip wrapped itself around them. 'What the—?'

He strained to pry them apart again. 'You can't do this!'

The underguard took him by the shoulder, pushing him towards the cave exit. 'You're under arrest. I wouldn't struggle if I were you; uncommon paperclips don't like to be pulled apart.'

Ivy got one last glimpse of her brother's features before he disappeared into the passageway. His brown eyes darted around wildly.

He was looking for *her*.

Chapter Seven

By the time the boy finally relaxed his grip around Ivy's shoulders, Seb's footsteps had disappeared. 'Get off me!' she spluttered, ripping his hand off her mouth. She inhaled deeply and scrambled away, sending a few loose suitcases flying. 'What is *wrong* with you?' she screamed. 'That's my brother!' She stumbled into the centre of the cave and made a beeline for the exit.

Her head was spinning.

Seb . . .

She had to get him back. She tried to think what her mum and dad would do if they were there, but the situation was so unbelievable she had trouble imagining them there at all.

'Where have they taken him?' she growled.

The dark-haired boy got to his feet, rubbing his shoulder where a large suitcase had just struck him. 'To the underguard station,' he said matter-of-factly, 'in the main cavern.'

Ivy came to a stop. *The underguard station* . . . She didn't even want to consider what might happen to Seb if Officer Smokehart got hold of him. 'Where's that?'

He considered her for a moment, cocking his head to one side. 'Tell me, why are the Ugs even after a commoner like you? It doesn't make sense.'

'I don't know what you're talking about,' Ivy said. 'And I don't care. Just tell me how to get my brother back.'

The boy rubbed his chin. '*If* I tell you,' he said carefully, 'you've gotta promise to do me a favour.'

'*What?*' Ivy balled her hands into fists. 'I'm not doing anything to help *you*.' She marched towards the exit, her face burning. It was that idiot's fault that Seb had been arrested in the first place – and he had the audacity to ask for her help!

When she got to the opening, she came to a halt. The passageway outside was shadowy and quiet. She wondered which way the underguard station was, or if it was even down there at all. She remembered Seb's wide eyes, searching for her as he was taken away. She clenched her teeth and turned back. 'What's the favour?'

The boy grinned. 'I need you to fetch me something from another cave down here. It shouldn't be difficult.'

'If it's not difficult,' Ivy said, 'why don't you do it yourself?'

He put his hands behind his back and rocked on his heels. 'I wish I could, but you see . . . my name's Valian Kaye.'

Ivy snorted. It made sense now. *Valian Kaye* – the third suspect on the underguard's list. *And a thief,* she recalled. That's why he'd been in the back of the under-guard's coach. He must have been arrested.

'They're looking for you too,' Valian reminded her. 'But your face isn't as well-known as mine and you have one other advantage: you're a mucker, and that means they can't track you.' He peeled off his gloves and stuffed them in his jeans pocket, flexing his fingers. 'That should slow them down a bit.'

Ivy's head felt woozy. 'A mucker? Wait. Slow down . . .' She could feel a sharp pain behind her eyes – the kind you get when you've been staring at something for too long. She wondered if the effects of the bike crash were catching up with her, or if her brain was just suffering from information overload. She reached for a nearby stack of leather trunks to steady herself. The hairs on the back of her hand stood on end as heat shot through her fingers.

Not that again . . .

She shivered and stepped away. Of course she needed to save Seb, but she also had to find out what was going on. 'If I go and fetch whatever it is you want,' she said sharply, 'then you have to tell me how to get my brother back, *and* explain about everything else – about the underguard, about 'muckers', about where this cave is, about why that suitcase was able to bring us down here. Do we have a deal?'

Valian tapped his foot. 'If I tell you all that, I'll be breaking the law.'

Ivy's thoughts returned to the underguard's *Notice to Arrest* message. 'I doubt that's a problem for you,' she remarked. 'And anyway, do you have a choice?'

He stared at her for a long moment without breaking eye contact. Eventually he said, 'Fine. Follow me.'

Apart from Ivy's footsteps, the narrow passageway leading off from the cave was unnervingly quiet. It was lit by the same glass discs and smelled faintly of incense. Ivy dragged her fingers over the grainy walls as she walked behind Valian, looking for signs of wires or plugs, but there didn't appear to be any. With a shiver, she wondered what was powering everything if it wasn't electricity.

Valian looked over his shoulder and noticed her examining the walls. 'They call this an arrivals tunnel,' he said. 'There's a whole network of them down here. We're under Blackheath, in London.'

Ivy froze. 'London?!' She tried to process that. Bletchy Scrubb was six hours' drive from London, so how had they come all that way in a . . .

47

'The suitcase,' she asked. 'How does it work?'

Valian's shoulders tensed. 'I can't tell you here. There might be an Ug waiting round the next corner. Follow me.'

They continued in silence for another ten minutes, snaking through a labyrinth of – as far as Ivy could tell – *identical* tunnels. She stumbled along, her mind full of questions. Eventually Valian stopped at an intersection of three passageways. He checked that they were clear before speaking. 'There's only time to explain it once, so you'd better keep up.' He pointed to one of the glass lights. 'Do you recognize this?'

Ivy stared hard at the object. It was about the size of a side plate, glowing with cool yellow light. There was a conical bit sticking up in the middle and a grooved lip around the edge. At first she couldn't identify it, but then she realized that if you took it off the wall and turned it on its back, it would look a lot like . . .

'A lemon squeezer,' she said, surprising herself. 'We have one in our kitchen at home.'

Valian pointed to the ceiling. 'And that?'

Ivy tipped her head back and gasped. Hanging from the roof of the tunnel by a short length of chain was a metal colander, the kind used to drain spaghetti. Silvery wisps of smoke leaked out of the holes and then dissolved into the air.

'Colander?'

Valian nodded. 'It filters the air down here so that we can breathe. The lemon squeezers give out light. They're a bit like lamps, except better for the environment – and no electricity bills.'

'They . . . *what*?' Ivy shook her head, resting a hand against the wall. 'How is that possible? The ones at home can't do that.'

Valian shrugged. 'That's because the ones at home are all *common*. The lemon squeezer and the colander here . . . They're both *uncommon*.'

Uncommon. The word struck a chord in Ivy's mind. The underguard who'd arrested Seb had mentioned that his paperclip was uncommon . . .

She looked down. 'Right . . .' she mumbled, trying to follow Valian's explanation. 'So if an object's uncommon, it means it can do something amazing. But how? Is it, like . . . magic?'

'Magic?' Valian gave a wry smile. 'Hate to ruin your fairy tale, kid, but magic doesn't exist.'

Ivy felt her cheeks flush. After everything she'd seen that morning, it wasn't *that* stupid a suggestion. 'OK, well then, what makes uncommon objects special? How can you tell the difference between that lemon squeezer on the wall and the one I have at home?' She swallowed as she watched the clean yellow light coming from its centre. 'I mean, apart from the fact that it's glowing.'

49

'For most of us, that's the only way you *can* tell,' Valian said. 'There are some people who can . . . Well, that's not important. As for what makes them special,' he continued, 'let me ask you a question: what's the most powerful force in the world, the most incredible and extraordinary thing in existence?'

Ivy frowned. She was no good at riddles and she certainly didn't have the patience for them right now. 'I don't know.'

Valian's dark eyes glittered. 'Us,' he said. '*We* are. Most of the time we die and go on to the next world, right? No problem. But sometimes we don't go on, we get stuck; or rather *part* of us – the soul, the spirit, the eternal bit, whatever you wanna call it – gets stuck . . . in an object.'

The hairs on the back of Ivy's neck stood on end. '*WHAT?*'

'Shh,' Valian whispered. 'Keep your voice down.' He glanced nervously down each of the three tunnels, then rummaged around inside his leather jacket. Eventually he retrieved a tattered roll of paper and opened it out in front of her. 'There's more. Here – read this.'

Ivy's heart was racing now. She could feel pressure building behind her temples again as she looked down at the piece of paper.

NOTICE OF THE PROCLAMATION OF THE UNDERMART OF LUNDINOR

At 12 midday following the day on which it is
announced by the four Quartermasters of the
Undermart:

All manner of uncommoners, alive or dead,
may take notice that in the Great Cavern of Blackheath under
the Olde City of London, and the passages, caves and chambers
adjoining is now to be held an undermart for Christmas Day
and the twelve days following, to which all traders may freely
resort to buy and sell according to the Liberties and Privileges
of the Great Uncommon Trade (GUT).

The notice was signed at the bottom in swirly handwriting: *Mr Punch, Quartermaster of the Great Cavern,
Guardian of Lundinor.*

Ivy raised her eyes slowly. The pain in her head was
getting worse. 'This doesn't help. I've never even heard
half of these words before. What does *undermart* mean?'

Valian rolled up the notice and stuffed it back into
his jacket. 'Undermarts are markets that only sell uncommon objects. There's one in the caves down here,
called Lundinor. We're sent these notices the day before
they open for trade.'

Ivy blinked. 'A market?' She didn't know what she was expecting, but it wasn't that.

'Classic mucker reaction,' Valian muttered, smiling.

'You keep calling me that,' Ivy complained. 'I don't even know what it means.'

'The people who are welcome in undermarts are called *uncommoners*,' Valian explained; he sounded bored. 'Everyone else is a *commoner*, or *mucker* for short because of that saying *common as*—'

'*Muck?*' Ivy guessed. 'How nice.'

His face darkened. 'Yeah, well, uncommoners don't like outsiders. You can't just join the Trade. You inherit the right to be an uncommoner through your blood-line. If your parents were uncommoners, then you will be too. There's no other way in, and that's the way un-commoners like it.'

Ivy was puzzled as to why Valian kept describing uncommoners as if he wasn't one of them. *If it runs through the family*, she thought, *then his parents must have been uncommoners too. He's not exactly an outsider.*

'Muckers are banned from undermarts,' he con-tinued. 'And if an uncommoner reveals anything about the Great Uncommon Trade to a mucker' – he ran a finger across his throat – 'the underguards get cranky.'

Ivy looked at him. It was obvious that he was risking his life by explaining all this to her, just so that she would retrieve something for him. She wondered, with a cold feeling of unease, what could possibly be that important.

All of a sudden something bright yellow and squealing came streaking down the tunnel towards them.

'Mind out the way!' called a shrill voice. 'Coming through!' A woman in a fluorescent workman's vest and knee breeches was riding something – Ivy squinted: was that a *doormat*? – like it was a skateboard, except that it didn't have any wheels and just hovered in mid-air. Valian dodged nimbly aside, but Ivy had to launch herself against the wall.

'Sorreeeee!!' the lady called as she zoomed past. 'I've just bought it! Haven't learned how to use the brakes yet!' Her voice followed her down the tunnel and out of sight.

Ivy winced as she straightened. Valian pulled up his collar and rolled his eyes. 'We need to go – *now*.'

Minutes later, they came to a stop in front of a mountain of rucksacks, all piled on top of each other like rocks after a landslide.

'Damn it.' Valian bent forward, picked up a bag and chucked it behind him, where it landed with a soft thud. 'Well?' he asked Ivy. 'Are you going to help? We need to get through these.'

She tentatively grasped the looped handle of the nearest rucksack. As her hand closed around it, a soothing wave of heat rolled up her arm like a warm breeze. She concentrated as she held on, trying not to let Valian see her reaction. She didn't need to be a genius to understand what was going on. Every time she touched something uncommon – whether it was the silver coin, Valian's suitcase, or any of the bags down there – she could *feel* that they were different.

The more she thought about it, the more uncomfortable she felt. It couldn't have been happening to the others; Seb hadn't mentioned anything about it after he came through the suitcase, and Valian didn't react when he picked something up.

So what was different about her?

'Don't be fooled by the huge number of bags down here,' Valian said after a few minutes. He heaved aside a heavy sack. 'Uncommon objects are still rarer than moon rock. A common person could go their whole life and never come across one. Uncommoners use special methods to find them. That's why Lundinor only opens three times a year; everyone spends the rest of the time getting hold of something worth trading. Right now we're in the middle of the winter trading season – that's when Lundinor opens, from Christmas Day till Twelfth Night.'

Ivy struggled for words; there was too much to say. The more Valian explained, the more frighteningly real Lundinor became. 'This whole thing is insane,' she said finally, dropping a bag on the floor. 'You know that, right? How come no one knows about this? Think of all the amazing things people could achieve using uncommon stuff. You could probably save lives.'

'Or end them.' Valian snatched at another handle. 'Part of the reason uncommoners keep the Trade secret is to prevent uncommon objects from getting into the wrong hands. There's a whole guild of traders whose job it is to conceal the uncommon world from muckers, just to protect them.'

He shoved a few more bags out of the way and then looked up at the shrinking pile. Behind it was a dark, square hole in the wall. A selection of leather belts hung from a row of hooks beside it. 'Elevation shaft,' Valian explained, pointing. 'No one uses it much any more. It'll be the safest way for you to travel.'

As Ivy considered the dark hole, her mind returned to her brother. She pieced together what Valian had told her. If, as a mucker, she was banned from under-marts, it was going to be harder than she thought to get Seb back. 'The underguards . . .' she said. 'They're like your police, right?'

Valian lugged a heavy canvas backpack out of the way. 'They're meant to be.'

Ivy pictured Officer Smokehart with his – she now guessed – *uncommon* toilet brush, and hoped Seb was all right. She reached down for the strap of one last rucksack; it was making a funny chattering sound. When she bent closer, she spotted something tied to it – a tortoiseshell comb.

'Careful!' Valian yelled. He grabbed the bottom of the bag and threw it onto his pile. As it hit the other bags, it made a strange clicking sound before falling silent.

Ivy stared at it. 'What the—?'

Valian reached into his jacket pocket and brought out his comb again. 'Remember this?' He stroked it gently, and in a startling instant the plastic teeth transformed into real gnashing canines and incisors, set into brown plastic gums.

Ivy shrank away, aghast.

Valian shrugged. 'It's an anti-pickpocket device.' He stroked the comb in the other direction and then tucked it back into his pocket. 'Objects have different uses when they turn uncommon,' he said, scrambling over what was left of the rucksack mountain. When he reached the rail of trouser belts, he threw one back to Ivy and took another for himself.

Ivy jumped up to catch it.

'Uncommon belts kinda do what normal belts do,' he called, fastening the buckle. 'They hold things up.' He raised the belt above his head and was instantly lifted off the ground.

Ivy felt dizzy as she watched him float up to the cave

roof. She looked down at the belt in her hands. Shifting all those warm uncommon rucksacks had left her palms sweaty, but there was something else she had noticed every now and then.

Whispers.

Careful not to let Valian see, she held the belt to her ear. If she listened closely, she could hear voices. She couldn't tell what they were saying – they seemed to hover at the very edge of her hearing – but she wasn't imagining it. If the heat she felt was real, then the voices were too.

She took a deep breath and clutched the belt tightly. She'd have to figure out what was going on later. Right now she needed to focus all her energy on rescuing Seb.

She peered over at Valian, who was sinking back towards the remains of the rucksack mountain by lowering the uncommon belt past his waist. Once safely down, he stepped over to the elevation shaft. 'Just copy me,' he called. 'We don't have much time.' He lifted the belt over his head and immediately rose up off the floor. Using his elbows to nudge himself clear of the walls, he headed into the shadowy hole and floated upwards.

After Valian's feet had disappeared, Ivy hauled herself up the rucksack hill and leaned out over the edge of the opening. There was only darkness beneath her,

heavy with the smell of stagnant water. Her face flushed.
She still couldn't believe this was happening . . .

'Hello?' Her voice echoed in both directions.

There was no response.

Chapter Eight

Cool air streamed through Ivy's wet curls as she soared up the elevation shaft, Granma Sylvie's bag rocking gently around her hips. The sensation was incredible.

I'm flying.

I'm actually flying.

She could feel her face glowing with exhilaration as she clutched the uncommon belt tightly above her head, marvelling at the fact that she didn't need to do anything. It wasn't as if she was hanging from the belt; the belt seemed to be holding her up.

A square of pale yellow light glowed above her – the entrance to another tunnel. As she floated up to it, Valian offered her an elbow and she pulled herself in, reaching down with her toes as she slowly lowered the belt.

I just flew. In the air. Using a belt.

She spotted a smirk on Valian's face as he returned his belt to another set of hooks on the wall. As she copied him, she tried to hide her amazement. She reminded herself that Valian had made no effort to stop Seb from being arrested. She shouldn't trust him.

He leaned back against the wall, stretching his shoulders. 'I can't go any further,' he said casually. 'Beyond this point I'll be recognized.' He gestured down the tunnel. 'When you get to the T-junction, take a left, then second right. After the cave filled with suit-carriers you go left, then down the passageway that smells of boot polish. That'll lead you into the main arrivals chamber.'

Ivy peered ahead. The thick gloom of the passageway was broken only by a few strips of weak lemon-squeezer light. She tried not to let Valian see her fear. 'Er – what exactly do you want me to get for you?'

'Just a candle.'

'*Just* a candle?'

Valian studied his nails. 'It's uncommon, OK? I need it to get into Lundinor, to visit someone who can clear my name.' He nodded in the direction of the main arrivals chamber. 'All you have to do is get into the cave. The candle trader has debts to settle with me, so you won't have to pay him; and you don't need to worry about finding him. He'll find you. He always does.'

Ivy didn't like being given orders by someone so suspicious. 'Fine. But first you have to tell me how to get my brother out. That was the agreement.'

Valian raised a hand. 'All right, I know. The under-guard station is in Lundinor, through the Great Gates. You'll find those in the main arrivals chamber – they're the ones with Sir Clement and Lady Citron, the founding traders of Lundinor, on either side. And next to them you'll see some ladders. They're the best way out of here for muckers – they're not used much any more so they won't be guarded. But first make sure you get my candle. Bring that back and I'll tell you the rest – how to break into the underguard station and get your bro out of there.'

Ivy huffed. She should have known there would be some security for him in the arrangement. 'Fine.'

Valian shrugged off his leather jacket. Beneath it he was wearing a black T-shirt with what Ivy assumed was the logo of a heavy metal band – it involved a rose wrapped in barbed wire. 'Here, take this.'

Ivy scowled as he thrust the jacket into her arms. 'Why do I—?'

'Because you'll need it, OK? You won't get very far in that coat. The Ugs have circulated your description, remember? They all know what you look like.'

Ivy groaned and reluctantly peeled off her duffel coat, depositing it in Valian's arms, then put her granma's bag over her shoulder again.

'Anyway,' he said with a hint of glee, 'you'll need to be wearing something a bit different in order to fit in.

Uncommoners all wear Hobsmatch.'

'What's that?'

Valian's eyes twinkled. 'You'll find out soon enough.'

Ivy fiddled with the strap of Granma Sylvie's handbag, repeating Valian's instructions over and over in her head. *Left, then second right . . .*

After the third turn, the tunnel walls started to shake with noise. Ivy fought the urge to turn back. The further she went, the louder the rumble of voices and shuffling footsteps became. Eventually she turned the final corner and was forced to grip the rock for support as a wall of sound rose up to meet her.

'*Whoa . . .*'

In front of her was another chamber, but this one was *gigantic*. The gaping roof glittered with red-brown stalactites, as long and jagged as giant fangs, and the walls were so high they disappeared into shadow. Against them were stacks of every type of bag imaginable: ostrich-leather handbags, sequinned purses, neoprene rucksacks, canvas sacks, duffel bags; even the odd cheap, rustling carrier bag tied onto the sides of larger cases. If the first arrivals chamber Ivy had crawled into was like a cloakroom fortress, then this one was more like the Colosseum.

On the floor hundreds of uncommoners bustled around, hopping over cases, bags swinging at their sides, some dragging children behind them. Ivy remained in the shadows of the tunnel while she observed them. She struggled to take in all the costumes: there was a lady in a silky kimono and herringbone tweed jacket; a man wearing breeches and a Hawaiian shirt; another lady in camouflage trousers, platform shoes and a baseball cap. Ivy watched wide-eyed as three kids wearing tight plastic raincoats over Roman togas chased each other through a group in petticoats and puff sleeves. Men in cycling shorts and sombreros stood next to others in top hats and tunics. There were fancy feathered collars, felt berets, shimmering Egyptian headdresses, fur stoles, medieval veils. It was as if everyone had taken bits of fashion throughout history and put them all on at once.

So this is Hobsmatch, Ivy thought. She didn't quite know what to make of it. The rich colours and elaborate designs were beautiful, but it didn't exactly look practical – all those ruffs and heels – and yet she guessed it suited uncommoners. They were collectors, after all. Hobsmatch must be a good way to show off.

She tried to pick out a few faces, though it was easy to get distracted. The people were as diverse as any she'd seen at an airport. And – her heart sank – none were carrying candles. Valian had said that this candle trader would find *her*. She wondered if she should go and wait somewhere.

Everyone was funnelling into the mouth of a tunnel in the far wall, positioned between two colossal iron gates. The vast hinges were set into the statues of two figures who held hands, forming an arch over everyone below. One was a stately man in a long-sleeved jerkin with a garland of oranges around his neck; the other an elegant woman wearing a tasselled dress decorated with lemons. Ivy stared at them. They looked grand, like the statues of ancient gods she'd seen on trips to the V&A with her dad. *The one with the oranges must be Sir Clement*, she thought, *and Lady Citron has to be the one with the lemons*. She wondered what her dad would make of them.

Between the two statues stood the Great Gates – which, according to Valian, meant the ladders would be close by. Ivy hunted around and, sure enough, spied a shadowy gap between two stacks of cases, where silvery rungs glinted against the wall. Her shoulders tensed. That was her and Seb's way out.

Turning up the collar of Valian's jacket, she curled her trembling hands into fists.

Here goes . . .

She stepped out.

It was like being trapped in the middle of an enormous school reunion where everyone had come in fancy dress.

'Kitty, I haven't seen you in ages! Your chain mail looks great – is it new?'

'How're the kids, Arthur? I heard your two'll be trading this season.'

'Ooh, yes. I saw those floods on the news. Must have been *terrible* for you down at the bottom of the country. How did your robes survive?'

Ivy slipped carefully between the puffed sleeves and flouncy skirts, a cold, heavy feeling settling at the bottom of her stomach like wet cement. *Keep it together,* she told herself. *This is real. You've got to rescue Seb.* She fixed her eyes on the ladders ahead.

'You read the *Chronicle* this morning?' Ivy heard one of the traders say. ''Eard there's been some sort of scandal at the Ug station. Something to do with the Wrenches.'

'Wrench? I haven't heard that name in years.'

'Well, it's hardly surprising . . .'

The name *Wrench* tripped alarm bells in Ivy's head, but the din of the crowd was so overwhelming, she couldn't think straight. A trader in an embroidered tunic and a kilt swished past carrying a basket of brass kettles. Everyone was hefting something – muddy bicycle wheels slung over shoulders, dusty wine bottles stuffed under armpits.

Suddenly something swooshed close to Ivy's head and she looked up as a dark shape passed over her.

It zoomed towards the Great Gates, before slowing down so that Ivy could identify it: *a man riding a flying vacuum cleaner.* She looked back up to discover a multitude of other traders flying in and out of the stalactites. Some were straddling broomsticks, mops or feather dusters, while others knelt on flying rugs or doormats.

'Hello, missy.'

Ivy froze as she felt a hand on her shoulder. She spun round and came face to face with a toothless, wrinkled old man.

'Bleedin' vacuum fliers,' he croaked, rubbing his hunched back. 'No care for pedestrian safety, absolutely none!' He was holding the broken pieces of a cardboard sign mounted on a long wooden stick. Ivy could just about make out what it said: INVISIBILITY CANDLES: 8 GRADE.

The man raised a fist towards the roof of the cavern. 'Broke three signs this week!' he shouted. 'If I ever get my hands on one of you ruffians . . .' He shook his head and turned his foggy turquoise eyes towards Ivy. 'Don't suppose I can interest you in a candle, dearie? Eight grade's an awful good price, honest.' As he smiled, his tanned skin creased like baked mud.

Ivy didn't say a thing. She didn't even move. *He'll find you*, Valian had told her. And here he was . . .

'Er – yeah, I need a candle,' she said, trying to keep her voice steady. In the pockets of Valian's jacket, her hands were trembling. 'It's for someone else. He said you had a debt to settle with him.'

The old man squeezed his lips together and frowned. 'A debt, you say?' He scratched his scalp. 'Who sent yer?'

Ivy hesitated and half smiled. 'Valian Kaye?'

The man spat in her face. 'Pah! Owe 'im a candle? 'E must be kidding. Boy's gone raving mad. 'E owes me objects to the value of fifteen grade!' He shook his head. 'Owe 'im a candle indeed!'

Ivy tried not to gag as she wiped the spittle off her cheek. *Lovely*. Valian had lied, but she still needed that candle. 'Wait,' she said. 'Maybe there's something I can give you in return.' She started searching through Valian's pockets. There must be something uncommon there—

'Ouch!' Ivy's fingertips burned as something bit her. She withdrew her hand and looked into the pocket. The lining was wriggling.

The comb! Of course.

'How about this?' Ivy pulled the comb out carefully and pointed it away from her, trying to keep control of the gnashing teeth.

The man inspected it from a distance, rubbing his chin. 'Not bad, not bad. But what would I use it for?' He signalled to the loose, tattered shirt he was wearing. 'I don't have no pockets.'

Ivy racked her brains. 'Er . . .' The man held her

gaze. His irises were swirly dark blue now, like a lagoon. 'Maybe you could attach it to the top of your sign to stop people flying into it?' she said hopefully.

The man looked angrily down at his broken sign and then, slowly, he smiled. 'You got yerself a deal there, missy.' He held out his hand, which was encased in a fraying grey gardening glove.

Ivy sighed with relief as she shook it.

The man glanced at her bare fingers. 'Best make sure yer wearing gloves in there,' he said, nodding towards the Great Gates.

'Yeah, thanks,' Ivy said dismissively, registering the advice at the back of her brain. She was more interested in getting the candle. After the old man had handed it over, she shoved it in her pocket, trying to ignore the fact that it was black and odd looking.

'Yer jus' gotta blow it out to use it,' the man instructed before turning to leave. 'It only works if you're touchin' it, mind. If you let go, you'll become visible again.'

Once the old man had disappeared, Ivy turned round and set off through the crowd. When the main arrivals chamber was well behind her, she sprinted down the last tunnel to Valian, anticipation surging through her. She had the candle; now she just had to make sure that Valian kept his side of the bargain. She was still determined to give him a piece of her mind when she found him. It served him right that she'd had to give away his comb. She felt the uncommon candle between her fingers as she dashed round the corner. 'Valian?' she hissed. 'I've got it!'

The tunnel was empty.

Ivy hurried to the end and called down the elevation shaft, but there was no reply. She ran back and looked down the two adjoining passageways.

'Valian?' she whispered. She didn't understand why he wasn't there. Then she spotted it: a shadow on the floor. As she drew closer, she realized what it was.

My duffel coat?

In the dust beside it lay the silver coin. Ivy picked it up and closed her fingers around it thoughtfully, letting the warmth surge through her. Valian must have found it and left it there for some reason.

She scoured the surrounding area and, in the next tunnel, found scuff marks on the floor and five long scratches down the wall.

Something had happened to Valian.

Chapter Nine

Ivy collapsed onto the dusty floor, feeling all her confidence ebb. Maybe Valian had been arrested, or maybe someone else had found him and he'd got into a fight and run off. Whatever had happened, Ivy doubted he was coming back. She was going to have to rescue Seb without his help.

After a few blank, cold minutes she reached for Granma Sylvie's soft leather handbag and sniffed. She knew what her granma would tell her, if she was there: *Get up, Ivy. You're all Seb's got. Come on, get up!*

Slowly she rose to her feet. To make herself feel more comfortable, she tugged off Valian's leather jacket and replaced it with her duffel coat. The wool still smelled like the vanilla air freshener her mum sprayed around at home. She tucked the silver coin into her pocket, ignoring the strange warmth spreading through her fingers, and tried to concentrate.

Think, Ivy. Think . . .

She went through Valian's pockets and got out the

uncommon candle. The old trader's sign had read: INVISIBILITY CANDLES.

Ivy examined it closely as it heated her palms. The candle looked like a blob of black pudding with a short wick that burned with a crystal-white flame.

How she had missed that it was already lit, she didn't know. She turned the candle around slowly, careful not to touch the flame. It didn't dance as it moved, like a normal one; it remained straight and unbroken. Ivy somehow suspected that if she did touch it, it wouldn't even feel hot – it hadn't damaged the inside of Valian's jacket, after all. She tried to recall the old man's parting instructions: *blow it out to use it; keep it in your hand at all times.*

Blow it out? Right . . .

It was worth a try. Ivy took a deep breath and aimed it at the flame.

Here goes nothing, I suppose.

The white spark wobbled and then faded. A puff of black smoke climbed up from the wick. It curled through the air with a low hiss, spiralling around Ivy. In seconds it had surrounded her in a wall of murky gas, but before she had time to panic, the wall dissolved, and her surroundings were visible again. The wick was left trailing an almost imperceptible wisp of grey mist.

Ivy stuffed Valian's jacket under her arm and pointed the candle ahead of her like a talisman warding off evil spirits. She wondered if it had actually worked; if she really *was* invisible . . .

She guessed there was only one way to find out.

The toes of Ivy's yellow wellies peeped out into the arrivals chamber, her body remaining firmly in the shadows of the tunnel. Her heart was thudding away inside her ribs. In front of her, buzzing with noise, were thousands of people who brought a whole new meaning to the word *stranger*. And she wasn't welcome here, she knew that.

She took a quick step forward while she still had a shred of courage, and began weaving her way through the crowd. Her eyes darted from face to face, checking reactions. It was the strangest thing she'd ever done in her life – making sure she was invisible. She could imagine Seb's face if she ever told him.

A minute went by. Then another. Not a single person made eye contact with Ivy. But that was almost normal. She was so small that not many people did notice her; not many adults, anyway. She couldn't assume that the candle had worked just yet. She had to make sure.

Over by a mountain of studded leather trunks, a man with oiled black hair and a twirly moustache was calling to the crowd.

'Feast your eyes on the latest Hobsmatch trends this season, ladies and gents!' He gestured to three rails loaded with strange garments. 'I've got the most talked-about looks from Paris and New York, straight off the Hobwalk.' He slid a floor-length mirror out from behind a rack of thick fur coats. 'Free to try and take a look!'

Ivy stopped when she saw the mirror. It was the perfect way to test her invisibility. She made her way carefully towards it, her eyes scanning the faces of the nearby traders. None of them seemed to notice her. When she was close enough, she stepped in front of the mirror, and then looked up.

And . . . nothing.

No Ivy. No candle. No leather jacket; no handbag.

Ivy waved her free hand around and jumped up and down. The trail of smoke from the invisibility candle left a scribbly pattern in the air, but it wasn't visible in the mirror, and neither was she. All Ivy could see was the reflection of the bustling arrivals chamber behind her and a woman in a large hat hurrying towards the mirror—

Oomph!

The woman smacked straight into Ivy. Ivy squeezed the invisibility candle tighter as she steadied herself, and quickly shuffled out of the way. The woman – dressed in ankle warmers, leggings and a padded leather jacket – looked as if she'd just woken from a dream.

'What the . . . ?' she muttered to herself, frowning

vaguely in Ivy's direction as she straightened up in front of the mirror.

Ivy's body tensed. She was invisible; the candle had worked – it must have. But now she had a new problem. If no one could see her, then it would only take one step out of place for her to be discovered.

Deciding to avoid the crowd as much as she could, she began skirting the edge of the cave, close to the towers of luggage. After a few moments she came across a group of children gathered around a man sitting on an upturned suitcase. He had long dark hair, a large nose, and wild, bushy eyebrows that moved up and down as he addressed his audience.

'The Fallen Guild came in the dead of night,' he was saying in a whispery voice. 'Six hooded figures, desperate for blood.'

The children gasped, eyes fixed on the ground in front of him. Ivy snuck closer to see what had captured their attention.

The man was holding one hand out in front of him, twitching his thin fingers in time with his words. 'They did not come for the blood of grown men,' he went on, 'for it was too bitter for them to drink.'

On the end of each of his fingers was tied a short length of white string, the kind you'd use to fasten a brown paper package. Ivy realized that something uncommon was being used when she looked down at the floor and saw six hooded figures rising from the dust. The stringless puppets appeared to be made of dirt, leaves and tiny pieces of rock. She blinked, astonished, as the puppets jerked and swayed in perfect synchronization with the five pieces of string, despite the fact that they weren't attached.

'Instead,' continued the puppeteer, 'it was the sweet, innocent blood of children that quenched their thirst.' His voice was dark and hollow. 'And do you know how they captured little children?' He twitched his fingers, sending the hooded figures rocking towards the children, their arms extended like zombies. 'They'd sing songs late, late into the night, when the children's parents were fast asleep and they were still dreaming. And the children would rise from their beds and go out into the street . . .' He spread a hand wide, nodding to the six creepy puppets. 'That's why the Fallen Guild named themselves after a song; a *Dirge*.'

The children screamed in terror and quickly hurried away. The puppeteer chuckled to himself as he removed the string from his fingers and allowed the hooded figures to disappear back into dust.

Ivy shivered as she swiftly moved on. She had assumed that the puppeteer was telling some sort of dark fairy tale, but now she had a horrible feeling there was more to it than that. She wiggled her fingers around in her pocket, feeling for the uncommon coin. She remembered that the word *Dirge* was written around the edge; she just didn't know why.

She gazed at the crowd. No matter how scared she felt, she knew she had to focus on Valian's instructions. Everyone's Hobsmatch was bulky and distracting, but if she could nestle alongside someone as they passed through the Great Gates, she might be able to get in undetected. She had to choose a suitable candidate. Some traders were too fast or too doddery; some kept stopping to talk to people or pick up extra goods. Eventually Ivy settled on a huge man in a purple turban; on one shoulder he carried a large cardboard box full of leather footballs – perfect for her to sneak under.

As she approached the gates beside him, Ivy counted at least a dozen underguards. She scanned their faces but couldn't find Officer Smokehart or the one with the grey moustache who'd taken Seb. She shuffled to a stop as the big man paused to take something out of his pocket.

Ivy's eyebrows drew together when she saw what it was: a pair of yellow rubber gloves.

She looked at the other traders. They were all doing the same: putting on a pair of gloves – from thick knitted mittens to fur-trimmed driving gloves.

'Stay in line, please!' one of the underguards called. 'Let's keep this orderly.'

Ivy remembered what the old candle trader had told her: that she must be wearing gloves in Lundinor. *Thank you, invisibility candle,* she thought as she carefully squeezed between the two lines to see what everyone was waiting for.

At the head of every queue, mounted on a table, sat a polished silver bell, each one supervised by a pair of underguards. Ivy had never seen bells that size before. They looked like you'd be able to hear them ringing a mile away. There was a symbol engraved on the front of each one: a swirling fingerprint.

The underguards appeared to be instructing each trader to ring one of the bells before passing through the Great Gates. It was too noisy for Ivy to hear what they were saying, but she could tell one thing:

They're checking for something.

Sneaking past them might not be as easy as slipping through the crowd.

She retreated behind Mr Turban, a horrible feeling knotting up her insides. As they approached the bells, she held her breath.

'Gloves, sir?' the underguard at their checkpoint asked. The man nodded. Ivy's heart was in her mouth as she watched him reach out and ring the large silver bell.

But the bell didn't ring.

It *spoke.*

'Thaddeus Kandinsky,' it said, in a high, sing-song voice. 'Sports equipment specialist trader. Primary undermart: Helsior in Norway.'

Ivy gasped. She was shaking now – but she had to keep it together.

The underguard nodded. 'Very well, sir. Come on in. Enjoy your visit.' He stretched over and handed Thaddeus Kandinsky a tea-stained old pamphlet the size of a postcard. 'You might find this useful.' Ivy saw what was printed on the front:

LUNDINOR
Farrow's Guide for the Travelling Tradesman

Thaddeus Kandinsky stuffed the guide in his pocket, right by where Ivy was hiding, and plodded through the checkpoint.

Following him closely, she had no time to feel relieved. Past the Great Gates was another tunnel ending in a large dark hole. Thaddeus Kandinsky was swept along by the crowd as they all funnelled through, and Ivy struggled to keep up with him. She stretched up onto her toes to try and see above the heads in front but it was no use. However, she did notice something curious. There were words carved into the tunnel walls:

Rules, Laws and Bye-laws

■ No goods may be traded before the raising of the
glove on Christmas Day or after the extinguishing of
Old Meg on Twelfth Night. Any outlawed transactions
which are discovered shall be investigated and the
perpetrators fined. Penalty: 50 grade

■ No uncommoner shall take the pitch, lodgings, spot,
corner or shop of another trader without prior written
consent from the trader – to be approved by a
quartermaster. Penalty: 30 grade

As Ivy's eyes scanned the list of rules and bye-laws, she grew more and more anxious. In a few minutes she'd be in Lundinor, in the very heart of this unbelievable place. She tried to prepare herself – maybe the undermart would have street stalls like Portobello Market, or even little shops like Covent Garden.

Except they're both common markets, Ivy reminded herself. She had to try to think more *uncommon*.

She glanced at the old guide hanging out of Thaddeus Kandinsky's pocket and wondered if it might help her find the underguard station. Hoping that Mr Kandinsky would understand, Ivy made a silent apology as she reached a hand towards the guide and gently tugged it free. The trader didn't feel a thing.

Stuffing the guide into her pocket, Ivy scurried away as the crowd fanned out onto a wide stone terrace that looked over Lundinor.

As Ivy caught sight of the view beyond, her legs went weak.

Lundinor wasn't just a market.

It was a *city*.

A sea of crooked rooftops, spires, towers and chimneys – belching everything from smoke to bubbles to glittering fireworks – stretched into the distance. The cave was so big that Ivy couldn't even see the surrounding walls. She crept to the edge of the terrace and looked down at the web of cobbled roads and shadowy alleyways, flickering with lights and movement.

No. Way.

It wasn't possible. An entire city hidden beneath London?! Ivy remembered what Valian had said about uncommoners protecting their secrets, but this was extreme. She wondered what uncommon objects they'd used to keep the place from being discovered.

All around her, uncommoners began making their way down to the cave floor. Those who had brought goods on trolleys and carts loaded them onto uncommon rugs to be flown down, while everyone else went down two large flights of steps chiselled into the cave wall on either side. Ivy searched around for someone to camouflage her, and found two tough-looking traders in kilts and judge's wigs heading towards the steps, carrying a grandfather clock between them. Ivy tiptoed over and carefully fitted herself beneath their cargo, crouching down as they moved off.

Once on the cave floor, she retreated to a quiet spot in the shadows of the stairs, where she tried to gather her thoughts.

OK, now what . . . ?

She needed a plan. Just then, she heard a crackling noise and looked down.

Wait – no!

The wisp of black smoke that had been trailing from the wick of the invisibility candle was now fading as a flame spluttered back into existence. The black wax, in some bizarre, reverse way, seemed to have shrunk. Ivy shook the candle and blew on the flame, trying in vain to put it out again.

Eventually she had to admit defeat. She turned her eyes away from the steadily burning white flame and looked out into Lundinor.

A chill swept over her.

She was visible.

Chapter Ten

Ivy knew she had to act fast. She tore off her duffel coat, half tripping over the sleeves as she tried to turn it inside out. The notice for her arrest had described her as wearing a blue coat; the red lining might make her less identifiable. She tossed what was left of the invisibility candle into Granma Sylvie's handbag, tugged the bottom of her jeans over her yellow welling-tons and tugged her hood up to cover her hair. With Valian's leather jacket tucked under her arm, she set off.

She headed towards the first buildings, which were small and crooked, with gnarled wooden beams and sloping snow-topped roofs, like houses on a Victorian Christmas card. The uncommon lighting made the place feel like a film-set. She looked around. No one seemed to be paying her any attention . . . for now.

She pulled out the pamphlet, opening it at the first page.

Ivy frowned. *OK* . . . She flicked through the rest of the guide. There was text on every page, but it was all written in gobbledygook. *Another language maybe?* The only part that was in English was the title on the cover. *Great.* Her shoulders slumped. She shoved it back in her pocket and sighed; she'd have to think of another way to navigate Lundinor if she was going to find Seb.

Her eyes scanned the market; there was only one road leading in – a wide cobbled street flanked by wrought-iron streetlamps. Cautiously she approached the nearest one. It was decorated with a wreath of berries, and a fist-sized bell hung from a hook at eye level. Checking that no one was watching, Ivy reached up and tapped it gently. Her fingers came away tingling with a pleasant warmth.

It's uncommon. Now what?

Unlike the bells by the Great Gates, there was no fingerprint symbol on the front. Instead, Ivy saw the image of a compass.

I wonder . . .

She grabbed the short length of rope that hung from the bottom and shook it gently. A voice rang out clearly.

'*You are on the Gauntlet, Lundinor,*' it said, immediately falling silent.

Ivy thought for a moment and then rang the bell again.

'*The Gauntlet, Lundinor,*' the bell repeated.

'Is that all you can say?' she whispered, hoping no one was close enough to hear.

The bell remained quiet. Ivy waited for a moment. Eventually it gave a small, purposeful cough. '*I'm only supposed to speak when you ring me,*' it said, in a hushed, slightly annoyed voice.

Ivy whispered an apology, stretched up and rang it again. 'Do you know where I can find the underguard station?'

'*Underguard station?*' the bell repeated. '*The closest one is on the other side of the cavern. An hour north of here. End of Runner Street.*'

An hour . . . ? Ivy's heart sank. She repeated the address in her head and wandered back onto the cobbles. Ahead of her, the Gauntlet seemed to stretch on for ever. Hulking grey stone buildings rose up on either side, lurching towards each other. Beneath them, the pavements were crammed with brightly coloured kiosks that spilled over into the road. Traders riding broomsticks, doormats and rugs flew over the rooftops, while the thud of a thousand footsteps made the ground shake. The noise would have easily drowned out Seb's loudest drum practice.

Ivy took a deep breath. The air was thick with

delicious smells, making her mouth water: sweet roast chestnuts, freshly baked bread and spiced fruits. *Just act normal*, she told herself. *Don't attract attention.* But it was almost impossible to contain her amazement. It was like stepping into the pages of a Victorian history book, except . . . with uncommon objects.

Traders shuffled around in all directions. Some sang out to passers-by, trying to drum up business.

'Lovegrove's Leather Dashers! Belts for all elevations! Best in Lundinor!'

'Sale on long-haul bags, ladies and gents: at least two grade reduction!'

Above Ivy's head, shop signs creaked as they swung to and fro. AL-DIN & SON FLYING CARPETS, OLD MR TANNENBAUM'S UNCOMMON DECORATIONS, ROY. G. BIV'S ART SUPPLIES, LIMELIGHTS' CITRUS LAMPS. She stopped by the open windows of one particular store and peered inside. There was a length of ribbon suspended across the glass that seemed to be moving of its own accord, twirling into a message.

Welcome to Gil's Glove Shop!
Proprietor: Gilbert Grandiose – Glove-Maker for All Ages

Behind the ribbon was a circular room fitted with glass drawers. The front of each displayed a glove – violet suede, lace-cuffed, buttoned, leather, cotton, rubber . . .

The room was dimly lit by half a dozen floating milk jugs. Ivy could tell they were uncommon – not just because they were hovering, but because, as they tipped over, a liquid gas poured out, glowing like stardust.

Standing in the middle of the room was a man with beady eyes and an absurdly huge white moustache which curled around his face, almost touching his ears. He wore an apron covered in oily stains and a name badge that said: GILBERT, THE ONE AND ONLY! There was a bobbing crowd of children in front of him, none of whom were wearing gloves.

'Now,' Gilbert said, sticking out his chest. 'Can anyone tell me what uncommon gloves are used for?'

One of the children – a stout boy in a Roman centurion's helmet – stuck his hand up. 'My mum says they're like her credit card because they remember every transaction she makes.'

Gilbert beamed. 'An excellent analogy, Louis. Uncommon gloves record the trades of whoever is wearing them. That's why uncommoners have to shake hands at the end of every deal. Is there anything else they do?'

A girl with a lilac bow in her hair raised her hand. 'The most important thing they're used for is to tell the underguard where you are at all times. That's why you have to wear them inside the Great Gates, even if you don't want to.'

'Correct,' Gilbert agreed. 'After you take the glove, the underguards know exactly where you are, *all* the time. That's how they catch criminals. Uncommon gloves are used for all kinds of official business, they don't just help you trade. They are the keys to all Lundinor.'

'But what does taking the glove actually *mean*?' asked the boy in the helmet.

One of the other children – a very small girl in a pale pink tutu – pointed up to a pair of long silk dress gloves. 'Can I just take those ones?'

Gilbert hushed the group. 'Taking the glove is a lot more special than that. You must be at least secondary school age – and be nominated by one of the four great quartermasters of Lundinor. It is a mark of your responsibility to the Trade and your promise to live by the rules of GUT law.' He held out his hands, encased in a pair of apple-green suede gloves. 'When you wear a pair of uncommon gloves for the first time, a bond forms between you and them. You keep the same pair of gloves your whole life. They are with you for every trade you make and' – he lowered his voice – 'they know if it is honest or dishonest.' He pointed to a spot on the wall.

Ivy followed his thin finger. Beside a drawer containing a pair of old leather boxing gloves was a framed poster. There was writing at the top and then a photo:

REMEMBER
If you perform an illegal deal according to GUT law, your uncommon gloves will leave a permanent mark against you.

She looked at the photo beneath. It showed a pair of yellow, rotten hands, the skin infested with maggots.

'The man in grey,' she whispered. She clapped a hand over her mouth as she backed away from the window. She hadn't meant to say it out loud. But . . . she had seen hands exactly like that this very morning, in the hospital. It felt like a lifetime ago.

Ivy continued along the street. Some things were starting to make sense. The man in grey was an uncommoner – an extremely shady one, if that glove poster was anything to go by. It couldn't have been a coincidence that he was poking around in the hospital that morning. Maybe he *had* been looking for Granma Sylvie – just like Ivy had suspected at the time. And that meant . . . she was in danger.

Ivy clenched her fists as she hurried towards the underguard station, weaving her way through the traders. When she had rescued Seb, they had to get back to the hospital as quickly as they could. Her heart pounded as she dodged and ducked past traders, desperately hoping she'd make it to the underguard station without being identified as a mucker. The crowd slowed as they approached a crossroads in the Gauntlet. Ivy tried to squeeze through, but the traders were standing shoulder to shoulder and she found herself stuck between a wooden cart heaped with old chairs and a kiosk with a yellow awning. She heard shouts up ahead. No one was moving.

She turned to the stall beside her. Its owner seemed to have disappeared, but Ivy saw that it sold *coins*. Hundreds of them – shiny copper, dull silver, six-sided, circular, all stored in little plastic pouches – hung from the metal poles of the canopy. Every face was engraved with a portrait, although Ivy wasn't familiar with any of the heads on show. She reached down into her reversed pocket and fumbled around for the silver coin. Her fingers tingled as they found it.

'Can I interest you in anything, little one?' A head of curly red hair popped up from behind the stall. 'Maybe a nice tuppence?' The lady took one of the pouches and pulled out a small copper coin. 'You can put the image of your sweetheart on it.' She flipped the coin over several times. With each turn the face changed. 'Can fit eight different pictures on this one – see? Much better than a common photo frame.'

Ivy blinked. *Eight different pictures . . . ?*

Just then the crowd started to move. She shook her head shyly at the stallholder and shuffled along. In her pocket, she turned the silver coin over and over between her fingers, thinking.

The coin is like a photo frame . . . Which meant that it held pictures of people. Ivy couldn't remember seeing a face on it before, but at the time she'd been more interested in the words around the edge. She hadn't bothered to flip the coin over and check it again. She needed to have a second look.

To her surprise she soon spotted a shop that seemed to be closed – the front windows were empty and the heavy glass door was shut. *Odd* . . . all the others were clearly open. Still, Ivy climbed the three black steps up to the front door. She looked around, checking that no one was watching, before retrieving the coin.

The portrait engraved on the front was of a hooded face in a tusked mask, most likely that of a man – the jaw was too large and square for a woman. Ivy flipped the coin over several times, but in the gloom she couldn't make out the other faces. She leaned back, angling the coin to catch the light.

All of a sudden she slipped and lost her footing. Her head struck the door, and then there was a crack, followed by a long groan as it swung inwards. Ivy tripped over Valian's jacket and fell head-first into the shop. The coin rolled out of her hand and onto the floor with a loud *thrum*.

Chapter Eleven

Ivy clambered to her feet, wincing. She wasn't quick enough to stop the door rattling to behind her. She squeezed her eyes shut, tensing as the sound reverberated around the room. After a moment's silence she slowly opened them again.

The shop was empty. Or at least – she corrected herself – empty of people. The small room was filled with row upon row of bells – gleaming brass bells, acorn-shaped wooden ones and stone bells with strange carvings on the side. Ivy had never seen so many different designs. She guessed that she was looking at a lifetime's worth of collecting.

She made a hurried search for the silver coin. At the very back of the room, beyond the bells, was a large counter and, behind that, a door. Ivy spotted something glinting on the floor beneath the hinged flap in the counter top. *The coin.* Maybe if she was really quiet, she could just nip over, pick it up and leave without anyone knowing she'd been there.

She tiptoed slowly into the room, gawping at the array of bells. Each one had its own wooden plaque mounted below it. There were tiny silver sleigh bells and huge brass ship's bells; bells from pet collars and bells from musical instruments. Some were extremely old. Ivy read one plaque that said ALARM BELL, 1901, but further along she spied a much less familiar WELL-WISHING BELL, 1642 and also a BELL OF TRUTH, 405 AD.

As Ivy passed, a few of the bells swayed on their hooks and whispered to each other.

'*Who's she?*' one asked.

'*What's she wearing?*'

A clutch of small gold bells twitched as Ivy ran her eyes over them. The plaque below read SINGING BELLS.

'*Any requests?*' they asked, in a single harmonious voice.

She timidly shook her head and scuttled on. At last she came to the desk. Upon it was one more bell – this one larger than the others and so highly polished she could see a perfect reflection of herself in it.

She looked awful. There was mud in her damp, frizzy hair and a web of thin red scratches on one cheek. She turned to read a hand-scrawled sign that was propped up beside the bell.

ETHEL DREAD'S HOUSE OF BELLS
RING FOR TRADE – OTHERWISE GET OUT

Ivy gulped. The owner didn't exactly sound friendly – perhaps that was why the shop had looked shut. As quietly as she could, she bent down and reached for the silver coin.

The bell on the desk twitched. '*Ethel!*' it squawked loudly. '*Ethel, get out here!*'

Before Ivy had time to run, the door at the back swung open and she heard the screech of a chair, followed by a groan and some footsteps.

'I'm coming, I'm coming! Bloomin' interrupting my lunch . . . You'd better have a good reason fer—' A sour-faced woman emerged through the doorway. She had dark eyes, a crooked nose and frizzy black hair that sprouted from under a flowery headscarf. She wore leather biker's gloves on her hands, dusty combat boots on her feet, and loose navy overalls covering the rest of her.

Ivy recognized her face immediately.

No, it can't be . . .

She rose slowly from the floor. Ethel took a step closer. 'And 'oo might you be, then?' she asked, in a thick Cockney accent.

Granma Sylvie's photo.

Ivy couldn't believe it: this was the woman in that picture – the one from Granma's life before the accident; the one she kept in her handbag. Ivy had seen it hundreds of times; this woman looked older, but it was definitely her – the same jaw, the same angular cheekbones, and the same sharp gaze.

When Ivy didn't answer, Ethel's eyes narrowed. 'Whatcha doing 'ere?' She reached over and pulled Ivy's hood back. Her hair bounced out from beneath it.

Ivy shot a look back at the silver coin. She hadn't been able to grab it. 'I, er—'

'Left something down there, 'ave you?' Ethel asked slowly. 'How's about I get it for you?' She bent down and snatched the coin up with her thin fingers. Standing straight, she opened her palm to take a look at it.

The bells started whispering as Ethel raised a hand to her chest and staggered away from Ivy. 'Where did you find this?' she hissed. 'D'you know what it *is*? D'you know what would happen to me if someone found that 'ere, in my shop?'

Ivy stumbled to find words, but no sounds came out. A cold, prickly feeling rose up through her chest and her throat tightened. 'I don't know anything about it,' she squeaked finally. 'Please, I'm sorry. I don't mean to be any trouble but I can't leave now. You see, I've seen you before, in a photo with my granma.' She scrabbled through Granma Sylvie's handbag, catching sight of the photo tucked away in the corner. 'Here . . .' She held out the picture with a shaking hand.

Ethel's cheeks flushed as she saw it.

It was exactly as Ivy remembered it from earlier that morning: the young Granma Sylvie standing with her arm round Ethel, both of them wearing fancy dr—

Ivy blinked. She took the photo back and stared hard at the image. 'Hang on . . . What was Granma Sylvie doing wearing Hobsmatch?'

Ethel peered into Ivy's face, a frown deepening across her forehead. After a moment's consideration she flapped a hand towards the windows. 'Shut the blinds,' she ordered. 'We're closed.' The bells hanging above the main window swung to the side, releasing a venetian blind that was fixed beneath them. It fell to the floor with a dusty thud. Ethel jabbed a finger towards the large silver bell on the desk. 'You!' she barked. 'Let me know if anyone so much as thinks about coming in.' She returned the silver coin to Ivy, looking at her anxiously. 'You'd better take that out back,' she said, pursing her lips. 'We'll talk there.'

The door at the rear of the shop opened into a dark storeroom. When Ethel switched on a lamp, Ivy saw that on one side were racks of bells padded with foam or cotton wool, while on the other were shelves of other objects – a trombone, an old-fashioned skipping rope, a set of skittles and a moth-eaten teddy bear. The place smelled like the inside of a rabbit hutch, and as Ivy crunched over the floor, she realized why: it was covered with a layer of pale golden straw.

Ethel shut the door behind her. 'You should sit,' she said, pulling up a velvet-cushioned piano stool.

Ivy took the seat gladly, her legs like jelly. Ethel drew up a wooden dining chair and plonked herself down. She nodded to the photo in Ivy's hand. 'Let me see it again.'

Ivy handed it over. She couldn't stop staring at Ethel's face. The lines around her eyes were sadder than Granma Sylvie's, but they were probably about the same age, Ivy thought. Ethel had slightly hunched shoulders, a wicked slash of a mouth and callouses on all her fingers. Her eyes were the colour of flint.

'How do you know my granma?' Ivy managed at last.

She couldn't believe it. Granma Sylvie's mysterious past was sitting directly in front of her. This woman actually knew Granma Sylvie. Ivy wondered what her mum and dad would say.

Ethel's eyes were shining. 'Is she alive?'

The question felt like a punch in the chest. Ivy nodded.

Ethel sighed and smiled. 'That's good to know. We was friends a long time ago.' She reached across and picked up a steaming bowl of something from one of the shelves. 'The best of friends.' She slurped up a spoonful of whatever it was. The noise echoed in the small room.

Ivy looked around at all the strange objects stored away in the semi-darkness. 'Wait . . . Did she know about Lundinor?'

'*Know* about it? Sylvie grew up in Lundinor, like me. Her family – the Wrenches – come from a long line of powerful uncommoners.'

Ivy sat up straight. 'But Granma Sylvie doesn't have any family other than us. She's never mentioned the Wrenches . . . She doesn't know about uncommoners.'

Ethel put down her spoon. 'Look, your gran is an uncommoner and so are you. Ain't she explained all this?'

Ivy's entire body went rigid. 'I'm—' She couldn't finish the sentence aloud. *I'm an uncommoner?* After what Valian had said, it did make sense – the right to be an uncommoner ran in a family. But Ivy wasn't . . . She couldn't possibly be . . .

She tried to clear her mind. This was too much to take in all at once. She looked back at the photo. Ethel had said that she and Granma Sylvie were friends once, but that was so long ago. 'What happened?'

Ethel stirred whatever was in her bowl, but she appeared to have lost her appetite. 'Nobody knows.' Her voice was cold. 'Twelfth Night 1969, Sylvie disappeared, along with the rest of the Wrenches. The entire family – Sylvie, her three brothers and her mother – vanished in one night. The underguard searched for them all for years afterwards but never found any trace. It became one of the greatest unsolved mysteries in uncommon history.'

'Twelfth Night 1969?' Ivy repeated. She had never forgotten that date . . . *the night of Granma's accident.* 'There was a snowstorm that night,' she recalled slowly. 'Granma Sylvie had a car crash that gave her amnesia. She doesn't remember anything about her life before the accident.' She gestured around the storeroom. 'She doesn't know about any of this stuff.'

Ethel's eyes widened. Her spoon was shaking in her hand. 'She don't know?' she whispered. 'But . . . ?' She looked down at the coin in Ivy's hand. 'Then whatcha doing 'ere, with that?'

Ivy tucked the old photo back into the handbag and unfurled her fingers so that the silver coin was lying flat in her palm. The heat soaked into her skin, making her fingers twitch. She wondered if the sensations were connected to her being an uncommoner – maybe it happened to others as well.

In the low light she could just about see the masked face on the coin. 'We found it,' she explained. 'My brother and me. We were at Granma's house this morning and there was this black feather writing on the wall.' She swallowed as her mind took her back. 'It said *We can see you now.*'

Something flickered in Ethel's stony eyes.

'What's wrong?' Ivy could tell that the message meant something.

Ethel's jaw was tense. 'There's only one organization that uses black featherlights: the Dirge.'

'The Dirge . . . ?' Ivy's skin prickled as she turned the coin over, remembering the creepy dust-puppets she'd seen in the arrivals chamber. The image on the other side of the coin changed to another hooded, masked face, this one with fangs. 'I read that word on the coin. What does it mean?'

Ethel turned away, staring into the lamplight. 'It's a long story; one that folk don't talk about no more.' She settled her bowl back on the shelf and sighed. 'Uncommoners belong to guilds. Each guild 'as a particular responsibility and a particular coat of arms. I belong to the Right Honourable Guild of Bell Traders, for example. The Dirge was an ancient guild of scientists 'oo studied uncommon objects. Their coat of arms showed a coin – an old crooked sixpence.'

Ivy looked down at the silver coin in her hand. When she'd first found it, she noticed that it was bent in the middle.

'In the beginning,' Ethel continued, 'the Dirge's research 'elped build Lundinor and many other under-marts around the world. They discovered 'ow to use uncommon colanders to filter the air, 'ow to carry 'eavy loads on uncommon rugs – it made 'em famous. But they soon became obsessed with unlocking much darker secrets – things to do with controlling the very essence of uncommon objects: human souls.'

Ivy had a sinking feeling. She didn't like the sound of where this was going.

'When everyone discovered what the Dirge 'ad been up to, a new GUT law was passed that forbade anyone from tampering with the uncommon part of an object. The Dirge were ordered to disband and, over time, their story became no more than a page in uncommon 'istory. Then, sixty years ago, when your gran and I were teenagers, they reappeared.'

Ivy gasped. 'What happened?'

'It started with the disappearance of a child,' Ethel

told her. 'A young boy no older than you was kidnapped in the dead of night from 'is room above one of the shops on the Gauntlet. 'Is parents found a crooked sixpence resting on 'is pillow and a black featherlight from the Dirge 'overing above 'is bed. The message claimed that the boy had been taken for research. When the coin was examined, it showed six disguised faces – the new members of the guild.' Ethel paused. Ivy could see the lines around her eyes more clearly than ever. 'Within weeks, children were going missing from all quarters of Lundinor. The underguard could find no link between the victims and didn't know where the Dirge would strike next. A campaign of other attacks followed – arson, theft and, finally, murder. A crooked sixpence was found at the scene of every crime. It became the Dirge's calling card.'

Ivy thought back to the black feather in Granma Sylvie's house and her hands shook. It suddenly felt dangerous to hold the crooked sixpence. She flipped her palm over and watched it drop to the floor.

'Nobody knew 'oo the six members of the Dirge were. They used code-names to keep their real identities a secret: Blackclaw, Ragwort, Wolfsbane, Monkshood, Nightshade and Hemlock; each named after a different poison.'

Ivy shuddered as she remembered reading some of those names on the crooked sixpence.

'The underguard 'ad difficulty finding 'em because it was said they met in a Hexroom – a chamber that can only be entered by uncommon means. Fear spread through the streets like a plague. In the end people were too scared to even say the Dirge's name and they became referred to simply as the *Fallen Guild*.'

'What happened to stop them?' Ivy asked. Something must have put an end to it all.

Ethel lowered her eyes. 'Everything culminated in a huge battle on Twelfth Night – the night Sylv disappeared. The Dirge 'ad rallied certain . . . people around 'em. An army, of sorts. They very nearly won, but at the last minute the tables turned and they were pushed back. Five of the six members managed to flee, but one was caught and unmasked. After that, the other five were never seen or 'eard of again.'

There was silence as Ivy allowed this information to wash over her. Ethel reached down and picked up the crooked sixpence, depositing it back in Ivy's lap. 'But if Sylv 'as been sent that coin, it can only mean one thing.'

'The Dirge are back,' Ivy finished with a gulp. 'That's what you were going to say, isn't it?'

Before Ethel could respond, a high screech filled the air. '*Ethel!?*'

Ivy flinched.

'*Underguard Sergeant to see you, Ethel! Ethel? Can you hear me?*'

The bell on the desk; Ivy recognized its voice.

Ethel sprang out of her seat like a jack-in-the-box. 'Put it away,' she whispered, looking at the coin. 'Find somewhere to hide.' She laid a hand on Ivy's shoulder. 'I'll do everything I can to 'elp you.' She turned towards the shop. 'I can always bloody 'ear you!' she yelled. 'And so can 'alf the street!' She switched off the lamp, then marched through the door and slammed it shut behind her. For the second time that morning Ivy was plunged into darkness.

Chapter Twelve

Ivy dropped to the floor, feeling her way forward. Ethel's story about the Dirge was still running though her head, but so was Ethel's last instruction.

Hide.

She crawled past what she remembered was a row of bells and headed for the furthest corner, disturbing the dusty straw as she did so. She had to pinch her nose to stop herself from sneezing.

Muffled voices came from the front of the shop; she could only make out the odd word.

'Ms Dread . . .'

There was a rustle and the screech of a chair being dragged across the floor.

'. . . trespassers. Uncommoners . . . haven't taken the glove. There is a warrant out for their arrest. A girl and a boy. Here are the details . . .'

Ethel muttered a complaint.

'We still need to search the premises. You never know who or what may stow away.'

Ivy started. *Search the premises?* But . . . they'd find her. She was in total darkness; she had no idea if there *was* anywhere to hide, let alone how to get there. She shuffled forward as fast as she could. Her heart was pounding.

The storeroom seemed to go on for ever. Eventually the underguard's voice faded away. Ivy began to wonder if there was a back door to the room or a hatch in the wall.

Ahead of her, she spotted a sliver of light coming up through the floor, illuminating a narrow shaft of dust. She inched towards it and rummaged around in the straw, to find that one of the floorboards had a hole in it about the width of her thumb. If there was light beneath her, she thought, there might also be a way out. She gave the floorboard a tug and felt it groan, but it seemed to be stuck.

She reached into the darkness next to her and ran her hands over one of the shelves. She needed a tool to lever the floorboard up. Wave after wave of tingly heat flowed into her fingers as they touched a number of oddly shaped uncommon objects. Eventually her hands met something cool.

Something common.

It was long and heavy, with a scratchy fabric covering. Ivy pulled it down to examine it in the shaft of light. The fabric was an old stained piece of canvas tied with string; wrapped inside it was a small paintbrush and a rusty hammer. She ran her fingers across each one. The string felt uncommon, but the paintbrush and hammer were cool to the touch.

She set to work wedging the hammer into the gap in the wood and pushing down on it with her foot, easing the floorboard away. There was a loud crunch and the board pulled free. Ivy hastily wrenched up the next board along, till the gap in the floor was just big enough for her to squeeze through. She swung her legs over the side, peering into the shadows below.

She didn't know for sure that it would be safer down there, but she didn't fancy her chances with the under-guard. She dropped Granma Sylvie's bag and Valian's jacket through first, before grabbing the canvas, string, hammer and paintbrush.

I'll return them, she decided as she tossed them down before jumping through the gap herself. She didn't want evidence of her escape to be left behind.

Her wellingtons thumped as she landed on a hard surface. She appeared to be in the foundations of the House of Bells – a concrete L-shape with bare bricks around it. In one corner, a wooden hatch swung from its hinges allowing a flicker of light through from the street outside.

There it was: her way out. Ivy slid the floorboards back into place over her head. The space beneath the building was tight, but she was small. With Granma Sylvie's bag over her shoulder, she wrapped the tools in the canvas, stuffed it into Valian's jacket and shoved them both under her arm, then dropped onto her hands and knees and shimmied towards the exit.

Before she had made it to the hatch, she heard a voice.

'Helping, please!' it whispered. 'Dear oh. Helping, please!' The voice was high pitched and muffled, with a distinctive lisp; it sounded like a little boy trapped somewhere.

Ivy stopped and looked around.

'Pleases me find you!' the voice insisted, louder. 'Mud in the stuck! Mud in the stuck!'

Whoever it was, they didn't seem to be talking in coherent sentences. Ivy scanned the ground, looking for mud. The concrete floor finished a short distance from the edge of the building, leaving a few inches of soil. Ivy crawled towards it.

'Yes, am I here!' The voice was so high now, it sounded like a whistle.

Ivy glanced at the patch of earth. She couldn't see anything trapped in it, but then she didn't know what she was meant to be looking for. She pressed her finger-tips into the nearest section. The soil was warm.

Something uncommon? It must be buried, Ivy thought, prodding it experimentally.

'Hee-hee! Tickles do you!' the voice said.

Ivy could feel the soil trembling as the voice spoke. She began digging. A metal object the size of a doughnut started to take shape in the earth.

Carefully Ivy picked it up and tried to rub off the remaining mud with her sleeve. There was a small gash at the top and a lever sticking out at the side. She tugged it experimentally. The object vibrated.

'Goodbye hello,' said the voice.

Ivy frowned and tugged the lever again. There was a giggle. Was she holding a bell? She ran her fingers round it once more. There was only one kind of bell she knew that was this shape. 'You're a bicycle bell . . .' she realized.

She heard a laugh. 'Yes, yes, found you. Your name's Scratch. What's mine?'

Ivy tried to make sense of what the bell was saying. 'Um, my name's Ivy. Do you mean that *your* name's Scratch?'

The bell tinkled. 'I do not mean what I mean, of course. Scratch got a back-to-fronted problem. Nice to Ivy meet you.'

A back-to-fronted problem? Ivy ran her thumb along the dent on Scratch's top. Maybe the damage prevented him from speaking properly.

Suddenly a creak sounded above her head: someone was walking about in the shop, directly above her. She turned towards the hatch.

'I've got to go,' she told Scratch. 'Sorry.'

'Go, wait! Please Ivy take Scratch! Me don't leavings here.'

'Shh . . .' Ivy didn't want whoever was upstairs to hear her. She gazed down at Scratch; the warm, tingly sensation in her hand was stronger now, as if she could feel the bell's desperation. 'OK, fine, I'll get you out of here,' she decided, putting him in her pocket. 'Just keep your voice down.'

Chapter Thirteen

Behind the House of Bells was a narrow alleyway that smelled of chicken soup and laundry powder. Bin bags were piled at the back doors of shops and dripping Hobsmatch garments hung from washing lines across the path.

Ivy looked in either direction but couldn't see movement. She was safe for the time being.

She paused, trying to decide what to do next. She was worried about what Ethel had said – both about the Dirge and Granma Sylvie's past life as a trader. Ivy didn't know if she should be happy or scared that she was an uncommoner. All she really felt was numb. More than ever, she wished her parents were there.

She tucked all these thoughts away in the back of her mind and tried to concentrate. The underguard station could be in any direction. She wondered if Scratch knew.

'Scratch, can you help me?' she whispered, taking

the little bell out of her pocket. 'Do you know where the nearest underguard station is?'

'Of course saviour helping, Ivy.' Scratch shivered. 'Why go wantings to there?'

Ivy peered down at him as she deciphered what he was saying. His speech seemed to be a mixture of opposites and jumbled sentences. 'My brother's in there,' she explained. 'I have to rescue him.'

Scratch went very still. 'Oh.' After a moment he gave a shudder. 'I where know Uglies station, but getting not in you out.'

Uglies. That was one word for them. 'You know how to get there, but not how to get in or out?' she guessed.

Scratch tinkled.

'*Right.*' Ivy smiled, pleased she was getting the hang of his speech. She readjusted Granma Sylvie's bag around her shoulder. Judging from the underguard's conversation with Ethel, the streets were packed with people looking for her. She wasn't going to get anywhere without being spotted. 'I wonder if I can get another invisibility candle . . .' she murmured.

'Why one another?' Scratch asked her. 'Again and candle use again.'

Ivy went still. '*What . . . ?*' She unzipped her granma's handbag and fumbled blindly for the black candle. When she brought it out into the light, she could see that the wax had regrown. It was now at least half as big as when she'd first been given it. Hope rose up inside her belly, blooming like a flower.

'What direction for the underguard station?' she asked, blowing out the candle flame.

Scratch squeaked. 'This corner's round, then wrong.'

Ivy puzzled through his directions. *Round this corner, then right.* She squeezed him gently. 'Thank you.'

They wound their way through the back streets of the Gauntlet and emerged further up the main road, where a series of cutlery traders were demonstrating the properties of various spoons and forks. Ivy didn't stop to see what an uncommon ladle was capable of; instead, she clutched the invisibility candle to her chest and ducked through the crowd, dodging feet and elbows. As she crossed onto the cobbles, a shadow fell across her path and she looked up to find a tall white obelisk standing proudly in the middle of the road. At eye level was a brass plaque. Ivy stretched up to read it.

The Great Cavern Memorial
In loving memory of the gauntlet
traders who were killed in the
Great Battle against the Fallen Guild
Twelfth Night 1969

Ivy studied the names – at least thirty of them, if not more. She swallowed. It couldn't just be coincidence that the Great Battle had occurred on the same Twelfth Night that Granma Sylvie had disappeared.

As she continued towards the underguard station, she tried to work out how she might rescue Seb, but her thoughts kept slipping back to the Dirge and that crooked sixpence. If the Dirge had sent the *We can see you now* to Granma Sylvie, it meant they'd been searching for her all these years.

Scratch quivered in her pocket. 'Ivy not almost far now there,' he whispered. 'Rounding of the corner.'

She made a sharp turn and then came to a halt. The street had opened out into a black marble courtyard filled with . . . Were those *gravestones*?

Ivy examined one nervously. It was engraved with a public notice:

UNCOMMON NEEDLES HAVE EYES.
ASK YOUR LOCAL OFFICER ABOUT NEEDLE CCTV;
IT'S PINPOINT ACCURATE!

The next one along read:

OBSERVE THE TRADING HOURS:
FIRST LIGHT TILL MIDNIGHT.
GUT LAW BREAKERS WILL BE TRACED AND PROSECUTED.

Ivy shuddered. It was eerily quiet. She regarded the surrounding buildings with their smooth granite walls and smoked-glass windows. If there was a design theme here, it was *darkness*. She could see only one set of doors in the entire square and these were iron, with a sign hanging from a hook above them. 'That's it?' she asked, her voice cracking.

Scratch only shivered. Ivy didn't blame him.

She made her way quickly across the courtyard, her wellies pattering over the marble floor. When she reached the station doors, she paused to read the sign hanging above:

FIRST COHORT UNDERGUARD HQ
COMMANDING OFFICER: LADY SELENA GRIMES,
QUARTERMASTER DE

Ivy grasped the strap of Granma Sylvie's handbag, trying to summon up some courage. She could hear the voices of her mum and dad in her head: *Come on, soldier, you can do this. We believe in you.* She swallowed the lump in her throat and pushed open the doors.

Ivy surveyed the interior of the underguard station with a deepening sense of horror. In addition to the expected underguards, she could see a skull-shaped vase filled with headless flower stems and a collection of large stone urns with the letters RIP etched on the front. There were thick black drapes hanging in the windows and a mahogany picture rail running around the walls from which dangled sepia photos of old bones. The smoke-filled air smelled of strange chemicals, whisky and furniture wax.

Ivy trembled as she went in. Fortunately there seemed to be plenty going on so one noticed when the front doors closed of their own accord.

A dark stone reception desk – unnervingly like a tomb – stood at the back of the room; on it was a black marble cherub holding a silver bell. Behind the desk, underguards in long dark cloaks swished about their business with feathers or toilet brushes.

Ivy felt Scratch shivering in her pocket as she scanned the far wall and counted three doors. The smoked-glass window of the one in the far right-hand corner was engraved with the word CELLS.

Ivy checked on the underguards as she snuck past them. It was still difficult to believe they didn't know she was there. *I'm invisible*, she repeated to herself. *I'm invisible*.

As she approached the door, she glanced back once more. Satisfied that the guards were all distracted, she reached for the handle.

Just in time, she heard it creak and leaped back—

The door burst open. Ivy ducked aside and pinned herself against the wall.

A willowy lady with sloping shoulders and a long neck came striding into the room. Her dark hair lay neatly plaited over her shoulder and she wore a floor-length grey silk dress with a purple sash across her chest, like some Roman emperor. 'There must be a mistake,' she said calmly. 'It can't be her.'

'I can assure you,' said a second voice, 'there is no mistake.'

Ivy identified the second voice instantly; her skin turned to ice as Officer Smokehart stopped right in front of her. He gestured to a framed picture behind the stone desk. 'The map doesn't make mistakes.'

Ivy scrutinized the picture curiously. Except . . . wait, it *wasn't* a picture; it *was* a map – she could see the image on its surface shimmering like a seashell. First it depicted a rugged coastline of white cliffs, then a patchwork of fields and rolling hills, and finally crisscrossing roads and concrete buildings. The map was *moving*.

Smokehart turned back to the tall woman. With her slanting blue eyes, thick lashes and high cheekbones, she looked a bit like a movie star. Around her wrist was a thin leather leash; a small, sandy-haired dog sniffed around the bottom of her dress.

'I've checked the records,' Smokehart insisted. 'Sylvie Wrench took the glove when she was eleven. She was visible on all uncommon maps after that date until Twelfth Night 1969, when she disappeared off the face of the planet. Our map hasn't been able to find her for over forty years, but it *can* see her now. She appeared this morning.'

The tall woman lowered her head, thinking.

'With your authority,' Smokehart continued, 'I will reopen the enquiry into Twelfth Night. Everyone knows what happened to Sylvie Wrench's father, Octavius, but the movements of the rest of the family have always eluded us. If we can piece together what really happened that night, we might be able to discover the whereabouts of the three brothers and the mother, and bring them to justice. This is the first opportunity we've had to—'

The tall woman raised her hand, her blue eyes widening as she interrupted him. 'This is the first opportunity we've had to stir up the past. Many uncommoners lost friends and family on Twelfth Night, fighting the Fallen Guild. Reopening the case is like baring old wounds. It is not a good idea.'

'Selena, listen to me. We could make history—'

'*Officer,*' the woman said sharply. 'You and I are colleagues, but please do not feel you have earned the right to address me as anything other than Lady Grimes. I am a *quartermaster.*'

Just for a second Smokehart's pale face flushed scarlet and little red dots appeared on his neck. Ivy remembered that it had happened before, when he had been pursuing her in that rain-drenched field. He bowed his head. 'Forgive me, Lady Grimes, but if you could just—'

Selena Grimes raised her hand again. 'You said that Ms Wrench is confined to a common hospital, yes?'

Smokehart gritted his teeth. 'Yes. She appeared on the map while travelling in an ambulance. I ascertained her address, and then, after my constable and I had searched her house, we went to the hospital to question her. Unfortunately the woman simply doesn't know anything. Purposefully or not, her mind has been wiped.'

Ivy's nostrils flared. How confused and scared Granma Sylvie must have been!

'Then she is hardly going anywhere,' Selena Grimes summarized. 'Place her under twenty-four-hour guard and question her again in a few days' time. Maybe whatever was used to wipe her memory was only temporary. There is no need to alarm the whole of Lundinor unless you have solid information *and* evidence.'

Smokehart grimaced. 'This woman has concealed herself for years – that's more than enough evidence to make her a suspect. I already have her grandson in custody. He may have valuable knowledge. I plan to start the interrogation immediately.'

Ivy's chest tightened. *Seb* . . .

Selena's mouth twitched. '*Officer.* While I admire your pursuit of justice, GUT law does not allow you to reprimand someone if they themselves are not under suspicion. If this boy is Ms Wrench's grandson, then he is an uncommoner; he is one of us. You must release him and allow him to roam Lundinor freely.'

She turned, her long dress billowing at her side. 'That is my final word. Oh, and I don't want the press getting involved – there'll be uproar.' She looked fondly down at her dog. 'Come along, little one.'

Smokehart followed as Selena Grimes swept towards the exit. His shoulders stiffened as the front door closed behind her with a thud.

Ivy gave a sigh of relief. She didn't quite know what to make of that conversation but she did know one thing: Smokehart's back was turned. This was her opportunity to sneak through to the cells, and she was going to take it.

The door opened into a gloomy slate-tiled corridor. Glass doors were set into the left-hand wall, each inscribed with a different underguard rank and name. Officer Smokehart had what appeared to be the largest room; a Sergeant Crabshorte was next, followed by a Sergeant Pike and a Constable Stormfront. On the opposite wall was a series of doors with only a small glass window at the top; a brown feather hovered outside at eye level.

Ivy approached the first cautiously.

'Be not uncarefully,' whispered Scratch. She felt him

vibrating in her pocket and gave him an appreciative squeeze. When she was in front of the first feather, it began writing:

Prisoner 4
Name: '2 grade' Lil
Crime: Fraud
Status: Awaiting sentence

Ivy peered through the glass and found a neon-lit square room beyond. A woman with scruffy red hair, in a tartan beret and football kit, was lying on a plastic bench, picking at her nails.

The next two cells were empty, and the one after that was filled with a strange green light that made Ivy feel dizzy.

'Ghoul hole,' Scratch explained in a tinkling whisper. 'Cell for special uses with muckers. Losing of memory inside, so Lundinor being ever forgotten.'

Ivy shivered. So if a mucker went inside a ghoul hole, they lost their memory. Wow – uncommoners really did go the extra mile to keep Lundinor a secret. As she approached the next door, the feather began writing:

Prisoner 2
Name: Valian Kaye
Crime: Theft of a bell from Ethel Dread
Status: Investigation pending

Ivy gasped. *Valian*. She could see him sitting on the edge of the bench, rubbing his bare arms as if trying to warm himself. His mouth was a tight line. Ivy bit her lip. If he was in there, he must have been arrested earlier and not run away. She wondered if he'd really stolen a bell from Ethel. She wasn't sure how she felt about him being locked up. Maybe he deserved it.

She shook her head. She didn't have time to work it out. She was here for her brother. She moved on to the next cell. When she saw who was in there, her heart pounded.

Seb.

He was scrunched up in the corner, his knees tucked under his arms, the lead from his headphones creeping down his chest. His grey hood was hanging low over his eyebrows but Ivy could still see his face. There were dark circles under his eyes and a bloody scratch across his cheek.

He looks terrible. She ran her hand across the glass. She needed to get inside.

The feather swished around by her head.

Prisoner 3
Name: Unknown. Grandson of Sylvie Wrench
Crime:
Status: Awaiting interrogation

Ivy examined the cell door. There was no handle, but she saw a small opening that looked like a keyhole. With the invisibility candle in her left hand, Ivy got onto her knees to take a closer look.

There must be some way to get it open.

She did a quick inventory of her tools. Granma Sylvie's handbag contained some bits of paper, a small packet of tissues, a silk scarf and a purse full of coins. The pockets in Valian's jacket were all empty. The only thing left was the grubby piece of canvas she'd taken from the House of Bells.

Inside was the small paintbrush, hammer and the uncommon piece of string that had secured the canvas. She ran her fingers across them thoughtfully, wondering if they might be useful. She had no idea how to pick a lock; in movies people used hairpins or wire.

She grabbed the uncommon string, wondering what to do with it. The heat coming from it was especially ticklish, like warm pins and needles under her skin.

She swung it around experimentally in front of her, but nothing happened. Something about it tugged at the corners of her memory . . . She'd seen someone using it before . . .

Of course, she realized. *The puppeteer.*

She tied the string onto her middle finger, just as he'd done. Immediately the string started to move of its own accord, snaking through the air like a white cotton worm. Ivy directed it towards the lock, where it slipped inside.

She wiggled her finger slightly. She could feel the string turning inside, as if it was made of steel.

Click!

There was a deep groan and the door edged open. Ivy tugged the string out of the lock and leaped to her feet.

It worked! She couldn't believe it. She cast her eyes along the corridor to check that she was still alone, stuffed the string inside the canvas and hauled back the heavy cell door.

Seb was on his feet as she burst in. He ripped his headphones out of his ears.

'Seb!'

'*Ivy?* Where are you?' He swept back his hood, frowning as his eyes strained. 'Is this some kind of trick?'

Ivy thrust the invisibility candle into Granma Sylvie's handbag, hearing the flame crackle back to life. She watched the air around her shift for a second, and then Seb blinked.

'Ivy!' He rushed forward and grabbed her, pulling her close. His top smelled of damp sweat. 'I can't believe you're—! How did you—?'

She pushed him away. 'There's no time to explain now; we have to get out of here.'

Seb's face darkened. 'Yeah, I know.' He looked into the hallway. 'Are you on your own?'

Ivy winced. 'Not exactly.' She held the door open. 'Come on – we have to be quick.'

Just then, she heard the clack of footsteps in the corridor. 'Wait,' she whispered, shoving Seb back inside. She caught a flash of black cloak as she heaved on the cell door, leaving it ajar. Her heart was in her mouth as she waited for the footsteps to fade.

After a minute they both crept outside. Ivy checked for patrolling underguards. The place was empty.

'We've got to find a way back to the street,' she said. 'There must be a fire exit somewhere.' She dashed along the corridor, away from the reception. There was a sign on the wall pointing to the ARMOURY, with the symbol of a toilet brush next to it. Ivy turned the other way, Seb hard on her heels.

'Mmmm hhmm mmm,' came a muffled voice.

'Ivy . . .' Seb whispered. 'Did you know that your pocket's moving?'

Ivy frowned and pulled Scratch out. 'Scratch, what's up?'

'Stables horses! Outing way through stables,' he said enthusiastically. 'Scratch outside from seen.'

Seb's jaw dropped. 'Ivy, did that thing just—?'

Ivy grabbed his sweatshirt. 'It doesn't matter. Look for the stables – *now*!'

Seb began checking every door. Ivy hurried after him, trying to guess where the stables might be. Ahead, the passage split in two. There was no time to check both – Ivy thought she heard approaching footsteps. She took a sniff and tugged Seb's arm, pulling him down the left-hand passage; the air smelled fresher in that direction. Soon she could hear thuds behind the wall and then, just once, the thrilling noise of a horse neighing.

'We must be close,' she said. 'There!'

Her spirits soared as she spotted a set of double doors with smoked-glass windows. Through them, she could make out a dark hall with a high ceiling and a row of shadowy stables on either side. On the wall was a set of flashing silver horseshoes. Above them, a sign read: LIGHTNING LUCKY HORSESHOES. An archway at the opposite end of the hall led out onto a road lit by streetlamps.

Ivy hissed. 'The exit's there – I can see it!'

Seb was at her shoulder. 'Ivy, wait. What if the door's alarmed?'

Ivy glanced at the large conch shell mounted on the wall above it. 'We'll just have to make a run for it anyway. I know where we're going when we get outside.' She could only think of one place where they might be safe. 'Ethel's. I'll show you . . .' She pushed the steel bar on the door. It creaked but wouldn't budge.

Seb came to help, but it was no good. His face flushed. 'It must be jammed.'

'What?' Ivy puffed. 'Someone will come along at any moment, I just know it.' She thought of using the uncommon string again, but this door had no keyhole. 'We don't have time.'

She felt Scratch trembling. 'Gloves uncommon what you needed.'

Seb drew back. 'Seriously, you're OK with that thing talking? It's creepy.'

Ivy ignored him. *Uncommon gloves.* She remembered what Gilbert Grandiose had said in his shop: *Uncommon gloves are the keys to all Lundinor.* Maybe they were literally like keys; maybe they opened doors . . .

'He's right,' she decided. 'We need an uncommon glove to open it.'

Seb jerked his head back. 'Wait – you understand what it said?'

Ivy stared back at him.

'OK. Well, where do we get those from?' he asked.

Ivy could only think of one possibility. When she told Seb, he exclaimed, 'No way! Absolutely not! That guy is the whole reason we're down here. We can't trust him.'

Ivy knew they didn't have a choice.

Valian rose from his bench slowly, his eyebrows raised.

'You've got to be joking. You two? *You* got inside this place?'

Ivy couldn't help flashing him a smug smile but it lasted barely seconds. 'There's no time,' she said. 'We need you to open the stable door.'

Seb grunted in agreement, but didn't seem happy.

Looking slightly dazed, Valian grabbed his leather jacket from Ivy as he sauntered out of his cell. His shoulders relaxed as soon as he'd put it on. Following behind, Ivy wondered whether she and Seb had done the right thing in freeing him, or if they'd live to regret it.

At least her idea worked: when they made their way back to the stables, the door sprang open easily to Valian's gloved touch.

Soon they were out on the road, heading for Ethel's. Ivy couldn't quite believe their luck.

Chapter Fourteen

They fell through the front door of the House of Bells like three skittles.

'Valian!' Ethel shouted as soon as she saw him. 'Ivy! Sebastian . . . ?'

Ivy shoved Valian off her and struggled to her feet. She was surprised that Valian had followed them all the way, especially after what she'd read on his cell.

Seb got up and brushed the hair out of his eyes, puffing hard. Ivy wasn't sure if he was out of breath because of the run or because of what he'd seen in the streets. She guessed the underguard hadn't exactly given him a tour of Lundinor on the way to the station. She had a lot of explaining to do. So much had happened in such a short space of time.

He looked warily at Ethel and whispered down to Ivy, 'How does that lady know our names?'

Ivy narrowed her eyes. 'I don't know . . .' She was

quite sure she hadn't told Ethel her name before she escaped earlier.

'I traced Sylvie's position using a map of mine,' Ethel said, locking the front door. 'I spoke to 'er 'alf an hour ago.'

'You've spoken to Granma?' Seb repeated.

That explains it, then, Ivy thought. Her stomach clenched as she remembered that Granma Sylvie had been visited by Smokehart. 'How is she?'

Ethel sighed. 'Bloody terrified, I should say. She's had God knows who down there this morning, trying to prise answers out of 'er.' She looked them both up and down, wiping dust off Ivy's shoulder and frowning at Seb's grazed face. 'Your gran's reappearance 'as started something,' she said in an ominous tone. 'Something that involves the Dirge. A lot of people may be in danger. I 'ave to see Sylvie and work out what's going on. And you're both coming with me. It's too risky to let you out of my sight.'

Ivy could feel the relief washing over her. 'We're going to see Granma Sylvie?' She didn't think she'd ever wanted to see her granma so much in all her life. And it was evening by now – her mum and dad might be at the hospital too.

Seb looked from one to the other. 'Er – you might have forgotten, but I've just been locked in a cell for three hours,' he said sharply, turning to Ethel.

'So who are you and how do you know Granma?'

Ethel placed a hand on Ivy's shoulder. 'Looks like you've got a tale to tell. Best go out the back for it.' She looked sternly in Valian's direction. 'This one and I 'ave business to discuss.'

Ivy was happy to leave the shop floor for the quiet of the storeroom, and for the chance to talk to Seb alone. She returned the canvas, hammer, string and paintbrush to Ethel's shelves and then got out the photo of Granma Sylvie and Ethel. 'Remember this?'

Seb's eyes widened. 'Whoa . . .' He dropped onto the piano stool in the corner of the room. 'No way. That's her. That's Ethel.'

Ivy sat down opposite him and told him what she'd learned in the last few hours.

'I don't know if . . .' Seb put his face in his hands. 'Do you really believe that uncommon objects contain part of someone's' – he tapped his chest – 'you know?'

Ivy nodded as she passed Scratch to him. 'I know it sounds weird, but it's true. How else do you explain it?' She watched carefully as Seb picked up the bicycle bell. There was no reaction. 'All uncommon bells can talk,' Ivy said. 'I think Scratch speaks funny because he got damaged.'

Seb gingerly turned the bell over, holding it a distance away, as if it might explode at any moment.

Scratch giggled. 'Do you think he can see?' Seb asked. 'It's not like he has eyes.'

'Scratch hearing you can,' Scratch whirred. 'Scratch seeing can also. Eyes don't need seeing to.'

Seb jumped. 'Uh – here, you have him back.' He leaned over and dropped Scratch into Ivy's lap.

She chuckled as she put Scratch back into the handbag. She caught Seb giving her a sidelong glance: the same list of questions was running through his mind as was running through hers. There was so much they needed to talk about – but for the moment she was just glad to sit quietly with him. She'd missed him, she realized. She wouldn't tell him that, obviously. But she had.

The silence was slowly broken by voices in the front of the shop. Valian and Ethel.

'What do you mean *every waking moment*?' Valian snapped. 'I'm not following them everywhere.'

'Oh yes you are,' Ethel replied. 'They don't know nothing about the Trade. They'll be eaten alive down 'ere. You're a scout. You're street-smart by nature and they need someone to protect 'em.'

Valian sighed. Ivy could hear him pacing. 'And if I do this, you'll drop the charges? Immediately?'

'Gone,' Ethel said simply. 'But I want the bell returned, mind you.'

There was a long pause. Ivy looked at Seb. She

could tell that he didn't trust Valian either. He obviously *had* stolen that bell.

'If you shake,' Ethel said, 'then this is a binding deal. Your glove is your word.'

'I know,' Valian groaned. 'Let's just get it over with.'

When Ivy and Seb left the storeroom, they found the atmosphere in the shop like ice. Valian was looking out of the window into the street, his arms folded. Ethel was sitting at her desk, tapping a feather on the table top, staring into space.

'Company's here,' Valian announced.

Ethel turned to Ivy. 'Yes – nice to see you both again. Everything sorted?'

Ivy shrugged non-committally; she heard Seb murmur something under his breath.

'No, no,' Valian said. 'I didn't mean *them*.' He stepped away from the front door as it sprang open, a black cloud rushing in.

The desk bell shouted, '*Officer Smokehart of the First Cohort of—*' Ethel laid her hand on top to silence it.

Ivy inched backwards. *Smokehart.*

'What in the name of the dead do you think you are doing, Ms Dread?' His voice boomed around the room, making all the bells shake. They started whispering feverishly.

'Harbouring criminals?' he continued. 'Deceiving officers? There's two charges right there.' He thumped his fist into his other hand as he marched in, followed by two constables, neither of whom Ivy recognized.

Smokehart scowled at her and Seb, and pointed a long gloved finger at Valian. 'And you must have aided their escape. Don't think I won't add it to your list of charges, boy.'

Valian took a step towards Smokehart, but the two constables blocked his path.

Ethel rose from her seat. She was only a wisp of a woman, and yet when she spoke, she sounded huge. 'You will do no such thing!' she exclaimed. 'I've dropped the charges against 'im. It was a mistake. There was no missing bell.' She swept out from behind her desk and walked right up to Smokehart.

Ivy tensed.

'No one in this room 'as done anything wrong, *Officer*,' Ethel insisted. 'I suggest, seeing as this is private property, that you kindly leave!' She jabbed a finger into Smokehart's chest. The bells on the walls gasped.

Smokehart stiffened as Ethel touched him and his face became speckled with red dots. Ivy was becoming more and more familiar with the reaction, even though she didn't know why it happened. 'Ms Dread,' the underguard said. 'You are treading a fine line. You do not want to make an enemy of the law.'

Ethel stood a little straighter. 'Prove it, then,' she said. 'Prove the crimes against 'em, if you can. If not, then clear off – or I'll be featherwriting to Lady Grimes about you.'

Smokehart tightened his fists. Ivy could hear the squeak of his leather gloves. 'Let me be clear about one thing,' he said, his voice sharp. 'I will get to the bottom of what happened to Sylvie Wrench and the rest of her godforsaken family on Twelfth Night. And you' – he gestured at the four of them – '*none* of you will stand in my way!' With that, he stormed out, his constables hurrying behind.

When he was gone – and only when he was gone – Ethel's shoulders crumpled and she gave a big sigh. Valian opened his mouth.

'You can keep your comments to yourself,' she barked, pointing at him.

Ivy gazed over at the front door. 'What's Smokehart's problem?' she wondered.

Ethel shook her head. 'Smokehart loves the law above all else. There is no good or bad with him, there are just law-abiders and law-breakers. It blinds him.' She signalled to the door. 'Come on, all of you – we've got to get to Bletchy Scrubb.'

Valian sighed and shoved his hands in his pockets. 'Where the hell is *Bletchy Scrubb*?'

'In the common world,' Seb declared cheerfully, slapping him on the back. 'You know – the place where carpets stay on the floor and gloves just keep your hands warm and stuff.'

Chapter Fifteen

'Not again,' Seb moaned as he looked down at the large bag that Ethel had opened on the floor. The material was thick and tufty, covered in a flowery print. Ivy thought it looked suspiciously like carpet, but she didn't want to say anything in case she offended Ethel.

The thought that she would soon see Granma Sylvie warmed Ivy's insides, but she still sighed as she got down on her knees: she remembered how confused she'd felt crawling through Valian's suitcase the last time. She thought about shrinking again. 'Isn't there another way out of here?'

Ethel threw a tasselled pashmina over her shoulder. 'There are other ways in *an'* out,' she said, 'but not for you. Uncommoners 'ave to 'ave taken the glove at least a year ago to travel via uncommon rug, and everything else requires a licence, for which you need to pass a test.' She ushered Ivy forward.

'But why?' Ivy asked. 'Surely if I can do this, I can—'

Ethel rolled her eyes. 'Dontcha think it'd look a bit suspicious to a mucker if they saw someone riding an uncommon vacuum cleaner over Blackheath?' She pursed her lips. 'You need special training to use uncommon objects outside of undermarts. That's left to Special Branch. They're underguard whose entire job it is to 'ide Lundinor from common eyes. It's for commoners own good, of course. Clements knows the kind of chaos there'd be if everyone started using uncommon objects willy-nilly.' She laid a hand on Ivy's back. 'Now no more questions. Let's go!'

Bletchy Scrubb hospital was lit up like a giant doll's house against the black sky. Ivy could almost peek into every room, where the greenish lights illuminated a doctor typing at a desk, or a hurrying nurse, or a hallway dotted with staff. The car park was emptier than it had been that morning. Ivy brushed herself down as Ethel rubbed soothing circles on Seb's back: he already looked nauseous. In the shadows beside them, Valian slunk out of Ethel's bag and snapped it shut behind him.

'Just take some deep breaths,' Ethel advised Seb. 'The feeling should fade after a few minutes.'

Seb frowned at her, his mouth pinched shut. Ivy was glad he couldn't see Valian grinning over his shoulder.

As they approached the main entrance, Ivy looked around. There were people going in and out, smoking in huddled groups or heading for the car park. The night air was still. Ivy could hear the drone of distant traffic.

She remembered the man in grey. 'I'm pretty sure there was an uncommoner here this morning,' she told the others. 'He was acting oddly and his hands were all shrivelled and rotten.' She saw Ethel give Valian an anxious glance. 'That means he must have made an illegal trade, doesn't it?'

Ethel pursed her lips. 'For 'ands to get that damaged you'd 'ave to make lots of illegal trades. Very illegal ones. Mem—' She hesitated. 'Members of the Dirge were known to do it on purpose, as a mark of loyalty.'

Ivy had already guessed that the man in grey was looking for Granma Sylvie; it made even more sense if he was a member of the Dirge.

As they went into the hospital, Ethel got out a piece of paper and glanced at it. 'It's ward six B.'

Ivy tried to picture the man in grey again. She hadn't seen his face because of his hat, but she remembered the way he moved: stealthy and quick. Calculated.

While Ethel went to ask a nurse for directions, she whispered to Seb, 'What if the man in grey was a member of the Dirge? What if he was the one who stole Granma Sylvie's notes? That way, he'd have seen her address and . . .' She shuddered. 'Maybe he went straight to her house and searched it while we were on the bus?'

Seb had his mobile phone in his hand. He shoved it back in his pocket and rubbed his neck. For a second Ivy thought he was going to tell her she was being paranoid again, but he only shook his head.

As Ethel came back with instructions, Ivy looked around, searching for signs of uncommoners. Through an open door she caught sight of an elderly lady unpacking a small suitcase. Ivy blinked, realizing that she was half expecting the woman to crawl inside and disappear.

Seb must have noticed, because he gave her a nudge. 'We're in the common world now, remember,' he told her. 'Everything's back to normal.'

Ivy felt a twinge of disappointment. *Normal isn't always best.* Using the invisibility candle *had* been pretty awesome.

For a moment she imagined how different her life might have been if her granma's amnesia had never happened. She might have grown up knowing about Lundinor, knowing just how amazing the world really was.

They found Granma Sylvie sitting up in bed in a private room; her white-blonde hair tumbled over her shoulders and her soft cheeks were pale. 'Ivy,' she croaked. 'Sebastian.' She held open her arms and smiled.

Ivy was shocked to see her looking so weak. It was as if she'd been sick for days. She noticed a plaster cast on one hand; on the other, a patch of white sticky tape held a thin tube in place.

'I'm so sorry,' her granma said as they drew closer. 'I'm *so* sorry.'

Ivy's vision blurred as she hugged her carefully. 'This is all my fault,' Granma Sylvie whispered.

Ivy stepped back; Seb eyed Valian suspiciously before pecking his granma on the cheek.

'Are either of you hurt?' She inspected them closely.

'I'm OK,' Ivy said, wiping away a tear before her granma noticed. She didn't want to make her feel worse. Seb just shrugged.

'What about you?' Ivy asked. 'Is it just your wrist that's broken?'

'Yes – my hip's only bruised, thank goodness,' Granma Sylvie replied.

'Sylv?' At the end of the bed, Ethel cleared her throat. She took off her flowery headscarf, and her spiky black hair sprang up. Ivy got a flash of the mischievous, daring young woman she had once been; it was easy to understand why Granma Sylvie had been friends with her.

Granma Sylvie blinked, staring at Ethel like she was a ghost. Tears appeared in the corner of her eyes. 'I don't remember your face,' she said softly. 'I'm sorry, Ethel. It's only your voice that's familiar.'

Ethel nodded slowly and steadied herself against

the bed. 'That's OK,' she said, as cheerfully as she could, though Ivy could tell that she was hurt. 'It's not all goin' to come back right away.'

Granma Sylvie brought a hand up to her face, rubbing her temples. 'I wish it would; everything feels so out of reach.' She turned to Ivy and Seb. 'When I returned from surgery, my head felt fuzzy and was full of strange images – words, faces and names – nothing that made any sense. I thought they were hallucinations caused by these painkillers they've got me on. That was until I got a phone call from Ethel.'

Ivy glanced over at her. 'A phone call?'

'I thought in the circumstances featherlight mail might be a bit scary,' Ethel explained with a shrug.

Granma Sylvie continued. 'Now I think the images must be memories.'

Ivy thought how strange it must be to have memories of Lundinor come flooding back after forty years.

'The amnesia is fading – just incredibly slowly . . .' Granma Sylvie frowned at Ethel. 'Everything is still mostly blank. There are some memories that seem stronger, a particular pattern my mind keeps returning to, over and over, though I can't make sense of it. First I see a woman with sad blue eyes, and then I hear the trickle of water followed by the sound of creaking gates. Then, finally, there's this big old house full of dark faces.'

Ivy had a sudden thought. She rummaged through Granma Sylvie's handbag for the old photo. Maybe it would help jog her memory.

She opened the inside pocket – and the hairs on the back of her hand stood on end as she came across something that felt unnaturally warm. Her cheeks flushed.

She wriggled her fingers around until they found a thin curved object; it felt like it had just been under a heat lamp. As Ivy brought it out into the glare of the hospital lights, she gasped, realizing what it was.

'Your bracelet, Granma Sylvie!' she exclaimed. 'It's uncommon.' Everyone looked at her. 'I mean, er – it must be, mustn't it?'

Ethel assessed her suspiciously. 'Give it here,' she said.

Ivy handed over the half-bangle. Ethel made a quick inspection, then passed it to Valian. 'You ever seen anything like that before?' she asked him.

Seb coughed. 'That's Valian, by the way, Granma,' he said, pointing a thumb at him. 'He's with Ethel, not us.'

Valian scowled at him, then turned to Granma Sylvie, who nodded back.

Ivy racked her brains while Valian examined the piece of bangle. 'Earlier,' she said, 'in the underguard station, I overheard a conversation between Smokehart and this woman . . . er – Selena something, I can't remember.'

Valian raised his eyebrows. 'Selena *something*? Ha! Don't let anyone hear you say that back in Lundinor. Her name's Selena Grimes. She's one of the four great quartermasters of Lundinor. They're the most powerful people in any undermart.'

Seb glared at him. 'Big deal. Go on, Ivy.'

'Well, Smokehart said that Granma Sylvie appeared on his uncommon map while she was travelling in an ambulance. It must have been when the bracelet was cut off?'

Her granma sat up straighter. 'Of course.' She beamed at Ivy, then looked at the piece of bracelet in Valian's hands. 'All these years I kept it on because it was the only part of me that was whole after the accident. I had no idea what it was.'

Ivy's insides turned heavy as she realized how Granma Sylvie was feeling. It must be like finding out that your favourite possession was a fake, or being deceived by a best friend.

'Must have some sort of memory-wipe ability,' Valian deduced, turning the bracelet over in his fingers. 'The underguard use uncommon whistles to wipe people's memories, but that's permanent. Maybe the bracelet only does it while you're wearing it.'

Ethel gave the object a sidelong glance. 'It didn't just hide your memories, though, Sylv. It hid *you*. That's what its real use is. No one can hide from the underguards when they've taken the glove. *No one*. You were the first ever to do it.'

'And the rest of our family . . .' Ivy added, though it felt strange to say *our*. But they were her family too, as well as Granma Sylvie's. She wondered what her mum and dad would make of it all. Her dad especially – he had uncles now. 'They all disappeared on Twelfth Night, your mum and dad and your three brothers,' she finished. She noticed Ethel and Valian shifting uncomfortably and wondered if they knew more than they were letting on. Before she could ask them, Seb raised his voice.

'Damn it. Where *are* they?' He stared down at his mobile phone screen before looking up again. 'I've been checking ever since we got here, but there's still no text or voicemail from Mum or Dad. Didn't Dad say he'd be here by now?'

Ivy checked the clock on the wall. It was eight-thirty. 'Yeah . . . he should be. And I thought Mum would arrive before him. Did they leave a message with any of the nurses?'

Granma Sylvie shrugged. 'Not that anyone's told me.'

The room fell quiet. Ivy studied her feet, going through the possibilities in her head. When she looked up again, she saw that the others were looking anxious.

'You don't think—' Before Seb had finished speaking, a jet-black feather appeared out of nowhere and hovered in front of his face. He tried to swat it away but it dodged his hand, flew over the middle of the bed and started writing:

You have something that is valuable to us.
Now we have those who are most valuable to you.
You have two days to give us what we want.
The clock is ticking.

The feather evaporated in a tiny cloud of black smoke, and in the same spot an alarm clock appeared and bounced onto the bed with a soft thud.

For a moment Ivy stood there, dumbstruck. Then she turned to Ethel, whose face looked like it had been drained of blood. She poked the clock, turning it over so she could see the front: the bells were spotted with rust, the glass dusty. The clock face was yellowed, painted with Roman numerals, and the black hands, each as thin as a spider's leg, pointed to just after midnight.

'Black hands . . .' Valian murmured.

'What did that—?' Ivy gasped. 'I mean, who was it?'

Seb suddenly grabbed the clock. 'Ivy, I can see Mum in it . . . and Dad.' She stepped closer and took hold of it too.

Within seconds, heat was shooting through her fingers; anguished voices echoed in her ears – cries of pain. She grimaced, trying not to drop the thing. Holding an uncommon object had never hurt like that before; like it was going to burn her. 'It's uncommon,' she exclaimed. 'What does it do?'

Granma Sylvie tried to reach out towards her. 'Ivy, be careful. Ethel – should they be holding that?'

Ivy looked at the glass front. Her freckled face with its wide pale-green eyes and stubby lashes stared back at her. A voice whispered her name: *Ivy . . . Ivy . . .*

Slowly the faces of her mum and dad appeared in the glass before her. After a moment their reflections changed. The shadows under their cheekbones darkened and their skin withered as if they were starving. It was happening to Ivy's reflection too – she watched the whites of her eyes yellow and her thick hair wilt and fall out. Her hands shook, making the image blur. 'What's happening?'

Ethel leaned across the bed. 'Put it down, Ivy. It's meant to scare you.'

'It's choking me!' Seb cried. 'The hands – they're strangling me! Dad too – and Mum! We're dying! I'm watching us all die!' He let go of the clock, stumbling back.

Ivy looked into the clock face and swallowed. Her skin had now rotted away completely and her eyeballs

146

had disappeared, leaving two dark holes brimming with squirming maggots. As she watched, the delicate black minute hand of the clock reshaped itself into a chain and wrapped itself around the reflection of her dad's decaying neck. Before long, the hour hand had choked her mum, who shriveled to a skeleton.

Ivy dropped the clock, the burning sensation disappearing immediately. The noises coming from the clock were silent.

Panting, she looked from Ethel to Valian. 'What *was* that?' she asked again. She felt like she'd just watched a scene from a horror movie. 'What just happened? Where are Mum and Dad?'

Ethel picked the clock up by one of the rusty bells

and held it gingerly out in front of her. 'Uncommon alarm clocks are used as fortune tellers,' she explained, her voice full of disgust. 'Depending on the grade, they can predict anything from a thunderstorm to the age you're gonna lose your eyesight. This one, 'owever, has black 'ands and that only means one thing . . .'

Ivy shivered. She had a horrible feeling she knew what was coming.

'Uncommoners call it being dealt the "hands of fate",' Valian finished. His face was serious. 'This alarm clock counts down to the date of someone's death.'

'Are you saying that Mum and Dad . . . ?' Seb shook his head. 'There's got to be some mistake. Are the clocks ever wrong?'

Ethel rubbed her chin. 'Wrong? No. As long as the 'ands remain black, then your fate is sealed. But the clock reads the future. If you change the future, then the clock will change too.'

Ivy saw that her granma was trembling beneath the covers. She laid a hand on her arm; it was covered in goose pimples. 'Who sent it?' Granma Sylvie asked Ethel.

Ivy didn't wait for Ethel to reply. She already knew the answer. 'The Dirge,' she said. The name seemed to hang in the air. 'The black feathers, the coin, the *We can see you now* – it's them, isn't it? They *are* back.'

148

Ethel lowered her eyes. Valian's expression was grim.

'Hang on,' Seb said, exasperated. 'Ivy told me that the Dirge were never seen again after Twelfth Night 1969.'

'They weren't,' Valian said, in a cold voice. 'Everyone believed they'd gone for good.'

Ethel nodded, her face pale. 'Except now, I think that was just a foolish hope. Somewhere in the world, one of the Dirge must 'ave been waiting for you to reappear, Sylv. As for what you 'ave that's of value to 'em, I don't know.'

She looked out of the window into the dark winter evening. 'One thing's clear: wherever the Dirge fled after Twelfth Night 1969, in whichever parts of the world they've been hiding, your reappearance may 'ave just given them the incentive to come together again.'

Chapter Sixteen

Valian paced up and down at the foot of Granma Sylvie's bed. Seb had collapsed into a chair, looking drained, while Ivy curled up next to Granma Sylvie, tucking a hand through her good arm.

'If the Dirge are about to re-form,' Ethel said darkly, 'then many people are in danger, not just the ones in Lundinor. Years ago, rumour 'ad it that the Dirge wanted to use uncommon technology to control the entire common world. Taking your parents may be just the beginning. We 'ave to do something.'

'We have to track them down,' Valian said sharply. 'All five of them. I always knew they'd never really disbanded. They've been here all the time, lurking in the shadows.' There was a flicker of something in his eyes – hysteria, maybe, Ivy wasn't sure.

'It's not about *them*,' Seb retorted. 'Our *parents* have been taken! We need to find them.' He looked helplessly at Ethel. 'Can't you – you know, use something uncommon?'

Ethel sighed. 'It's not that simple, love, I'm afraid.'

Seb dropped his head into his hands. The sarcasm was gone. Ivy realized that he was in the same state of panic and desperation as her. She tried to think. 'The black feather wrote: *You have something that is valuable to us,*' she reminded everyone. 'Does anyone know what the Dirge are talking about?'

Valian shook his head. Ethel shrugged. 'It could be anything. The Dirge did everything in secret. No one knew any of their real plans. It was all rumour and speculation.'

Granma Sylvie sighed. 'It's useless me trying to remember. I have no idea.'

Ethel reached for the uncommon alarm clock again. 'By the looks of this you've got till the stroke of midnight on New Year's Eve to get an idea,' she said, not unkindly.

Two days to change the future, Ivy thought. That was it.

'We need a plan,' Ethel went on. 'There's no use moping around 'ere, the three of you, trying to figure it out. We need answers and there's only one place we're gonna get those.' She straightened, her hands on her hips. For the second time that day Ivy got the impression of a formidable woman; a warrior, with the battle lines drawn on her face to prove it. 'Ivy, Seb? You're coming back to Lundinor with me. I 'ave old friends there – people I trust – you can stay with them.'

Seb looked at Ivy. 'I'm not so sure that's a good idea. We don't fit in there. Won't we be in more danger?'

'There'll be no arguments about it,' Ethel insisted. 'If your parents 'ave been kidnapped by the Dirge, you're not going to save them from this hospital room. Besides, who's gonna protect you 'ere?'

Ivy snuggled closer to Granma Sylvie. She didn't want to leave her again, she really didn't. *But Ethel was right.* They couldn't just hang around the hospital for two days waiting to see if Granma Sylvie remembered anything. Her mum and dad were going to die if they didn't act.

Her granma frowned. 'I – I don't know . . .'

Ethel gestured around the room. 'You're safe 'ere, Sylv. The underguard 'ave already been to question you and left with nothing. The Dirge won't come after you again until the deadline's up.'

Granma Sylvie put a hand on Ivy's shoulder. 'If only I could remember . . .' She sniffed and wiped her eyes. 'What have I done? What *did* I do?'

Ivy's spirits continued to plummet. Ethel and Valian were looking at each other bleakly; whatever they were thinking, it wasn't good. Ivy had to hope she could save her mum and dad by working out what it was the Dirge wanted from Granma Sylvie. The trouble was, she didn't have a clue where to start.

She glanced over at Seb. Sometimes, when she was upset or worried, she'd look at her mum or dad and all her worries would just fade away.

Seb's head was lowered. Ivy couldn't see his eyes – but it didn't matter because she had already noticed the two dark patches that had formed on his jeans. He was crying.

Chapter Seventeen

Ivy rolled her shoulders back and groaned. Her whole body was still sore from yesterday's bike crash, and the lumpy mattress she was laying on only made things worse. She looked around at the walls of an unfamiliar bedroom. There was a single window draped with spotty yellow curtains, and an empty fireplace set between two wardrobes painted in peeling duck-egg blue.

Only the chimney breast had been wallpapered – a thick white paper veined with hundreds of different fold-lines. As Ivy watched, one corner of the paper peeled away from the wall with a loud crumpling sound and folded over into a triangle. She sat up in bed, looking on with wide eyes as the rest of the wallpaper did the same, lifting and folding, crimping and twirling. Ivy had once seen a boy at school do origami, but it had never looked this fast or intricate. In the end, the paper had rearranged itself into a vase of huge white orchids perched on the mantelpiece.

'Whoa . . .' Ivy whispered. Impressed didn't even cover it.

'You're awake then?' Seb asked from above her.

'I'm awake,' she called, yawning. They were in bunk beds. Ivy had a vague recollection of climbing some creaking wooden stairs and being escorted into the bedroom by Ethel and a kind man with a doughy face and blue eyes.

'I've been awake for an hour, listening to music,' Seb continued. 'Couldn't get back to sleep. And it's not just because this mattress seems to be filled with marbles. I can't stop thinking about Mum and Dad . . .'

Ivy's stomach turned over. For a second – for a tiny blissful second – she'd forgotten about the Dirge and the parent-napping. Her heart sank as she saw her duffel coat hanging over the back of a chair by the bed; on the cushion was Granma Sylvie's handbag, Scratch and the uncommon alarm clock.

She let her head fall back against the pillow as the vision of her parents' decaying faces swirled in front of her eyes.

The bunk bed creaked. Ivy watched Seb's legs swing over the edge, and then he landed with a thud on the polished floorboards. 'I've been thinking,' he said. 'That thing the Dirge want . . . it must be something Granma had before she disappeared on Twelfth Night 1969, so we have to find out more about her life when she was here.'

'Ethel was her closest friend,' Ivy reminded him, 'but even she doesn't know what they're after, so . . .'

'So we'll have to do some digging,' Seb decided. 'There must be other traders here who knew Granma.'

Ivy looked closely at her brother. There were dark circles around his bloodshot eyes, and after the rain yesterday, his thick blond hair was a mass of bedraggled curls.

'We're Mum and Dad's only hope, Ivy.' He grabbed a towel hanging over the end of the bunk bed. 'I'm gonna go wash my face. Let's start as soon as you're ready.'

There was a small bathroom leading off the bedroom. While Seb was getting ready, Ivy sat on the edge of her bed, thinking. So much had happened yesterday that she hadn't had time to address what was going on with *her*. She picked up Scratch and gazed at him. Her palms tingled pleasantly.

'Scratch,' she whispered. 'I need to ask you something.'

Scratch stirred. 'Ivy mornings.' He sounded as if he was yawning. 'Helpings Scratch can will.'

'Do uncommon objects ever feel . . . warm at all? Kind of like body temperature.'

'Guessings the object what depends it. Normal to no.'

Ivy bit her lip. 'It's just . . . Whenever I touch something that's uncommon, it feels warm, like it's been left out in the sun; and then the feeling spreads and starts to tickle . . . And then sometimes, if I concentrate really hard, I kind of' – she hesitated – 'hear voices coming from it . . .'

Scratch was still. 'Ivy,' he said quietly. 'Scratch meanings to know.' He turned warmer, vibrating strongly in her hands.

'What is it?' She could sense his fear. 'It's OK, Scratch. You can tell me.'

The bell spoke softly. 'Ivy beings a . . . a *whisperer*.'

'A what?'

'A whisperer.' Scratch sounded terrified. 'Whispering gift of sensing soul a part trapped inside.'

He fell silent for a moment. How strange it must be for him, she thought; after all, *he* was uncommon. She tried to still her hands, but she was too overwhelmed. Whispering seemed like a very dangerous gift; a gift she hadn't asked for. 'Do you know anything else about it? Like, can I turn it off?'

Scratch quivered. 'Strong must beings Ivy's whispering, voices hearing because only if strong. But . . . Scratch does understandings not enough: whispering beings impossible to children.'

Ivy tried to decipher what Scratch was saying. He was talking fast, sounding nervous, which made it more difficult for her to understand. 'Whisperers are normally adults, then?'

'Yes's. Running it through family normals. Bad things to whisperers happen long ago.'

'Bad things?' Ivy asked uneasily.

'Whisperers forcing to work,' Scratch said. 'Chased whisperers throughout history. Must be whisperers quiet.'

Ivy held her breath. Being a whisperer sounded like more of a curse than a blessing. She would have to be careful who she told. Before she could ask Scratch any more, Seb burst through the door.

'Bathroom's free,' he said, swinging a towel over his shoulder. He was wearing a fresh hoodie and jeans, and his trainers had been cleaned. Ethel must have been back to Granma Sylvie's house and picked them up last night.

'I hope you actually washed,' Ivy said with a frown. He never did at home. His bedroom always smelled of sweat.

Seb threw the towel at her bed. 'I hope you can actually reach the basin, titch.'

Valian was waiting on the landing when they emerged from their room. Against the light from the second-floor window, his slim, black silhouette looked like a ninja. Ivy saw that he was scowling.

'You're still here?' Seb grunted. 'Aren't there some other people you can go and annoy?'

Ivy headed towards the stairs. 'He has to be here,' she said.

'Don't think I don't have better things to do with my time than babysit you losers,' Valian muttered, following them. 'But I shook on it with Ethel, so I have to be your bodyguard till the end of trade. *Every waking moment*, she said. Brilliant.'

Seb looked at him. 'Do you see us bringing out the party poppers?'

Ivy gritted her teeth. Valian was going to get in the way of their digging, and besides, she didn't trust him. The way his eyes had lit up yesterday when they'd been talking about the Dirge . . . Just the thought made her skin crawl.

As they went downstairs, Ivy stuffed her hands into her empty coat pockets. She'd left Granma Sylvie's cumbersome handbag and all its contents in the bedroom, along with the uncommon alarm clock and Thaddeus Kandinsky's useless guide. She almost put Scratch in her pocket, but in the end it seemed safer for him to stay behind.

Down in the hall, Ivy quickly remembered everything from the previous evening – the threadbare patterned carpet, the worn leather sofas, the set of sun-bleached watercolours. It looked like a crummy seaside hotel, badly in need of refurbishment.

Valian gestured around. 'Welcome to the Cabbage Moon Inn,' he announced sarcastically. 'Best guestrooms in the land.'

They walked into a large dining room that echoed with the clink of glasses and laughter. Delicate paper snowflakes dangled from the ceiling and wreaths heavy with berries hung on the walls. Ivy could smell bacon and baked beans. Long wooden tables seated all manner of Hobsmatched guests, and behind a bar at the back, the doughy-faced man was busy polishing some cutlery.

'That's the innkeeper, Mr Littlefair,' Valian whispered in her ear. 'Old friend of Ethel's.'

Ivy did a double take as she approached the bar. There were bottles and flasks of different coloured fluids, some steaming and bubbling, and above, where the pint glasses and wine glasses would have been stored in a normal pub, hung rows and rows of spectacles, sunglasses and reading glasses.

'Why is th—?'

Her question was lost as Seb bumped into her, knocking her aside.

'Mind out!' he called, ducking his head and swatting at something. Ivy looked up and saw a meringue-topped pie crust bouncing through the air. 'Don't tell me you eat stuff that moves now,' Seb groaned. 'Doesn't that give you indigestion?'

'*That* is Lemon Meringue Sky,' Valian corrected him. 'A speciality in Lundinor. You should try some.' He nodded at the nearest table, which had been taken by a large family wearing matching zookeeper uniforms.

In the middle were bowls of cinnamon porridge and cereal, racks of toast and tiny jars of jam. 'Breakfast comes with the room so you might as well eat.' He pointed to a table at the back. 'There's space over there.'

Ivy flashed a look at Seb. She wondered if he had any appetite; she certainly didn't. Still, they could try asking the diners about Granma Sylvie.

She glanced back at the family in zookeeper uniforms. The youngest, a toddler with an Elizabethan ruff around his neck (which also doubled as a bib), was throwing something lumpy and glittery at his siblings. Ivy couldn't believe that this – that Lundinor – was part of normal life for some families.

As they headed across the room, a few dishes caught Ivy's eye. There were pies with jumping crusts, muffins that sprouted fresh strawberries and even pots of honey that buzzed like a hive itself. 'I didn't expect food to be uncommon,' she admitted.

'It isn't,' Valian told her. 'What they prepare it with is – ladles, terrines, ovens, hot plates – they make normal recipes turn out crazy.' He whipped a paper napkin off a table and laid it out on his other hand. 'Special Branch are always arresting uncommoners for cooking with uncommon objects outside undermarts. It's illegal, but so tempting.'

Ivy frowned as she watched him take item after

item off people's tables, laying them delicately on his serviette, as if it was some kind of buffet.

She looked at the other customers. By the far door a group of men in football shirts, fishing waders and feathered hats were toasting each other with champagne glasses full of something green and sparkling. On the benches opposite them, a couple of traders in base-ball caps and choirboy robes shared a dark bottle of something that appeared to be smoking. Ivy wondered what uncommoners' lives were like when they weren't in Lundinor. 'Where do uncommoners live the rest of the year?' she asked.

Valian pinched a slice of toast and deposited it on his napkin. 'Same places muckers do. Your neighbour could be an uncommoner – you'd never know. Uncommoners learn to live secret lives, keeping their collections hidden. Special Branch monitor the use of uncommon objects outside undermarts. Lundinor's only open three times a year; most uncommoners have regular jobs the rest of the time. The big traders spend months building up their collection or getting someone to do it for them.' He pointed to his chest with his thumb, carefully balancing his mountain of food. 'That's my job. I'm a scout. People pay me to find stuff for them.'

Seb smiled. 'Oh, of course. I should've guessed you were the lynchpin that holds everything together.'

Valian gritted his teeth. 'You don't understand anything. Uncommoners have a vital role in the world. It's their responsibility to keep commoners safe from uncommon objects. Sometimes Special Branch have to interfere and then wipe everyone's memories afterwards; sometimes it's just a simple case of covering something up. It's a fine balance.'

Seb sighed. 'Come on, Ivy. Let's sit down.' He stretched his leg over the bench and took a seat. At the far end of the table sat an old lady with white hair. Valian muttered something before slinking over to the bar with his stolen breakfast.

The old lady shuffled up as Ivy took a seat next to Seb. Ivy liked the look of her immediately. She wore spectacles and a voluminous powder-blue dress that, along with her straw bonnet, made her look like Little Bo-Peep's grandmother.

'Morning, dears,' she cooed. She reached for the handle of her teacup but missed.

Seb chuckled. Ivy elbowed him in the side. 'Morning,' she said, giving her brother a stern look.

'I think I saw you two come in last night,' the lady twittered. 'You're staying in the room next to me. I'm Violet.'

Ivy looked into her cornflower-blue eyes, which appeared cloudy behind her thick glasses. She doubted she could see anything at all.

'Not many people arrive *after* the start of Trade these days,' she continued. 'Heard there's going to be some sort of flash sale today at the Wanderer's Warehouse on Makeshift Avenue. I expect you're here for that.'

Ivy gave an awkward cough and looked at Seb. It wasn't as if they could tell anyone what they were *really* there for.

Just then, a girl wearing a pale pink ballet tutu and a tattered waistcoat approached the table. 'What'll it be then?' she asked, a feather poised in her hand.

Ivy looked at Seb.

'Um, can we just have a drink?' he asked.

'Of course,' the girl said. 'Hundred Punch OK?'

Ivy shrugged. 'Sure.'

The girl winked and laid two pairs of spectacles down in front of them before heading back to the bar.

Ivy stared at them, puzzled, while Seb rubbed a hand through his hair. 'This day is only going to get weirder, isn't it?' he muttered.

Violet smiled kindly. 'First time drinking from glasses, eh?' she guessed. 'Just open them up – they'll do the rest.'

Frowning, Seb carefully opened out his spectacles – half moon, with golden frames. Once the second arm had been fully extended, the glasses leaped up off the table and transformed into a drinking goblet – the lenses spiralled into a tall glass trumpet, while the frames

164

formed a handle. Seb almost fell off the bench. 'Whoa!'

Ivy studied the sunglasses in front of her. She opened them carefully and watched, astonished, as they morphed into a smoked-glass goblet.

The girl in the tutu came over with a large porcelain jug, poured a fizzing transparent liquid into both glasses and left.

Ivy looked at it nervously. 'Bottoms up, I guess,' she said before taking a sip. The Hundred Punch was the strangest, most amazing thing she had ever tasted. At first it was cool and sweet and fizzy like apple-ade; then it became thick and foamy and tasted of buttery shortbread; then it went warm and gooey and filled Ivy's mouth with the sharp tang of rhubarb. 'It's like three flavours in one,' she exclaimed.

Seb nodded, his mouth twitching into a smile.

'Actually there's a hundred,' Violet explained. 'That's where it gets its name from. A hundred different tastes, a hundred different ways to make you feel better.'

Seb smacked his lips. 'Mine's super sweet, like liquid candyfloss.'

Grinning, Ivy took another mouthful and let the

tastes roll around her tongue. 'I think my one might be apple pie – or maybe apple and rhubarb crumble . . .' She felt light and happy, as if she was about to fly away on one of the bubbles. Seb laughed at her, making her snort into her goblet.

Her exhilaration was short-lived. All at once she remembered why they were there: *Mum and Dad.* How could she enjoy herself while they were in mortal danger? Just thinking about her parents locked away somewhere made her want to cry. They might not even be together.

She looked over at Violet. Maybe this was a good time to start investigating. 'Er – what is it you sell?' she asked.

'Me?' The old lady's cheeks turned pink. 'You really want to know?'

Seb stared at Ivy and shook his head, but she ignored him.

'Yeah, really.'

Violet beamed. 'I'm a button trader,' she said. 'Violet Eyelet's Button Apothecary – you'll find me on the Gauntlet, just past Dragon Lane.

'Buttons do all kinds of things,' she continued. 'I love buttons – always have. I'd rather have a button than anything.' She reached into a pocket and brought out an avocado-green plastic button with ridges around the edge. 'They treat ailments, mostly. There's a button for everything these days. All you have to do is put it in your top pocket and the problem goes away. I've been using this one for a few days now to treat a little twinge in my left knee.'

Seb fought to keep his face expressionless. Ivy couldn't tell whether he was about to laugh or gasp with shock.

'Not many uncommoners use them any more,' Violet went on. 'I guess people think they're old fashioned, or . . . what is it they say? Alternative?' She fished around in another pocket and brought out a second button. This one was ivory-coloured, with three holes and an old trail of pink thread. 'This one works a treat for restoring health. The number of holes equates to the number of times you can use it, so this has three good uses. Here you go.'

Ivy stuttered, 'Oh – oh no, you don't have to . . .'

Violet Eyelet shook her head. 'No, no, don't be silly. You keep it. Payment for listening to me go on.'

Ivy smiled and took the button gratefully, stowing it away in her jeans pocket. She looked at the soft creases in Violet's face and wondered how old she was.

'I'm Ivy, by the way,' she said. 'This is my brother, Seb. We're not here for that sale thing you were talking about. We're here to find out more about our granma. She used to be a trader here, years ago.'

Violet managed to get a grip on her cup and took a

sip of tea. 'Anything I can do to help?'

Seb leaned forward. 'Yeah, actually. Her name was Sylvie Wrench. Do you know anything about her?'

Violet's face lit up. 'Sylvie! Well, knot my cottons! She's back? Is she OK?'

Ivy winced. 'Yeah, sort of.'

'We were never meant to be friends, Sylv and I,' the old lady said. 'Octavius Wrench – Sylvie's father – he didn't like his workers mixing with his children. It wasn't seen as proper.'

Ivy straightened. 'Wait . . . You worked for our great-grandfather? Is that what the Wrenches sold? Buttons?'

Violet chuckled. 'Octavius Wrench interested in buttons? No, no. I was only able to sell buttons *later*. When I first took the glove, I became a scout; it was the easiest way to build a career in those days. Most people scouted for one of the big companies; I chose the Wrenches because they paid well and let you keep anything they didn't want. Octavius never wanted buttons – he thought they were useless.'

Seb asked, 'Do you remember when you last saw our granma?' Ivy could see him trying to connect the dots.

'Of *course* I do. I had to give enough underguard statements on the subject. It was back in sixty-nine; Twelfth Night . . . a few hours before the Great Battle. I'd just dropped off my last haul of scouted objects at the Wrench Mansion. Sylvie and I crossed paths as I was leaving.' She shivered, sending her glasses slipping to the end of her nose. 'Creepy place, their house; always used to turn my stitches wonky, if you know what I mean. I'm quite glad it's disappeared really.'

Ivy thought she'd misheard. 'Sorry – *disappeared*?'

'Oh yes. The Wrenches were incredibly secretive. They didn't trust anyone; that's why they built their mansion with uncommon bricks so no one outside the family would ever find it. Uncommon bricks like to move, you see, so the house never stayed in the same place.' Violet took another sip of tea. 'Only members of the Wrench family knew how to find the secret entrance. I had to be escorted blindfold every time I went to drop off my scout haul. Sylvie did it occasionally – that's how we became friends.'

'Do you know *why* our granma disappeared that night?' Ivy asked hurriedly.

Violet shook her head, glancing around warily. 'It's not for me to speculate,' she whispered. 'I'm just glad she's OK.'

Ivy turned to Seb, her eyes wide. 'What about the mansion? There might be answers there.'

'No one has seen it since Twelfth Night 1969,' Violet told her. 'The underguard looked for years but even they had to give up.'

Ivy had a pretty good idea who'd been involved in that search. *Smokehart.*

'The house was designed so that any member of the family could find it easily,' Violet said. 'Theoretically it should still work for you two. Why don't you ask Sylvie?'

'She's forgotten everything,' Seb explained. He propped his chin on his hand.

Not everything, Ivy remembered. Granma Sylvie did have memories returning – they were just very vague. She tried to remember what her granma had said. *A woman with sad blue eyes, the sound of water . . .*

'Is there a map of Lundinor we could look at?' she asked. 'I think I've got an idea.'

Violet brightened. 'There's a street map on the side of the featherlight mailhouse in the centre of town, though I don't know how up to date it is.'

Ivy got to her feet and turned to Seb. 'Come on,' she said. 'There's no time to lose.'

'Wait. Before you go . . .' Violet lowered her voice. 'Sylvie was a good friend of mine, but not many people around here will tell you the same. Especially now. Something's got the underguard riled and there have been whispers about the Fallen—' She broke off and shook her head. 'Well, let's just call them whispers about terrible things; things that would make the toughest of traders wish to stay silent.'

Chapter Eighteen

'The street bell said to take a left here,' Ivy reminded the others as she turned the corner. Seb was striding beside her, with Valian plodding along behind them like an unwanted smell.

They came to a paved square dotted with café tables and traders leisurely sipping fizzing drinks – Hundred Punch, Ivy guessed. In the middle was a spindly red-brick tower that stood over thirty metres tall. There were holes in the walls that looked like small dark windows.

'That must be it,' Ivy figured; 'the featherlight mailhouse.'

Seb craned his neck. 'It looks like it's gonna fall over any second.'

Ivy saw that the slate roof tiles were shaking and sliding over each other. Hundreds of different-coloured feathers flew out of a large hole where the chimney would be.

Valian shouldered his way past them. 'Well, it's

old enough. And so is the poor guy who runs it. Albert Merribus, he's called. He must have been mail-master for nearly half a century. The map's on the other side.'

As they got closer, Ivy heard the bricks crunching and cracking, as if they too were moving. She watched an uncommoner approach one of the dark windows and stuff his hand inside. He retrieved a feather, which he then used to scribble something in the air. When he'd finished, the feather disappeared back through the hole.

Ivy replayed Granma Sylvie's memory sequence in her head. She'd have to search the map thoroughly, but this might just work. Right now her parents could be— But she couldn't let herself think about it. Just then, she heard high-pitched voices.

'Go on, throw it at him. I bet you can't make that third hole on the right.'

'Yeah? Watch this!'

As they rounded the tower, Ivy saw a group of children holding something in their hands – though she couldn't quite see what.

'Here goes!' One of the boys took aim and lobbed whatever it was at the tower. Ivy thought she saw a flash of shiny plastic before the object hit the wall with a squelch, turning into yellowy-green goo on impact.

'Ha! Told you. Hear that, Merribus!' the boy called,

cupping his hands around his mouth. 'You're safe *this* time!'

Anger bubbled up inside Ivy. She herself hadn't come up against bullies before, probably because nobody was going to pick on Seb's little sister (his arms were bigger then anyone else's at their school). But whoever the old man inside the tower was, he didn't deserve this.

'That's horrible!' she shouted, unable to bite her tongue. 'Stop it!'

One of the boys started to taunt her, but when he saw Seb and Valian come up on either side, he reconsidered and made a run for it. The others scarpered after him.

Ivy shook her head and turned back to the tower. The map was easy to spot, although it wasn't what she had expected.

'So . . . it's made of rubbish,' Seb said in a flat voice. 'How eco-friendly.'

Ivy looked closely. The map was constructed from odd twigs and branches, tea bags, paper and glass – all nailed or tied with twine to the wall. Street names had been painted on in black paint, and there were deep white scratches in the bricks behind the map, as if the objects had been dragged over them again and again.

'The map changes,' Valian explained, seeing her expression. 'Things move in Lundinor, so they move on this.'

Ivy stepped back to try and get her bearings. 'The Gauntlet's here' – she pointed, spotting a long straight road running through the centre of the main cavern – 'so Ethel's must be about there . . .' She stretched up on tiptoe to indicate a spot a couple of metres above her head. But she was looking for something else.

'Seb, see if you can see any water on the map – a lake or a pond or anything like that.'

He scanned the wall. 'You wanna tell me why?'

'It's what Granma Sylvie remembered,' Ivy replied. 'She had a memory of a gloomy old house full of faces – that must be the mansion. But before that, she said she heard the sound of water. So maybe the two are connected?'

Seb shuffled from side to side, peering at the top of the map. 'I can't see anything that looks like a lake. There's some sort of pond up there, and maybe that old kettle with the streamer hanging down is a fountain, but I can't be certain. This place is huge. We've got more chance of finding a needle in a haystack than the Wrench Mansion.'

'Wrench Mansion?' said a deep voice. 'Ha!'

Ivy froze. It had come from a small window only a metre away from her head. She approached it cautiously.

'Er, hello?' She laid her hands on the unsteady bricks and peered into the hole. 'Do you know something about the Wrench Mansion?'

The hole wasn't big enough for her head to fit through, so she had a restricted view. She caught glimpses of a messy office, the air filled with floating feather down and scraps of paper. There were ink splodges on the floor and mugs of old tea on the wooden desk. The place smelled of tea bags and mouldy cheese. 'Anybody there?'

A gruff voice answered, 'I'll tell you something about the Wrench Mansion . . .' Suddenly a face appeared through the window. Ivy sprang back as she saw a wild mane of white-blond hair, a grizzled chin, pockmarked cheeks and fierce blue eyes.

'No point bloody looking for it,' Albert Merribus growled. 'It's only gonna be found when it wants to be. I've had enough of you young fame-hunters trying to locate it. All anyone's ever discovered is that it must be north of here, because that's the direction the feathers fly in.'

Ivy searched for a response. 'I, er—'

Suddenly a voice like an ice storm swept in from somewhere over Ivy's shoulder.

'*IS THERE ANYTHING THE MATTER HERE, MERRIBUS?*'

Ivy turned to find herself face-to-waist with Officer Smokehart. She looked helplessly for Seb, who was retreating round the tower, his eyes wide. Valian was nowhere to be seen.

'Have these two been hassling you?' Smokehart asked Merribus. He lowered his head towards Ivy's. She could see the reflection of her pink freckled face in his dark glasses.

Merribus grumbled.

'Trust me, Albert,' Smokehart went on, 'this is Ivy *Wrench*. She doesn't deserve any chances, so don't hold back.'

Ivy clenched her fists and stared him down. He was just like one of those bullies. 'It's Ivy *Sparrow*,' she said through gritted teeth.

'Thanks for the concern, Officer, but there's nothing to report this time,' Merribus said finally. He scratched his chin as he peered at Ivy. She noticed that he was wearing navy felt gloves. 'They were looking for an address that's impossible to find, is all. Waste of their time and mine. Now, good day!' And with that, Merribus and his explosion of white hair disappeared inside the tower.

Smokehart's thin lips curled into a snarl as he rounded on Ivy and Seb. 'I'm watching you,' he said. 'Both of you.' And his voice cut like a knife.

Chapter Nineteen

Ivy scuffed the toes of her wellies over the cobbles. Seb was standing beside her, his hands stuffed into the front pocket of his hoodie. The pond he had spotted on the map had turned out to be a public toilet – which wasn't the greatest surprise, as all the street bells they'd asked for directions had repeatedly told them that there was no pond in Lundinor.

'What do we do if the fountain's not here?' Seb asked as they trudged down another street. 'Mum and Dad . . .' He couldn't finish.

Ivy was trying to keep calm. *Two days.* That was it. She could almost hear the uncommon alarm clock ticking past with every pace she took.

She heard footsteps behind her and turned. *Valian.* She scowled at him. She'd like to know what he'd been up to back there – vanishing as soon as Smokehart appeared. She wished Ethel had never shaken his hand. That way, at least she and Seb could hold a conversation in private.

'That last street bell said it was just up here on the left,' she reminded Seb. She hoped it really was. At least the street bells had actually heard of a fountain – though Ivy knew that the sound of water could have come from anything.

They had reached a busy street lined with shops selling everything from uncommon feather dusters to snow-globe cameras and everlasting baubles. Ivy couldn't hear water anywhere.

'It must be around here somewhere,' Seb said determinedly. 'Let's split up.' He tugged Ivy to one side. Valian followed. 'That means you go in the opposite direction,' he told him.

Valian shrugged and headed away from them.

Ivy looked around. She didn't really know what she was looking for. The only fountains she'd ever seen had been huge things like the ones in Trafalgar Square.

'What if it's just a small one; something you'd have in your back garden?'

'Or,' Seb said, stopping abruptly, 'in your wall.' He pointed and hurried on. 'Come on!'

Ivy dashed after him. He'd turned down a narrow path between two shops.

'What do you think that is?' Seb asked, gesturing towards one of the shadowy walls.

Ivy squinted. Hidden behind a tangle of weeds in the brickwork was a tall, arched metal panel. Ivy assumed from its distinctive pale green colour that it was made of copper, like the Statue of Liberty. At the bottom was a semicircular basin, with a chipped spout above it.

'A fountain,' she observed, brushing back the trailing plants. 'But it's empty. It can't have been used in years.'

Ivy wondered if she could use her whispering to test a theory. She laid her hand against the fountain. Unlike the surrounding air, the metal was the temperature of warm breath. If she blanked out every noise around her and focused on it, she could even hear soft whispers.

'It's uncommon,' she told him. 'I'm certain of it.'

Seb was looking at her strangely. 'Right . . .'

Ivy ignored his expression and scooped some of the mud and leaves out of the basin. At the bottom was a strange sundial, with initials for the four directions of the compass.

'What clues do we have?' she asked. 'Let's go through them again.'

He sighed. 'Granma Sylvie remembered hearing water, and then she saw the house . . .'

Ivy touched the large *N*. 'The feathers fly north,' she said, as if in a trance. 'That's what Merribus said.'

'But this fountain's dry,' Seb pointed out, 'and hasn't been used in ages.'

It hasn't been used, Ivy thought. *Of course.* 'We need

water! Seb, see if you can get some from the street. It doesn't have to be much.'

Minutes later, Seb returned with a grubby black bucket. Valian was beside him.

'I hear there's no need for us to continue searching,' Valian announced with sarcastic cheer. 'You've found a fountain?'

Ivy sighed and snatched the bucket, then looked up and down the alleyway. It was empty and the fountain couldn't easily be seen from the street. Satisfied that they were unlikely to attract attention, she held the bucket over the basin.

Unable to cross her fingers, she made a wish and poured the liquid in slowly.

They waited in silence for a minute, but nothing happened.

'Well, that was an anti-climax,' Seb said, rolling up the sleeves of his hoodie. 'Do you think we need to do something else, maybe?' He dipped his fingers in the water and swished it around. The sound bounced off the opposite wall.

'I think you just did something,' Ivy said. 'We needed the *sound* of water, remember?'

She felt the air around her shiver as if a truck were passing by. Something in the ground rumbled, deep and low. She shot a look to either side. 'Can you two hear that?'

Seb nodded.

Ivy glanced at her feet. The earth between the cobbles was trembling.

'It's coming from the fountain,' Valian told them, his eyes fixed on the pale-green archway.

All at once the brick wall on either side of the fountain shook violently, sending cement dust up into the air. The metal basin screeched as it drew away from the wall. Ivy reached out for Seb's arm, steadying herself. 'What's happening?'

He pointed to the arched surround. 'Ivy, look!'

The metal was glowing as if being heated in a furnace. Gradually it formed the long iron bars of a gate. With a sharp screech, two cast-iron posts emerged from the bricks on either side. The gate between them

was shrouded in cobwebs, and at the very top was a single word in wrought iron: WRENCH.

Ivy stumbled backwards. Valian's eyes were gleaming. 'No way,' he breathed. 'No way. You've actually found the Wrench Mansion. It must be because you're related; I don't know why else it would open for you.'

Seb rubbed dust out of his eyes. 'This can't be the Wrench Mansion; it isn't a house. It's just a gate.'

He was right. No matter how hard Ivy looked, there was nothing behind the gate except what had been there before. A brick wall.

Valian smiled mischievously. 'Why don't you open it and see?' He stepped back and gestured for Seb to do the honours.

Seb rolled his eyes. 'Fine.' He laid both hands on the ornate iron bars and pushed.

Ivy was right behind him. As the gates parted, she saw a line of pitch-black, which expanded as the gates swung open, revealing a muddy pathway on the other side.

'Valian's right,' she exclaimed, laying a hand on Seb's arm. She peered into the gloom. The path was littered with leaves and bordered on both sides by an overgrown lawn. In the distance she could see a dark structure looming against an evening sky. A chill swept over her as she watched. It was like looking through an arched window into another world.

Valian touched the gate carefully with his gloved hands. 'I can't believe it. This place hasn't been opened since Twelfth Night 1969.' He stepped through the gates.

Seb thrust a hand in front of him. 'Hang on – we don't even know what's in there. I mean, look at the place; it's like Dracula's holiday home.'

'That doesn't matter. There are gonna be more clues in there than you'll find out here. You've got less than two days to save your parents, remember?'

Ivy peered through the gate, focusing on her mum and dad, wherever they were. She suspected that she and Seb would have to take risks if they wanted to get them back. *We're coming to get you, Mum,* she said to herself. *Just hold on, Dad. We're coming.*

Chapter Twenty

Once they were on the path the air became cooler. Ivy pulled her coat tight around her and looked up at the full moon. They couldn't be underground in Lundinor any more. She wondered if the mansion was in London – or, indeed, in another part of the world. She smelled fresh pine and guessed that the dark shadow in the distance was a forest.

Set up on the hill, the mansion stood four storeys high. Hunched stone figures perched on the corners of the mansard roof and the leaded glass windows glittered in the moonlight. Ivy looked back at the gate as they walked away. It formed part of an iron fence that ran round the lawn. She couldn't see anything beyond it.

Valian strode up the hill as if he had a train to catch. His eagerness made Ivy uneasy. She looked at Seb and wondered if he too was worrying about Valian's real motives – and about what they were going to find inside Granma Sylvie's childhood home.

The front door was, unsurprisingly, black. Seb examined the small stained-glass window set into the top. 'It's of a crow decapitating a snake,' he said. '*Homely.*'

Valian tried the door handle first, but it wasn't till Seb touched it that it decided to move. A long hiss escaped as it opened up.

Inside, they found a thickly carpeted entrance hall overlooked by two galleries, with a grand staircase and an ornate moulded ceiling. Uncommon lemon squeezers glowed into brightness as the three of them made their way in and gazed around. The walls were covered with dark oil paintings. Some depicted the house itself, while others were portraits of finely dressed ladies and gentlemen. Ivy felt their yellow eyes boring into her as she turned. *A house of faces*, she thought. *That's what Granma Sylvie described in her recurring memory.*

The air smelled musty; the whole place was still and empty. Ivy ventured towards one of the portraits. Forty years of dust had settled over the faces of the subjects, so she pulled down her sleeve and stretched up to rub it off.

'Careful,' Seb warned, coming to join her. 'This place doesn't exactly say *make yourself at home.*'

'No,' Ivy admitted. *But it was Granma's home once.* She swept her sleeve over the painting till six pairs of eyes peeped through the dust at her. She knew one pair very well. 'There she is,' she said, clearing the dust off Granma Sylvie's face. She must have been about Ivy's age when the portrait was done. Her golden hair was shoulder length, her eyes amber, and there were deep dimples in her cheeks.

Seb rubbed more dust off the bottom of the frame and saw a label. '*The Family Wrench, 1960,*' he read. 'That's nine years before they all disappeared.'

Ivy looked at the frame. It had six names written on it. She tried to match everyone up. Granma Sylvie's three brothers were beside her: Cartimore, a blond, plump-cheeked pig of a boy; Silas, raven-haired and sickly, and Norton – scruffy-looking, with two teeth missing. Ivy shivered as she studied their dull eyes and pinched expressions.

Granma Sylvie's mother, Helena, was the smallest figure in the picture. She had tightly curled mousy hair and wide, almond-shaped eyes, like Granma Sylvie, except that Helena's were blue. There was something haunted and lonely about them that made Ivy feel sad.

Sad blue eyes . . . Recalling Granma Sylvie's memories again, Ivy realized she must have been seeing the face of her mother.

In the centre of the portrait stood Octavius, Granma Sylvie's father. He had a strong, imperious face with a wide jaw and jutting cheekbones. Above his thin mouth rested a waxed black moustache.

'So that's the relatives,' Seb joked, his eyes wide. 'Can't exactly see Mum and Dad inviting them over for Christmas.'

Ivy agreed. Still, she tried to take note of all of their faces so that she could describe them to Granma Sylvie. She wondered how she was doing in hospital and hoped she hadn't had any more visits from the Dirge.

'Hey, look,' Seb said. Beneath the portrait was a chest of drawers, on top of which rested a rotary-dial telephone, a glass ashtray and a stack of newspapers – all covered in at least two centimetres of furry dust. Seb shook one of them clean and read the date: *4 January 1969.*

4 January . . . Ivy wondered if there was anything significant about it. 'That's from the day before Twelfth Night,' she realized.

The paper was called the *Barrow Post.* Ivy leaned over to read it. She deduced it must be an uncommon publication because it was priced at 0.2 grade.

'*Candidates Promise Fallen Guild Crackdown,*' she read, her voice echoing through the hall. '*In the final push before tomorrow's elections, the two leading candidates in the race for Quartermaster of the Great Cavern – Octavius Wrench and Mr Punch – have been speaking in the Market Cross. Wrench today promised to drive out corruption within the underguard by bringing in his own team of investigators to help deal with the Fallen Guild.*'

Seb looked up at the portrait. 'Octavius was running for Quartermaster,' he said. 'I guess he must have lost. Didn't you say that Mr Punch is the Quartermaster now?'

Before Ivy could answer, she spied Valian scuttling up the main stairs towards the gallery. 'Aren't you meant to be our bodyguard?' she called.

Valian turned round, his face flushed. 'I thought we should probably split up to search the place for clues. It'll be quicker.'

Ivy exchanged a suspicious look with Seb.

'Let him go,' Seb said quietly. 'It'll smell better without him around.'

Once Valian had disappeared upstairs, Seb folded up the edition of the *Barrow Post* and stuffed it into his hoodie pocket. Ivy searched through the chest of drawers. There were a number of other items – a pair of polished brogues, a horsehair hairbrush, some unopened letters addressed to Master Norton – but nothing of any real interest, until . . .

Ivy gazed at the bottom drawer. Unlike the others, it had a keyhole. She gave it a yank but it didn't budge. *If only I still had that uncommon string.* 'It's locked. Do you think you can break it open?'

Seb rolled up his sleeves and got down on his knees. 'Maybe.' He looked underneath the chest and gave it a thump, then pulled hard on the drawer handle.

Eventually the drawer snapped open and a cream paper envelope fluttered out. Ivy snatched it up off the floor. Her fingers sizzled with heat immediately. On the front, in scratchy black ink, was written:

Send to:
The Private Study of Octavius Wrench,
The Wrench Mansion

There was a slightly smudged ink stamp on the top right corner that said DIRECT MAIL.

'It's uncommon,' Ivy said.

Seb went still. 'How do you know that? You did it before with the fountain. Am I missing something?'

Ivy pushed a tangle of curls behind her ear. She had to tell Seb; he was her brother. She looked at him seriously. 'Promise you won't make me feel like a freak if I tell you?'

Seb frowned. 'Uh, *OK* . . .'

'The thing is,' Ivy said quietly, 'well – when I touch something uncommon, I can kind of sense it. First my skin goes really warm and tingly where I've touched it and then' – she hesitated – 'I hear these whispers coming from it.'

'What? How does that—?' Before Seb could formulate a question, Ivy recounted everything Scratch had explained to her that morning.

'*Whispering*,' Seb repeated when she'd finished. 'Right.' He gave her a thin smile. 'And there's me thinking this couldn't get any weirder. I mean, I'm no expert, but hearing voices in your head—'

Ivy stamped her foot. 'Seb! They're not in my head! And anyway, you promised not to make me feel like a freak.'

He held up his hands. 'OK, OK.' He pointed to the envelope. 'Well, look, if it's definitely uncommon, then what do you think it does?'

'I don't know.' She turned it over. It wasn't sealed. 'Maybe we should read what's inside? It might be a clue to what happened on Twelfth Night.' She slid her fingers under the flap on the back and opened it.

And suddenly the room was spinning.

'Seb!'

'Ivy?!'

The hallway – with its grand staircase and dark oil paintings – was swept away. Ivy felt herself rotating. She didn't want to reach out with her arms in case she hit something.

After a few seconds the spinning slowed down and a new room came into focus. Ivy fell to her knees and closed her eyes to let the dizziness subside. Her stomach was doing somersaults.

'Ivy?' Seb's hand was on her shoulder. 'You need to see this.'

Slowly she opened her eyes and struggled to her feet.

They were in a lavishly furnished room lined with mahogany bookcases and glass cabinets. Pale silvery light fell from a set of uncommon milk jugs hovering in the centre of the ceiling.

Seb took a few steps forward. 'Where are we?' He ran his fingers along the top of a studded green leather chair tucked under a desk. They came away covered in grey fur.

Everything in the room was covered in such a thick layer of dust and cobwebs that Ivy could barely make out individual objects – a crystal decanter and matching glasses; an ivory tusk displayed in a glass cabinet. No one had been there for a very long time.

She scanned the walls and spotted a single portrait hanging between two bookcases. 'Octavius Wrench,' she said, recognizing him from the portrait in the entrance hall. She re-read the front of the envelope. '*The Private Study of Octavius Wrench.* Do you think this is it?'

'Must be. The books are all about the history of Lundinor or uncommon stuff.' Seb looked around the room. 'It's weird that there isn't a door anywhere. That envelope must be the only way in or out. Maybe if you open it up, it takes us out again . . .'

Ivy considered the envelope carefully. Seb could be right. Common envelopes open, so uncommon envelopes might just open different kinds of things. 'Let's look around for more clues before we go,' she suggested. 'We might be close to something.'

Seb nodded and headed towards the bookcases on the other side of the room.

Ivy took a few shaky steps forward. She leaned against a wooden chair back, trying to steady herself. She could be imagining it, but the walls still looked like they were spinning . . . or maybe it was just the wallpaper.

The wall beside her was covered in thick, emerald-green paper decorated with vine leaves. Ivy traced one of them with her fingers. There was a loud *pop!* and the vine she had been touching sprang out of the paper and reached for her.

She jumped back. 'Seb! Over here!'

As he scurried over, a sound like the popping of a hundred champagne corks filled the room, and every vine started crawling out of the wall, unravelling and twisting itself into a rope.

Seb raised an eyebrow. 'Cool. Even better than the origami wallpaper in our room.'

The ropes had soon formed a large rectangular door with an oval doorknob. Eventually they creaked to a stop and, with a click, the door fell ajar.

'Not *another* doorway,' Ivy groaned. She felt like they'd had their fair share already. They'd better take a careful look before they stepped through.

Seb laid a hand on a leafy green frond. 'Seems OK. Let's see where it leads.'

'Wait—!' Ivy started, but it was too late. The vines scratched and crackled as the door opened and Seb stepped through.

A cloud of rust-red dust rose into the air and Ivy put a hand over her mouth. 'Seb!' she spluttered.

'I'm OK,' he coughed. 'You can come in.'

Ivy heaved a chair over from the study and used it to wedge the door open before tentatively crossing the threshold. 'Where are we?'

They had emerged into a small circular room. It appeared to be empty. 'I don't know,' Seb said. 'But there's loads more doors here.'

Ivy squinted, wiping the dust out of her eyes. Through the haze she could just see that the room wasn't in fact circular. It had straight walls, with a door in each. She turned slowly on the spot, counting. Altogether, there were . . .

'Six,' she said. Her voice ricocheted around the chamber, making her jump. Two of the doors were made of stone, one was stainless steel, while another was crafted from old splintered wood. The fifth had been carved from some kind of glittering rock that Ivy had never seen before. Each door had the same design drawn upon it. A dinner-plate-sized image of a coin – *the crooked sixpence.*

'The Dirge,' Ivy realized, with a shiver.

Seb's shoulders tensed. 'What did you say?'

Suddenly Ivy was spotting clues everywhere, like spiders waiting in the shadows – six doors, for the six members of the Fallen Guild, each door with a word engraved above it.

'The code names,' she said aloud. A sense of dread swelled inside her as she read them. '*Monkshood, Ragwort, Wolfsbane, Nightshade, Hemlock . . .*' She froze. 'Seb – Ethel told me about this place. It was called the Hexroom. It's where the Dirge used to meet.' The very thought made Ivy's skin crawl. She wondered what number of evil, whispered conversations had taken place here years ago.

She stopped when she was facing the open door they'd come in through – the one made of vine leaves. She slowly pushed it to, just enough to see behind it. The reverse of the door was crafted from stone and bore the image of a crooked sixpence, just like the others. The head on the sixpence was the same one she'd seen on the coin from Granma Sylvie's house – a hooded face with a large square jaw. A mask covered the person's eyes and nose, ending in pointed tusks at each side of the mouth. Chiselled into the bricks above was another code-name: *Blackclaw.*

Seb gasped. 'Wait – does that mean what I think it means?'

Ivy nodded slowly, still in a daze. She glanced towards the study. 'There's only one reason why Octavius Wrench would have a secret door that led to the Hexroom.'

Seb turned towards her, his eyes wide. 'He was a member of the Dirge . . . Granma's dad was a member of the Dirge.' He started pacing. 'I don't get it. Do you think she knew? Do you think anyone knows?'

Images swept through Ivy's mind: six hooded figures emerging from the shadows, each wearing a different mask . . . She grabbed her brother's arm. 'Seb, we need to get out of here.'

He went still. 'Yeah, yeah we do.' He headed towards the door of vines, pushing the chair away. Ivy took one last glance around as she followed. She looked down at her wellies, which had left footprints in the dust. It lay in an unbroken sheet across the Hexroom – except in two places. There was a bare triangle at the foot of two of the six doors, as if they'd recently been opened. One was the stainless steel one belonging to Wolfsbane; the other was the wooden door belonging to Ragwort. Ivy barely had time to register the information, let alone figure out what it meant, before Seb called out urgently to her.

'Come on! Quickly.'

At that very moment, the air was pierced with a long, high-pitched howl. The sound bounced off all six walls of the Hexroom and echoed around Octavius Wrench's

study. Every hair on Ivy's body stood on end. 'What was that?' she whispered. It sounded like an animal, an angry one. As the howl filled her ears again, she tried to pinpoint where it was coming from.

Seb tugged her sleeve. 'There.' He pointed over at the Wolfsbane door. There was a line of sickly green light around the edges and Ivy could hear scratching behind it. Her mouth went dry as the smell of damp dog crept into her nostrils. She thought she recognized it.

'Whatever's behind that door,' she said, 'I think it might have been there yesterday morning, during the break-in at Granma Sylvie's.'

Seb grabbed her arm and they ran.

Chapter Twenty-one

Ivy scrambled back into the study, tripping over the thick carpet. She grabbed Seb's sweatshirt with one hand and tore open the uncommon envelope with the other. The room spun. Mahogany bookcases and silvery milk jugs disappeared – until the murky hallway of the Wrench Mansion zoomed around them.

Ivy bent forward, heaving air into her lungs. That had been *way* too close. Whatever was down there, it had almost caught them. She looked up into the gloom of the hallway, surprisingly relieved to be back there. She and Seb had reappeared at the foot of the stairs. Valian was nowhere to be seen. Ivy wondered what he'd been getting up to.

For a moment she stood there while she tried to think. She and Seb were still panting for breath. It was the only noise breaking the silence until—

'I'd bet my claws you thought I couldn't follow you here, didn't you?' asked a voice.

Ivy spun round.

Standing on the other side of the hall was a *giant wolf*. Its pelt was shiny black with flecks of silver, and there was a diamond-encrusted pet collar hanging loosely around its neck. Ivy stiffened. The beast's eyes were blood-red with a small white pupil, like that of some demon robot.

'Now, isn't this interesting,' the wolf purred. It curled thick, leathery lips around each word. 'I wonder what you're both doing back in your ancestral home . . .'

A prickle ran between Ivy's shoulder blades. *It can talk. The wolf can talk.*

'Have you hidden it *here*? I wonder.' The wolf's voice was expressive but hoarse, like a Shakespearean actor with a sore throat.

Ivy forced her shaking hands into fists. 'L-leave us alone,' she stammered.

Seb lunged in front of her. 'Shoo! Get out of here! Go on – go!'

The wolf raised a tufty eyebrow. '*Shoo?*' It threw back its head and opened its considerable jaws, laughing. Ivy couldn't help but notice the rows of razor-sharp teeth.

'Ivy—' Seb stumbled on the carpet.

She looked frantically around the hall. There was no way out. The wolf was standing between them and the front door. Their only option was to run up the stairs and hope it wasn't fast enough to catch them.

It swished its long tail. 'I'll ask you once more, little

children.' It lowered its head and its voice deepened. 'Where have you hidden it?'

Ivy cried out. She couldn't help it. The creature was monstrous; whatever she'd been expecting to find here, it wasn't this.

The wolf's ears pricked up like great hairy antennae. 'Oh dear, are you crying because the big bad wolf asked you a question? How does the story go . . . ?' it asked, chuckling. 'The big bad wolf will blow your house down if—?' It shook its head. 'No, no, that's not the one. How about: the big bad wolf will eat your grandma if—? Nope, that's not it. Ah, yes, I know. What about: the big bad wolf will skin you alive if you don't tell him where you've hidden his mistress's property?' It bared more teeth. 'Now, that's much more accurate.'

Ivy gulped in terror. She wanted to move – she knew she should move – but she just couldn't. If she turned and ran, the wolf would catch her – it was twice her size, with rippling muscles and long claws; of *course* it would. She remembered measuring the paw-prints in Granma Sylvie's kitchen against her hand and decided that she was definitely facing their owner.

Something clattered on the gallery. The wolf looked up as a dark figure shot across the landing.

Valian.

Ivy recognized his nimble figure, but his face was unusually puffy and red and the sleeves of his leather jacket had been pushed up to the elbow. He launched himself off the stairs and landed in a crouch. In his hand he was swinging what appeared to be a large brown elastic band.

'*Ivy, Seb!*' he yelled. '*The door!*'

Ivy hesitated. How could they get to it? There was no way—

Valian released the elastic band. It shot towards the wolf like a dart, snapping into different shapes as it did so. First it made a circle, and a pair of brass cymbals appeared in the centre; then it formed a long curved shape, and a trombone appeared. Instruments continued popping out of it – drums, trumpets, violins. They crashed into the wolf in a screeching, squawking, tooting riot, and then started playing *on* its body.

The cymbals clashed around its head; the drumsticks beat its back. The wolf thrashed to and fro, and Ivy wondered whether she and Seb might manage to run past before it got free.

Seb was obviously thinking the same thing. 'Ivy – go!'

He pushed her, and suddenly she was running as hard as she could. Valian and Seb reached the front door first and opened it so she could go straight through.

They sprinted down the hill towards the gate without looking back. Ivy's wellies slapped down on the path, resonating out into the night.

Valian threw open the iron gates, and they hurtled through – only to meet a brick wall on the other side. Rebounding off it, Seb turned and shut the gates with an almighty clang. For an instant Ivy thought she glimpsed a wet black nose fading through the gates like a ghost, but perhaps it was just a shadow.

The gate-posts vibrated before sinking back into the bricks, and within seconds the pale-green fountain had re-formed.

Ivy eyed Valian as the three of them leaned over, panting. She remembered that he'd been out of breath even before the wolf showed up.

She straightened and looked around. The fountain was back in place, the basin full of dry leaves, as if there had never been any water in it. The alleyway appeared to be in a different part of Lundinor. There was no one around.

She tried to gather her thoughts.

Granma Sylvie's father, Octavius, was Blackclaw, a member of the Dirge . . .

She didn't know what implications that had for getting her parents back.

A giant talking wolf was there during the break-in at Granma Sylvie's . . .

Which meant that it probably worked for the Dirge. Ivy wondered if it had been following them.

Valian was up to something at the mansion . . .

She couldn't figure him out. One minute he was saving them, the next he was abandoning them. And he kept disappearing. It was like that was the only thing he knew how to do.

In her mind's eye she saw the thin black hands of the uncommon alarm clock ticking away. All she knew for certain was that she didn't have much time to work it all out.

Chapter Twenty-two

The Cabbage Moon Inn was quieter than it had been at breakfast. The dining room smelled of lemon washing-up liquid and tea. A few members of staff were mopping the floor, or wiping down tables.

Still weary, Ivy slumped into a chair in the far corner. As Seb and Valian took a seat opposite, the innkeeper, Mr Littlefair, came over.

'What can I get the three of you, then?' he asked in a jolly voice. 'You look like you're thirsty.'

Ivy considered ordering Hundred Punch, but instead opted for water. Seb ordered a Coke and Valian chose something called a Bugtop.

After the man had moved on to the next table, Ivy folded her arms and leaned forward. 'Can we have some privacy, please?' she asked Valian.

'Yeah,' Seb agreed. 'Go be someone else's bad smell.'

To Ivy's surprise, Valian seemed more than happy to leave them. Once he was out of earshot, she leaned closer to Seb. 'I don't trust him. He was up to something in the mansion – I just know it.'

Seb's eyes followed Valian across the room. 'Why did Ethel choose *him* to look out for us? We don't know anything about him. Where's his home and family? He doesn't seem to have any friends; that says a lot.'

Ivy nodded in agreement – though she doubted they could give Valian the slip in Lundinor. She turned her thoughts back to the mansion. 'What we learned about Octavius Wrench . . .' she whispered, not daring to voice the terrible truth. 'Apart from being horrifically awful, does that help us with Mum and Dad at all?'

Seb frowned. 'Maybe Granma stole something from him . . . And now he wants it back.'

Ivy shook her head. 'He can't want it back. There's no way he'd still be alive today – Twelfth Night 1969 was over forty years ago.' She thought for a moment. 'Do you still have that newspaper?'

Seb stuffed a hand into his pocket. 'Yeah . . .' He sounded surprised to find that the paper had actually made it back with him.

Ivy spread it out on the table. Seb shuffled round so that they could read it together:

Whoever wins the election for quartermaster, the task ahead is a formidable one. In the last six months 97% of assaults on uncommoners in undermarts were made by members of the dead community. Notably, selkies account for over half of these, closely followed by creeps and ghouls. In every case, the crooked sixpence of the Fallen Guild was found at the scene. Many people are questioning the nature of the partnership between the dead and the Fallen Guild, speculating that the Fallen Guild have been offering more than grade for the services of members of the dead community. Whatever is truly behind their allegiance, it can only be fuelling rumours of a dead uprising. So far only three members of the dead community have been prosecuted. Underguards claim that not enough witnesses are coming forward to give evidence.

Octavius Wrench's manifesto outlines stricter penalties to deal with the races of the dead. He said today: 'Evil-doers will be rooted out by any means necessary. Members of the dead who continue to disobey our laws will be expunged.'

The current Quartermaster standing for re-election, Mr Punch, responded, saying: 'Yes, there is evil at work within Lundinor, but the way to overcome this is not by perpetuating fear, but by strengthening our communities and working together to make the undermart a safer place. Our ancient traditions are built on communication and trust, and if we each hold fast to these, we will prevail.'

Polls suggest that Wrench has a narrow lead over Mr Punch going into tomorrow morning, but everything could change on the day.

Ivy swallowed. 'Did you read that bit at the end?'

'Hang on, I'm not as fast as you.' Seb was still focused on the foot of the page.

Mr Littlefair set two pairs of spectacles down on the table, which instantly transformed into pint glasses. He filled them with water and Coke respectively before moving on. Seb looked up. 'Thanks.' He grabbed his drink and took a long slurp. 'I don't get it. Octavius Wrench was standing for election to fight the Dirge, but *he* was one of them. And what's all that stuff about the races of the dead?'

Ivy remembered the portrait of Octavius in his study. She wondered how she and Seb would even begin to tell Granma Sylvie that her father was responsible for the kidnapping of children and the deaths of innocent people. It would break her heart. Even Ivy felt ashamed, and Octavius didn't exactly feel like part of her family. 'Maybe he was on a power trip.' She recalled how Ethel had described the Dirge: secretive, calculating and ruthless. They had fooled everyone. It seemed likely that they'd infiltrated as much of Lundinor as they could.

'Do you think this all has something to do with why Granma ran away on Twelfth Night?' Seb asked. 'She might have found out about Octavius being in the Dirge and been too frightened to stay.'

Ivy picked up her glass. 'That doesn't sound like

Granma Sylvie.' The Granma Sylvie she knew would never have run away from anything. She was always telling Ivy to face her problems head on. 'There must be something else we're missing.'

As she took a sip of water, Ivy cast her eyes thoughtfully around the dining room. She spotted Violet Eyelet sitting in a booth opposite, eating a piece of cake topped with glowing orange cream. As she looked on a group of tall men and women swept in, heading for a table in the centre. The ladies wore long taffeta gowns, while the men were in trousers or floor-length tunics. They glided over the floor as if they were on wheels.

'Seb . . .' Ivy whispered, unsettled by this. 'Look at them. Is it just me or is there something not quite . . . ?'

She didn't need to finish her sentence. Before taking their seats, they all removed their various overcoats, capes and hats. As one of the women's long skirts lifted, Ivy realized that there was nothing between her and the floor.

Nothing. As in absolutely nothing. Just air.

Ivy couldn't take her eyes off them. She watched one man with curly black hair lay his cavalier's hat down on the chair opposite. Instead of reaching *over* the table, however, his hand went straight *through* it.

She grabbed Seb's arm. 'Did you see that?'

Seb was transfixed. 'Yeah. Whatever uncommon thing he's using, we need to get us one. We could pretty much walk through walls with that.'

On the other side of the room, Violet Eyelet caught their eyes. She looked at the floating uncommoners and then came shuffling across the dining room, cake plate in hand.

'Try and take some deep breaths,' she told them. 'It's always a shock the first time you realize they're dead.' She sat down next to Seb, her huge skirt billowing up like a marshmallow.

'Dead?' Seb batted the skirt out of his face. '*What?!*'

Ivy looked back at the group: the innkeeper had

already taken their orders and now they were chatting as they waited for their drinks.

'What do you mean *dead*?' she asked.

Violet smiled nervously as she put down her plate. 'Well, the thing is, Lundinor isn't just home to *living* traders; it opens its gates to dead ones too. When an uncommon object is formed, only *part* of a soul gets trapped inside; the rest turns into one of the dead. There are hundreds of different races.' She lowered her thick spectacles to study the floating figures. 'I think those might be ghouls. You can always tell because ghouls can't be earthed – they wear long clothes to *cover the gap*.'

Ivy went rigid in her seat. No one else in the dining room seemed the least bit concerned about the ghouls; indeed, they looked quite friendly.

They can't be dead, she thought. *They're walking around.*

'Oh, I know it seems rather creepy,' Violet went on. 'Believe me, when I first found out about the dead, I kept looking over my shoulder, expecting things to jump out of shadows. But it isn't like that; at least, not any more. The dead and the living mix together happily now. When I was a little girl, it was exciting finding out about the dead – about all the new races being discovered, and what they could do. A new list was published every year in *Farrow's Guide for the Travelling Tradesman*.'

Seb, who was looking rather pale, swallowed and raised his empty glass. 'Excuse me?' he said, looking up. Ivy turned round and saw Mr Littlefair.

'Can I get some of that Hundred stuff please?' Seb asked. 'The one that makes you feel good?' He ran a shaky hand through his hair and stared at Ivy. 'I never thought I'd ever say this and mean it, but *I see dead people.* I need sugar to help me deal with that.'

Ivy smiled weakly, knowing exactly how he felt. *I can handle this,* she told herself. She'd got over uncommon objects; she could deal with dead people . . . walking around. She looked at the newspaper article and picked out the phrase *members of the dead.* 'Were the dead ever involved with the Dirge?' she asked Violet.

'The D—?' Violet clamped her lips together. 'You mean, the Fallen Guild?' she whispered.

'Yes,' Ivy said, forgetting that no one used their true name. 'Did the dead ever have anything to do with them?'

Violet's spectacles dropped further down her nose as she bent her head. 'Yes, of course. Many of the races of the dead worked for the Fallen Guild when they were at their most powerful. It was just one dead attack after another back then. On Twelfth Night 1969, it was the dead that fought on the side of the Fallen Guild – but no one talks about that any more. It was a long time ago.

The dead have been law-abiding citizens for decades; they've tried to put the mistakes of the past behind them.'

Ivy remembered what Ethel had said about the Dirge raising an army of sorts. She must have meant an army of the dead. She pictured a troop of zombies staggering towards her, and shuddered. It was easy to see why everyone was so eager to believe that the Dirge had gone.

Ivy heard something fizzing, and turned to find Valian standing beside her, a tankard of frothy black liquid in his hand. It smelled like aniseed. 'Thought you might like some company.' He squashed into the booth beside them.

Seb grabbed his pint glass right after the innkeeper had filled it with Hundred Punch, and started slugging it down, glowering at Valian as he did so.

'The thing to know about the dead is that they're just like the living – some are good, some are bad,' Valian explained.

Great, Ivy thought. *He's been listening, then*.

'Mostly they're hired to do illegal stuff, 'cos they don't mind breaking the rules and it's difficult to impose GUT law on creatures that can move faster than light, or disappear, or fly.'

Ivy thought back to the talking wolf in the Wrench Mansion. She had thought she'd seen it poke its nose *through* the iron gates. 'That wolf,' she said to Valian. 'Was it dead?'

'Yes.'

'A dead wolf?' Violet mused. 'Ooh, it must have been a grim-wolf. They're meant to be very shy.'

Ivy was fairly certain 'shy' wasn't the right word to describe it.

'The question isn't what the wolf is,' Valian said. 'It's *whose* it is. It must have been working for somebody.'

'For the Dirge,' Ivy said coldly. 'It was there, at Granma's house yesterday.'

'Members of the Fallen Guild were at Sylvie's house?' Violet exclaimed. 'No, there must be some mistake. They disbanded decades ago. It's not possible.' She shook her head, her glasses wobbling.

Seb ignored her and leaned forward. 'The wolf said that it had a mistress,' he remembered. 'So one of the members of the Dirge must be a woman.'

'*Wolfsbane*,' Ivy remembered. 'That was the door it came out of in the Hexroom. And it asked us where we'd hidden *it* – whatever it is the Dirge want from Granma Sylvie.'

Violet muttered to herself while pushing cake crumbs around her plate. 'The Fallen Guild . . . all those years . . .'

Ivy watched the crumbs curiously. They reminded her of something. 'The dust on the Hexroom floor . . .' she said. 'It had only been disturbed in two places. One was outside the Wolfsbane door, but the other was in front of the wooden door belonging to Ragwort. I think they're the only doors that have been opened.'

Seb placed his glass down on the table. 'Wolfsbane and Ragwort.'

Ivy shivered. 'Do you think *they* took Mum and Dad? Do you think they're both still in Lundinor?' She looked around the room.

'You've already seen one of them,' Seb reminded her. 'That man with the creepy hands in Bletchy Scrubb hospital.'

The man in grey. Ivy didn't think Seb had been listening when she told him she suspected he was a member of the Dirge. 'If Wolfsbane is a woman, then the man in grey must be Ragwort,' she said.

'Exactly. And right now they could be anyone. We can't trust men or women, dead or not, or people wearing gloves. That's, like, everyone in Lundinor.'

Ivy glanced warily at Valian and Violet. They couldn't trust *anyone.*

Chapter Twenty-three

In the dusty case of the uncommon alarm clock I see Mum's face appear out of the darkness. Her eyes are squeezed shut in pain, her lips black. Her wispy brown hair begins to whiten and her face lengthens into that of another . . . Dad. His glasses are smashed, his blue eyes wide with fear. There is blood streaked across his cheeks. For unbearable moments I watch him – until finally his mouth rips open in a scream, tears falling freely to his chin. The spindly hands of the uncommon alarm clock begin to whirl, blurring his face. They whir around, getting faster and faster. The air rushes out of my lungs. Panic begins to fill me like rising water. I can't . . . move . . .

This is it. I haven't been able to save them . . . My parents are going to die.

The alarm clock rings—

'Ivy? Ivy!'

Seb's voice pierced Ivy's mind. The alarm clock dissolved into darkness. She struggled for air.

'Ivy, wake up!'

Groggily she opened her eyes and heaved herself upright. The bedroom light was on. Seb was standing in front of her, already dressed. She rubbed her eyes. 'What time is it?'

Seb shook his head. 'It's early,' he said. 'Are you OK? It sounded like you were having a nightmare.'

Ivy glanced at the uncommon alarm clock on the chair by her bunk. 'I'm fine – it's just . . . we don't have much time. There's only one day left.'

Seb reached for the clock. In the quiet of the bedroom they could hear it ticking. 'Every step we take, it's like I can feel it getting closer,' he murmured. 'I keep wanting to shout at someone, you know? I want to ask *why* this is happening to us. What did we do to deserve it?'

Ivy felt angry too, but she had tried to push the feeling away. Her mum had told her once that anger could burn you up if you weren't careful.

Seb put down the alarm clock. 'We have no time to lose. I'm gonna go and ask some questions. Someone must know something about Granma that'll give us a clue. I'll meet you back in the dining room in an hour.' He paused. 'You know how Dad always says, *We just need a bit of luck*? Well, that's what I feel like right now.' He sighed as he opened the door. 'Do you think he's OK – I mean, wherever they've got him?'

Ivy shook her head. It was bad enough that her mum and dad weren't there. The idea of them locked away somewhere in the Dirge's control made her go cold inside. 'Hey,' she said. 'Keep an eye on Valian.'

Seb's mouth drew into a line. 'I'll try and lose him the first chance I get.'

After the door shut behind him, Ivy sat up in bed, thinking. Seb was right. There was no way they'd solve this without a bit of luck. Luck was the only reason they'd found the Wrench Mansion in the first place, and even after their visit yesterday, they still knew very little about what was going on; they were no closer to rescuing their parents.

Ivy threw back her duvet and got up. As her feet touched the floor, her skin prickled. She had the distinct – and very strange– feeling that something was watching her. She looked around, but there was nothing but old furniture and shadows. The uncommon wallpaper had rearranged itself into an ornate lamp, which was standing proudly on the floor. Ivy sighed. She hadn't woken up properly.

Before heading downstairs she put Scratch in her pocket. It would be nice not to be totally alone; for some reason talking to Scratch yesterday had made her feel better. Maybe it was because he was one of the few uncommon objects in which she could see all that was good about Lundinor. She stuffed Thaddeus

Kandinsky's copy of *Lundinor: Farrow's Guide for the Travelling Tradesman* in her pocket too. After Violet had mentioned it yesterday, Ivy thought she'd have another go at reading it.

She entered the dining room expecting Valian to be waiting for her, but he was nowhere to be seen. Mr Littlefair told her that he had followed Seb outside earlier.

Ivy gazed around the room. A couple of traders were gobbling down the last of their breakfast, while two waitresses were busy clearing up after the main rush. A half-empty dish of what looked like custard was making strange whistling noises in the corner.

Ivy went back to the door. There was no point waiting around. She would see what she could learn on her own and meet Seb in an hour.

Out on the Gauntlet she reached into her pocket and pressed the lever on Scratch's side. 'Any advice where to go?' she asked. The street was already filling up with uncommoners. Traders were rolling back awnings, sweeping tables clean and unloading their wares.

'Trying the other quarters?' he suggested.

Ivy dodged a small, portly man carrying a bundle of hay on his shoulders. 'The other quarters?'

'Undermarts always be quarters divided into,' Scratch said. 'Why that's four quartermasters in charging.

Lundinor quarters namings: the Great Cavern – beings of the biggest – the East End, the West End, and then of the Dead End.'

Remembering the ghouls in the dining room, Ivy gulped. 'The Dead End?'

'Yes, yes,' Scratch said. 'Tradings for the dead there happens.'

'Right.' Ivy ran a hand through her curls. *Best to avoid that one then.* 'What about the other two?'

Scratch jingled. 'Expensive beings the West End. All sellers furniture, of boutiques fashion and cafés. Opposite beings the East End.'

Ivy stopped at a crossroads and felt a sudden chill. She looked over her shoulder, sensing someone following her, but she could see no one. She shook her head before continuing. That nightmare she'd experienced was just making her paranoid.

She wondered where the Granma Sylvie from that old photo would have gone when she was in Lundinor. The Wrenches seemed quite posh – their house was huge. But Ivy had the feeling that Granma Sylvie wasn't like them. She'd been best friends with Ethel, after all. 'Which way to the East End?'

Scratch nudged her hand. 'Leftings.'

As Ivy walked, she saw that the drains at the side of the road were glossy with moisture. It looked silver, like snail slime. She wondered if it rained in Lundinor.

Maybe there was something uncommon that could do that . . . It was odd to have drains underground otherwise.

She passed a young man in a cloth cap, galoshes and kipper tie, who was selling uncommon tea-strainers – the kind Ivy's mum used. The man held the strainer in front of him and gave it a gentle tap. With a scraping sound, the object stretched to the size of a washing basket. Now, every hole was filled with a rolled sheet of canvas.

'Uncommon tea-strainers!' the man called. 'Great for storage – hold all your important documents in your pocket.' He slotted a roll of paper into an empty hole. The tea-strainer promptly returned to its former size with a clean *snikt*. 'Only two grade! Best you'll find in Lundinor!'

The man's stall was full of strange trading memorabilia – chalkboards, scales, old gloves, tin signs. Hanging from a pole at the top was a print of a poem entitled 'Grading'.

1 and 2 are easy to view,
3 and 4 take a bit more,
5 is a search,
6 is a quest,
Finding 7 demands your best.
8 is every true scout's dream,
While 9 has only thrice been seen.

But the find that beguiles all trading men is that rarest of rare – the Great Grade 10.

Ivy watched as a smartly dressed man bartered for a tea-strainer. No money changed hands; only objects. The stallholder handed over one of his tea-strainers, while the man tendered a spoon and two feathers in return. Afterwards they shook hands.

She puzzled over it as she continued. Uncommon objects must be exchanged, she figured, not bought. They were graded one to ten and then swapped. A bit like comics or trading cards.

As she turned a corner, she got a whiff of something nasty – sewage or overflowing rubbish bins – but it was gone in a moment, as if carried away on a breeze. At the end of the road a crowd had formed. Beyond them, some uncommoners in long white robes were singing.

Ivy moved in closer to listen.

'. . . *let yourselves be light, from now on our troubles will be out of sight . . .*'

The choir was performing *Have Yourself a Merry Little Christmas*, a song Ivy had heard on the radio at home. Each voice seemed to soar, lifting Ivy up with it. The tune reminded her of Christmas Day: her mum laughing while cooking lunch and her dad cracking jokes as she and Seb helped him set the table.

All at once Ivy noticed that there was something odd

about the singers. Their skin appeared to be glowing, and when she checked the ground beneath them, their white robes faded into thin air.

Scratch tinkled in Ivy's pocket. 'Spectres beautiful,' he said to her. 'Favourite they Scratch are.'

So that's what they are, she thought. *A race of the dead.* She had to admit that spectres didn't look scary at all. She wondered if she'd got the wrong impression of the dead. Maybe what Valian said was true. The dead were just like the living. Most were good, but there were also a few bad apples.

She got *Farrow's Guide* out of her pocket and looked around: she was heading down a dimly lit street bordered on one side by a shallow trench of stagnant water. It smelled foul, like rotten vegetables, so Ivy assumed it was some kind of sewer. She held a sleeve over her nose as she continued.

There were no stalls here; the pavements were empty. Ahead, on the cobbled road, stood a cement mixer, a heap of broken masonry and a pile of sand. Someone had evidently been making some repairs. The shops were all shut. Hand-scrawled wooden signs announced: *Closing Down Sale* or *Moving* or *Find Our New Store in the West End!*

Ivy looked at the drain and wondered if the smell had driven everyone away. Rivulets of soapy water still ran between the cobbles; maybe someone had been trying to clean up. She turned her attention back to *Farrow's Guide.* There must be a reason why it seemed like utter nonsense; she had no idea how it was meant to be helpful otherwise.

Or do I?

'Maybe it's a code,' she whispered to herself. That way, if the guide got into common hands, no one would be able to read it. She turned to a page in the middle and tried to spot a pattern in the first line of text.

Seva ŋr chak tec halbeht ŋitŋiots pep theede . . .

She groaned. It was impossible. It was like someone had got the guide and shaken it up so that the letters fell into all kinds of random places. Everything was upside down and back to fr—

Ivy quickly reached into her coat pocket. 'Scratch,' she said. 'Can you read this to me?'

She held him above the page. Asking a bell with no eyes to read something was probably the stupidest thing she'd ever done, but Scratch had said that you didn't always need eyes to see.

'Scratch readings is back-to-fronted problem too,' he admitted.

'That's perfect,' Ivy encouraged. 'Just read exactly what you see.'

'Huh-hum.' Scratch coughed before beginning.

'Entrance to the Dead End of Lundinor is only possible via the Well at the World's End, the deepest point in the Blackheath caverns. Once here, the answer to a simple riddle gives traders access to the markets on the other side.'

It worked! 'Go on,' Ivy said. 'You're doing really well.'

Scratch vibrated. 'Common races of the dead you may meet on your travels are: one, ghosts (also known as wisps, geists and gwei). Ghosts represent only a vague trace of a soul, and have no powers to substantiate. They are the least powerful of the races and are characterized by their dizzy, disorientated characters, which make them unsuitable for serious roles in trade. Because of their fleeting form they can travel huge distances in seconds, and before the advent of featherlight mail in the seventeenth century, ghosts were used to pass messages over long distances. The Great Chinese Whisper Calamity of 1549 is said to have been caused by one particular gwei who failed to deliver a message accurately because, as one witness reported, he was "not all there".'

Ivy felt more hopeful. Just think what else the guide might contain! She would ask Scratch to read the maps next, and then anything that might tell her what the market was like back when Granma Sylvie was trading.

'Two, Eyre Folk,' Scratch continued with a jingle. 'Easily recognized by their pale skin and inhuman speed and strength, Eyre Folk are likely to be responsible for the common *"vampire" myth because of their uncontrollable tendency to "spook" – a physical reaction to a heightened emotional state, during which their skin appears to sweat blood.'* Scratch suddenly stopped. 'Ivy, Ivy. Everything not some right.'

Ivy heard a splash. She looked back at the drain and spotted a stream of thick, slimy water flowing into the road, oozing towards her. It had a familiar silvery sheen.

'Ivy, get here out!' Scratch shouted, shaking violently. 'Get here out!'

'Wh-what's happening?' Ivy stammered, stuffing Scratch and the guide into her pocket as she ran. She checked back over her shoulder. The glistening trail had slithered across the cobbles after her and split in two, pinning her in on the opposite pavement.

She hadn't been imagining it; something *had* been following her.

Slime.

Only, it's not just slime, is it?

With a sound like a burp, a large dark *thing* rose up out of the gloop. The back of Ivy's neck prickled as the creature made its way towards her, dragging its huge body over the cobbles. It was roughly person-shaped, with broad shoulders and a scaly lower half that disappeared into the sludge. Its skin was covered in long dripping hair the colour of seaweed; it looked like something out of an old monster movie.

Ivy hurriedly weighed up her options. There was

no escape route – the shops were closed; the street was deserted. She wondered if she could outrun the creature. It was taking a long time to reach her, sticking to the part of the road that was wet. Maybe it could only move on water. Ivy glanced over her shoulder at the pile of sand beside the cement mixer. Could she somehow use the sand against this monster . . . ?

Before she could make a move, the slimy water around her sizzled, and a huge brown wave roared up out of it – two metres tall and full of floating plastic bottles, seaweed and driftwood. Ivy covered her eyes with her hand as spray pelted her face. The stench of salt filled the air. She blinked, lost her footing and fell to the ground.

The water made a loud sputtering noise. Then Ivy heard a voice; it sounded like it came from underwater.

226

'Little girl,' it said, bubbling away, 'where have you hidden it?'

Not this again. 'Hidden *what*?' she rasped, struggling to her feet. 'What do you want?'

She stretched up on tiptoe, trying to see over the wall of water that surrounded her. It was no use. Everything behind it was blurry and distorted. Except for . . .

Just then, from within the sheet of water, a face emerged, followed by a body. Ivy saw a pair of hollow muddy eyes and rows of teeth like a shark's. 'The Great Uncommon Good,' it said, frothing at the mouth. 'You know where it is.' It smiled devilishly, showing off those teeth. 'Tell me.'

Before panic overtook Ivy completely, she heard the cement mixer rattling beside her and remembered the sand. She just had to be within reach . . .

'Well, little girl,' the creature bubbled. 'Can you answer my question?'

'What makes you think I have it?' Ivy said, inching backwards. She could feel the edge of the sand pile behind her.

'Don't play games with me,' the creature hissed.

Scratch was trembling in Ivy's pocket; she hoped what she was about to do might save them both. She dug the toe of her welly into the sand, then kicked as hard as she could.

A cloud of sand lifted into the air, covering the

monster. It roared angrily before its face disappeared. For a brief second the wall of water surrounding Ivy flickered.

'*HELP!*' she shouted, dragging air into her lungs. '*SOMEBODY HELP ME!*'

Suddenly there was another voice: 'Ivy!'

'*Help!*' she screamed. She tried to see through the water. *Seb?* No. The voice had sounded different . . . stronger. 'Valian?' she called.

'Stay there,' he replied. 'Don't move!'

'Ivy! I'm here!' Now *that* was Seb. *Yelling.*

A narrow gap appeared in the water; something small and glittery shot through it. Ivy looked down. A candy-pink yo-yo had landed by her foot. 'What am I meant—?'

'Don't speak!' Valian shouted. 'Either of you. Selkies can only read your mind while you're talking!'

Selkies . . . ? Ivy shivered. *That name was familiar.* She'd read it in the newspaper they'd found in the Wrench Mansion. It had said that selkies used to work for the Dirge.

She crouched down and carefully picked up the yo-yo, keeping one eye on the selkie. It was staring at her with wide, hungry eyes, as if she was the prize turkey on display in a butcher's window.

Ivy was so terrified, she barely felt her whispering work when she touched the toy. It was uncommon, but she had no idea what it did.

The selkie's eyes focused on the yo-yo. Ivy was about to try throwing it as you would a normal yo-yo when an ear-shattering scream resounded along the street. The wall of water vibrated like a hurricane had just hit it. Ivy dropped to her knees, her hands clamped over her ears. It felt like they were burning. She winced and tried to look up, her eyes watering from the pain.

The selkie's throat vibrated as it screamed, its jaw hanging open. Her head pounding, Ivy imagined what an uncommon yo-yo might do. *They go away and come back to you . . . They work with gravity . . . You throw them . . . They spin until they hit the ground . . .*

Wait – they spin . . .

She removed one hand from her ear, flinching as the piercing scream broke through. Looping the string around her finger, she aimed the yo-yo at the selkie and flicked her wrist.

A cyclone burst out of the pink yo-yo, pulling the wall of water round in circles. In an explosion of foam, the selkie was sucked into the whirlpool. Its cries started to break up as its body flashed in and out of view.

In between the selkie's scream, Ivy caught Valian's voice.

'On three!' he shouted.

On three? Do what *on three?*

'One . . .'

Ivy panicked, looking around. Maybe he'd thrown her something else to use.

'Two . . .'

There was nothing: just water, a very angry selkie and the yo-yo.

'Three!'

At the last second she did the only thing she could think of: she let go of the yo-yo.

The selkie scream was cut off, and she saw rushing water and bubbles. The yo-yo rose above her head, taking the whirlpool with it. Below, she could finally see through to the street. She dashed underneath the water and out the other side.

Valian was standing there, soaking wet and covered in slime, holding a bath plug suspended from a length of silver chain. 'Get back,' he warned sharply.

Seb dragged Ivy away from the maelstrom. She looked over her shoulder as Valian took aim and threw the bath plug into the centre of the whirlpool.

The selkie gave one last stomach-curdling scream, and then, with an almighty guzzling sound, the whirlpool disappeared into the ground. The bath plug and the yo-yo hit the cobbles with a thud.

Ivy's legs almost gave way as she tried to stand.

Seb bent down to help her. 'Ivy, are you all right?'

'What's the Great Uncommon Good?' she spluttered. 'That's what the Dirge want. That's what they're after.'

Chapter Twenty-four

A long grey feather bobbed in the air in front of Ivy's eyes. She tried swatting it away, but it swooped under her hand and started writing.

'Great,' Valian groaned, at her shoulder. 'It's from Ethel.'

Ivy had no idea how he knew that – maybe Ethel only used pigeon feathers. Whatever the feather was, it started writing:

Valian Kaye,

You and I had a deal. I have already fulfilled my half of the agreement; in return you were meant to keep Ivy and Sebastian safe.

But what's this I hear about a selkie attack . . . in the STREET! And where were you?

Utterly reprehensible behaviour.

You call yourself a scout . . .

Ivy turned away as the feather continued its message, but she saw Valian rolling his eyes as it went on and on.

She sat down on a bench beneath one of the street-lamps. Seb hid a grin at Valian's misfortune as he slumped beside her. They were back on the Gaunt-let and the air was filled with the enthusiastic calls of traders, the babble of chatter and the swish and shuffle of Hobsmatch. The noises of Lundinor were becoming more familiar to Ivy and, after the terrifying cries of the selkie, they sounded warm and friendly.

'I'm sorry I didn't get there sooner,' Seb said, staring into his lap. 'I noticed you'd taken Scratch with you – that's how Valian tracked you on one of his scout-ing maps. I don't wanna think about what would have happened if we hadn't got there in time.' He turned to look at her. 'It was stupid of me to go off like that this morning. We have to stick together.'

Ivy sniffed. She could still taste the selkie slime. 'That's one of the last things Dad said to me,' she said. *'Make sure you and Seb stay together.'*

'I hope Mum and Dad are together, wherever they are.'

Ivy looked into her brother's big green eyes. She'd never noticed the similarity before, but now she realized they were exactly like hers.

'At least now we've got another clue to help save them,'

she said. 'What do you think the Great Uncommon Good is? That's what the Dirge want.'

Seb shrugged. 'It sounds like something famous, something historical. Wolfsbane and Ragwort must have sent the selkie after you to see if it could read your mind and find out where it is.' He shivered as he finished.

'What's wrong?' Ivy asked.

Seb lowered his head. 'It's just – what we read in that newspaper about the Dirge causing an uprising of the dead . . . It's happening again.'

Before Ivy could say anything more, Valian came striding over. 'I am *sick* of those lectures.'

Seb looked up. 'All right, whiny. You didn't *have* to read it.'

Valian gave him a sarcastic smile. 'Actually I did. Featherlight doesn't go away unless you've read it all. It just keeps re-writing the message in front of you.'

He brushed down his leather jacket, grimacing as his hand came away shiny with gloop. 'You two need something to defend yourselves with in case there's a next time. I'm not getting another earful from Ethel. Come with me.'

He led Ivy and Seb through the Great Cavern and into the East End. It was a lively place full of the noise of trade, where the air smelled of cooked meat, tar and ale. Ivy tried to banish her memories of the selkie.

Scratch had stopped shaking in her pocket; it was time for her to stop shaking too.

Instead, she considered the clue to what the Dirge were after. *The Great Uncommon Good* . . . Seb was right: it *did* sound historical – like an ancient legend. She wondered what or who the Great Uncommon Good was.

The East End streets were crooked and winding, littered with plastic packaging, cardboard and beer cans. Some shops had smashed windows boarded up, while others had put up fairy lights and scrawled cardboard signs.

'One shiny new straddlebroom!' a trader with a thick accent shouted. 'Only one point two grade, ladies and gents – cheapest in Lundinor!'

'One grade ha-ats, one grade ha-ats – change your guise in moments, one grade ha-ats!' sang another.

Valian stalked confidently through the crowds and then turned off onto a quiet side street. As she followed, Ivy began to reconsider his motives. She hadn't trusted him, but he'd risked his life to save her from the selkie . . . She had so many questions.

'What's the Great Uncommon Good?' she asked him.

'No idea.' He shrugged. 'Where did you hear that?'

Ivy glanced at Seb. 'The selkie mentioned it – it asked me where I'd hidden it.'

Valian frowned as he led them into a narrow alley.

This one was filled only with shadows, rubbish bins and the putrid smell of rotting fruit. 'I wouldn't take any notice of a selkie. They've been banned from under-marts for hundreds of years because they like violence.' He stopped and turned to the closest building, exploring the brickwork as if searching for something lodged in the cement. 'Selkies can read minds; they can tap into your darkest secrets and deepest memories, and you only have to be speaking aloud to give them access.' He glanced at Ivy. 'You got off lightly. Normally selkie victims look like they've been attacked by a shark. Whatever the thing said, it was probably just trying to keep you talking for longer.'

So it could read my mind, Ivy thought. But why did the Dirge think she knew where the Great Uncommon Good was? It didn't make sense.

At last Valian's fingers stopped; he pressed his nails into the cement and waited. 'Try to be nice,' he told Ivy and Seb. 'Despite appearances, this guy's actually a decent contact. He's a scout like me.'

Suddenly a loud crack reverberated along the alley-way. The bricks trembled, sending out sprays of sand. 'Stand back,' Valian commanded, shouldering them away.

Ivy stared as a diamond-shaped section of wall dissolved into mist and shadow. She stepped backwards, grabbing Seb's hoodie as she did so. There was a lot of coughing, a loud hiss, and then a dark figure formed in the mist.

'Young Valian Kaye,' the figure said – it was an amused male voice. 'Nice of you to stop by for a visit.'

Valian coughed and looked away.

'How's business?' the man asked, his face still shrouded in darkness. 'It's got to be a difficult time for an independent scout at the mo. In fact, the last time I saw you, weren't you trying to flog assassin shoelaces to a couple of gwei?'

Ivy listened carefully. The man definitely had an accent, but she couldn't quite place it. All at once he stepped forward into the dim streetlight, grinning. His crooked teeth, sandy hair and pale skin were blackened with something like soot, and beneath a tatty waistcoat he wore a once-white shirt over faded jeans. On his head was a red and blue jester's hat. Ivy looked down at his feet. His muddy trainers didn't touch the ground.

Her stomach flinched. He was floating. Which meant . . .

He's dead.

'Well then, Kaye, introduce me,' the man said, nodding towards Ivy and Seb.

Valian shifted uneasily. After telling him their names, he pointed at the dead man. 'You two, this is Johnny Hands – a ghoul with a special gift for matching weapons to owners.'

Ivy shuddered. *A ghoul.* Just like those traders in the tavern.

Johnny Hands smiled wickedly and then made a little bow, removing his jester's hat as he bent forward. 'Pleased to meet you,' he announced. Ivy caught his eye, and his grin widened.

Valian stepped forward. 'You know why we've come.' He beckoned to Ivy and Seb. 'They need something to protect themselves with; something that won't be detected on common land.'

Johnny Hands scratched his filthy chin. He looked Ivy and Seb up and down and then reached into the black mist behind him, bringing out three packages, each wrapped in stained muslin and tied with string.

'This one for the boy.' He handed Seb the largest of the three packages. It was long and thin, like a ruler. 'Not very subtle but it'll do some damage if you're attacked.'

Seb took the package and studied it, looking both confused and fearful.

'You're a little trickier . . .' Johnny Hands narrowed his eyes at Ivy. 'Something small like you perhaps? Or something quick and lethal?'

Lethal? Ivy couldn't believe he was saying this. She was *eleven*. What did she want with a lethal weapon? Then again, it would be helpful if she came face to face with another selkie.

The ghoul glanced at Valian for a second. 'Perhaps . . . something you are familiar with.' He handed Ivy the smaller of the two remaining packages. It was round and fairly heavy, like a cricket ball. 'And this one's for you . . .' he finished, handing the third package to Valian.

'I didn't ask for anything,' Valian protested. 'I just wanted weapons for these two.'

Johnny Hands raised a glove. 'I know, I know, but you'll understand when you see theirs.'

'What have you been up to, Hands?' Valian growled.

'I'll just put it on your tab, yes? Great. No need to shake.' Johnny Hands quickly stepped back into the darkness.

Ivy watched as, one by one, his features were enveloped by the mist. If he really *was* dead, then he might have been trading in Lundinor for decades; centuries even – to her knowledge, there wasn't an expiry date on death.

'Mr Hands – wait,' she said, trying to keep her voice level.

He paused, only his face still visible. 'What is it?'

Ivy swallowed. 'I was wondering, have you heard of the Great Uncommon Good?'

He cocked his head. 'A whisper here and there, yes. It is a legend. A very ancient one.'

'Can you tell us anything about it?' Seb asked, stepping forward. 'Anything at all? It's important.'

'Alas, no.' Johnny Hands winked as his face was finally absorbed into the shadows, leaving just his lips behind. 'You'll need to ask something much older than me,' he whispered. 'And I'm five hundred and forty-two.'

Chapter Twenty-five

The desk bell announced their arrival. '*Miss Ivy Sparrow! Mr Sebastian Sparrow! Mr Valian Kaye!*' It paused, and then screeched, much louder, '*ETHEL?*'

Ivy heard the clink of metal and the groan of something heavy being moved in the storeroom.

'Aha!' Ethel came striding through the door. She was wearing a stained cotton apron and held some yellow wadding in her hand. Ivy caught the acrid whiff of chemicals and guessed that Ethel had been polishing her bells. 'Decided to show your face then, have you, Kaye?'

Valian shuffled in. The bells on the walls immediately started muttering rude things about him. Ivy struggled not to giggle – she didn't want to make it worse; he'd already been cursing her the whole way there.

It was Ivy who had insisted they go and see Ethel. Seb had been right about the Great Uncommon Good – it sounded historical because it was. Ivy didn't know anything older than five hundred and forty-two, like

Johnny Hands, but she did know someone who might. She glanced at Ethel's bells as she made her way around the shop. Some of them dated back over a thousand years.

While Ethel made tea, the three of them sat around the desk with their packages from Johnny Hands laid out in front of them. The bells were chattering quietly to themselves, gossiping about everything from Ethel's choice of headscarf to the previous customer. Ivy spotted several that she hadn't noticed on her last visit, all locked away in glass cases. The most interesting were two matte-black ones that looked like they might have been carved from coal. Ivy read the label. It said: HELL'S BELLS.

'Bleedin' selkies,' Ethel cursed. 'I don't mind the dead, but never been fond of selkies – too many teeth than is good for a person.' She came through the doorway with a tray and gave Valian a sharp look. 'Still no reason to get them weapons, though.' She pursed her lips but looked down curiously at the three packages. 'Well then . . . You'd better open them up.'

As Ethel set the cups down on the table, Ivy reached forward and began undoing the string around her package. Seb followed suit.

'Nice,' he exclaimed when the muslin fell away. 'That dead guy knows me pretty well.'

Drumsticks. Wooden ones. He picked them up gingerly. 'What do you think they do?'

Ivy looked at her parcel. In the middle of the cloth lay the pink yo-yo she had used earlier to fight the selkie. She turned to Valian. 'I thought this was yours . . .'

'It was.' He glared at his package. 'I expect that's why I've been given this. Compensation.'

'Whoa!' Seb cried. 'Ivy, look!' He was swooshing his drumsticks around, air-drumming over the counter-top. With every beat, a thud sounded on the other side of the room. The blinds in the front window rattled as something wacked them. 'This is awesome. I can hit something from metres away!' He tried sliding the drumsticks up the sleeve of his hoodie. 'And no one would ever know I was carrying them.' He dropped them back out again and began slicing them through the air, aiming for different places on the far wall.

'Careful with those,' Ethel warned. 'You might knock—'

Too late.

Seb thrust both drumsticks downwards, as if smashing a cymbal at the finale of a particularly long riff. At the far end of the shop, a head-sized hole erupted in the wall, showering crumbs of plaster into the air.

The surrounding bells shrieked.

'Ah!'

'Look what you've done!'

Two bells squealed, 'Our wall!' as if they were about to burst into tears.

Ethel headed over to the hole, tutting and shaking her head. 'Now you've done it!' she exclaimed. ''Ow am I meant to fix this?'

Ivy sighed. 'Nice one,' she hissed at Seb. 'We're supposed to be here asking about you know what.'

There was a whispered chorus of 'You know what' from the bells. Ethel stopped inspecting the hole and turned to Ivy. 'What's a you-know-what?' she asked, hand on hip.

Ivy hesitated. 'Er . . .' Maybe she should just come out and say it. 'Have you ever heard of the Great Uncommon Good?'

'The *what*?' Ethel frowned and stepped closer. 'Where did you—?'

Suddenly a furious scratching exploded from the hole in the wall. It sounded like something was stuck inside, trying to get out. The bells squealed and whispered feverishly; Ivy shivered. The noise reminded her of the black feather scratching its message into Granma Sylvie's wall. 'What's that?' she said. 'It's coming from inside the wall.'

Everyone turned to look at the hole. After a moment the scratching stopped. They waited a while longer, but nothing happened.

'Try saying it again, Ivy,' Ethel said, her eyes on the wall.

Ivy wasn't sure what she meant. 'The Great Uncommon Good . . . ?'

243

As if on cue, the scratching, shuffling noise started up again.

'What's going on 'ere?' Ethel asked, pushing a gloved hand into the hole. She grimaced as she reached in, searching. Suddenly she went still. ''Ang on. There's something 'ere.' When she pulled her arm out again, she was holding a wooden box.

All around the shop, the bells were silent. 'Never seen this before,' Ethel muttered. As she headed over to the counter, the box started rocking and shaking in her hands. Ivy realized that the box must have been making the scratching sound; Ethel looked like a juggler trying to control it. 'There, there now,' Ethel soothed. She set it down on the counter-top and inspected the outside. Ivy did the same.

'You'd better lean back,' Ethel said. 'Just in case.' The box went still as she opened it. Inside was a lot of stale-smelling straw, which she pulled out in hand-fuls. Underneath lay two fragile-looking pottery bells, the red-brown colour of clay. Ivy drew closer to take a look at them. They were damaged – their surfaces were cracked and scratched, and covered in water marks.

'Must've been 'ere for years,' Ethel decided, scratching her head. 'Probably something my parents collected.' She looked up at Ivy, Seb and Valian. 'They ran the 'Ouse of Bells before me.'

Ivy watched as Ethel lifted one of the bells out of

the box. It swung a greeting, but no voice rang out. Ivy leaned over and examined the other bell. It looked like it had once been painted, but the design had been washed away. 'Why can't it talk?' she asked.

Ethel peered inside them both. 'No clangers,' she said briefly. 'They've been taken out.'

Ivy brought a hand to her mouth. There was something horrific about a talking bell with no clanger – like a person with no tongue.

'Tortured,' Ethel murmured as she rested them gently down on the counter. 'Must 'ave been. I've heard reports of it happening to bells before. The Dirge were known to do it.'

Deep in Ivy's pocket, Scratch shivered. She felt a stab of anger. 'That's so cruel. Why?'

Ethel ran her fingers across each bell's damaged surface. 'They must have information the Dirge didn't want anyone else to know.' She looked closer at the decoration on the outside. 'They look like story bells; they're designed to recount whatever tale is painted on their surface.'

Valian scrutinized them suspiciously. 'So what story was it? It must have been pretty interesting for your parents to have hidden them in the wall.'

Seb inspected them from a distance, still looking embarrassed by the damage he'd caused. 'They moved after Ivy said *The Great Uncommon Go—*'

Before Seb had even finished his sentence, both bells were swinging wildly.

'OK, OK,' Ethel hushed, stroking them. 'It's all right.' She pulled up a chair and sat down, stirring her tea. 'Story bells . . .' She frowned as she stared into her cup.

Eventually she looked up. 'My parents used to tell me this fairy story when I was a girl,' she said, as if just remembering. 'It was about five uncommon objects thought to be grade ten or beyond.'

Valian raised an eyebrow. 'Some fairy story.'

Ivy remembered the poem she'd read in the street that morning. *The Great Grade Ten* . . . No one had ever found one before.

Ethel coughed disapprovingly before continuing. 'The story went that thousands of years ago, a group of muckers discovered five truly extraordinary uncommon objects, which they used to wield great power in the common world. The very first uncommoners fought those muckers and won. They managed to get the five objects to safety, where they were hidden for hundreds of years – until the next common fool tried to get 'old of 'em. The uncommoners always prevailed in the end. That's why, according to the fairy story, the five objects occasionally appear in common stories – ancient mythology and the like. The story was called "The Great Uncommon Good".'

Ivy tensed.

'That's not good,' Seb said. 'That's definitely *not good.*'

Ethel sipped her tea. 'Like I said, it's just a fairy tale. I think these bells must have told the story before they were tortured. That's probably where my parents got it from. But why the Dirge would want to—'

'That selkie,' Valian interrupted, visibly shaken. 'It asked you about the Great Uncommon Good?'

Ivy nodded. 'It thought I knew where one of them was. The Dirge *must* be looking for one of the Great Uncommon Good,' she told Ethel. 'That's what Granma Sylvie's stolen from them. And now they want it back.'

'*What?*' Ethel's face drained of colour. She looked at each of them in turn, and then down at the two story bells. 'These five objects – *if they really exist* – they'd be extremely dangerous in the 'ands of the Dirge; dangerous to every single mucker and uncommoner on the planet.'

Just then there was a noise in the street outside. Ivy heard voices shouting and hoofbeats ringing on the cobbles.

Valian got up and hurried to the window, pulling back the blinds. 'It's just Ugs,' he murmured. 'Must be some kind of emergency – they've got the coach out.' He continued watching a moment longer and then turned back. 'Weird . . . They've stopped right outside the—'

'Sweet Clements!' Ethel leaped to her feet, sending her chair flying. She held a hand to her chest as a brilliant green parakeet feather flicked through the air in front of her, writing.

Ivy read through the message at lightning speed.

Ethel,
*   Come quickly. Violet has been attacked. The underguard are on their way, but I need your help.*

Derek Littlefair
Proprietor of the Cabbage Moon Inn

Chapter Twenty-six

Ivy followed Seb as he elbowed his way through the crowd that had gathered outside the Cabbage Moon. 'Excuse me!' he shouted, swiping aside a blue tutu. 'We need to get through!'

Ivy felt a chill as she passed the underguard's black coach. There was someone in the back, but the nodding feathered hats and glittering headdresses obscured her view.

Inside the inn Valian and Ethel slammed the door behind them, shutting out the buzz of the crowd.

'Derek?' Ethel screeched into the empty lounge. 'Derek! Where are you?'

A door in the far wall swung open, and they all dashed through, finding themselves in a long galley kitchen. Bowls of freshly prepared vegetables sat next to stone jugs steaming with hot liquids. A pot of Bugtop – Ivy could tell by the aniseed smell – sat frothing on the stove, while above hovered jars, bottles and jugs containing jams, stews and soups.

At the far end stood the doughy-faced innkeeper, Mr Littlefair, fanning himself as he answered questions from a rotund man in underguard uniform. It was the constable Ivy had seen on the doorstep of Granma Sylvie's house. And if *he* was there, it was likely that he'd be joined by—

'Smokehart,' she breathed. The tall, pale officer was standing by the oven with a feather in his hand. Beside him, Violet Eyelet sat slumped on a chair. Ivy winced as she saw that her face was wet with tears. The spectacles hanging round her neck were smashed and her huge dress had been badly singed. Her white hair wobbled as she gestured with her lace-gloved hands.

As Ivy drew closer, she heard what Violet was saying.

'Like a hundred little black moths it was, at first. I thought they'd all got stuck in the room, so I went to the window to let them out, and then' – she sniffed, wiping her eye with a lace handkerchief – 'they kind of swarmed together into a great cloud and turned into darkness; pure darkness with a hundred eyes.'

'Violet!' Ethel hurried over, ignoring Officer Smokehart, and threw both arms around her. 'Are you OK?' She pulled away and assessed her.

Violet sniffed. She looked woozy and disorientated. 'I thought I was a goner, Ethel, honestly. I'd forgotten to put on my specs and stumbled into the wrong room upstairs.' She poked around in her pocket. 'It's all right – I've taken a button for the shock.'

Ethel rubbed her shoulder encouragingly. 'Derek,' she called. 'Best brew up some fresh Raider's Tonic for Violet's injuries.'

Mr Littlefair nodded. 'Right-o!' he said, and started pulling jars out of cupboards, mixing something on the worktop.

Smokehart cleared his throat. 'Ms *Dread*.' His voice sliced through the air. 'As you can see, I am in the middle of an investigation.'

Ethel grumbled but stepped back.

'Now, Violet,' Smokehart began. 'You said that the room you found the creature in was the one next door to your own?' He turned to the innkeeper. 'Who is staying there at the moment, Mr Littlefair?'

Mr Littlefair gulped. 'Just some other paying guests.'

'Indeed.' Smokehart lowered his feather. 'But their names?'

The innkeeper wiped a hand down his apron and looked at Ivy and Seb guiltily. 'Well, er . . . Ivy and Sebastian Sparrow.'

Smokehart's shoulders stiffened. '*Sparrow*?' He quickly spun round to find Ivy and Seb standing behind him.

Ivy shuddered. There was nowhere to go. She winced as he shouted.

'*YOU!*' The feather in his hand shook. 'Grandchildren of Sylvie Wrench. I might have known it.' He threw the feather over his shoulder, where it disappeared into thin air, and marched towards them.

Ethel reacted fast. 'Now wait just a moment.' She jumped into his path, arms spread wide. 'Just because the creature was in their room, it doesn't mean—'

'Ms Dread.' Smokehart smiled at her and pressed his fingers together. 'Do you know what it was that attacked Ms Eyelet?'

Ethel pinched her lips together, falling silent.

'I thought not. It was a wraithmoth.' He let the name hang in the air for a few seconds. Violet squeaked and brought her handkerchief to her mouth. Mr Littlefair stepped back against a cupboard, fanning his flushed cheeks.

'Wraithmoths are one of the few races of the dead who haven't been seen since the Fallen Guild were in power,' Smokehart reminded them. 'And who, I wonder, is the only person ever to be convicted as a member of the Fallen Guild?'

Every face in the room turned towards Ivy and Seb. Ivy could feel their eyes boring into her.

'Octavius Wrench is the name you're all searching for.' Smokehart moved Ethel aside and continued towards Ivy.

'Do you know what finally happened to your great-grandfather?' he asked her.

Ivy glanced anxiously at Seb as he reached for her arm. Everyone must already know the truth about Octavius. She wished someone had had the courage to tell them before.

'No? Then let me enlighten you . . . After Octavius Wrench lost the election on Twelfth Night 1969, an army of the dead took to the streets of Lundinor, led by six masked figures with rotten hands and black hoods. We all knew who they were.'

The Dirge, Ivy thought. *And Octavius was among them.*

'I was only a constable at the time, but the entire underguard force – myself included – stood against them. We were completely outnumbered: many good people lost their lives. At the last minute, back-up arrived from other underguard forces around the world. The increase in emergency bag-travel even sparked a geothermal disturbance, creating a temporary snowstorm over London. Only then did the tide start to change.'

Ivy wondered about Granma Sylvie's accident that night, in the snow. She must have fled Lundinor during the battle.

'Five of the hooded figures escaped,' Smokehart recalled, 'but one fought till the bitter end. When this sixth one realized he wasn't going to win, he ran into a shower of uncommon bolts and was killed. He was unmasked right there in the street, for everyone to see. Nobody could believe who it really was: *Octavius Wrench*, one of the pillars of the uncommon community.'

Ivy's mouth was dry. She didn't know how she was meant to feel about Octavius Wrench. Surely you weren't automatically bad just because someone in your family was.

Smokehart jabbed a finger at Violet Eyelet. 'Back then, the Fallen Guild used wraithmoths as spies because they lived in the shadows and you never even noticed they were there till it was too late. Maybe you'd feel a chill, or as if someone was watching you.'

Ivy remembered having that exact feeling that morning, in her room. *The wraithmoth must have been there.* The Dirge had sent it to spy on her, no doubt.

She straightened as Smokehart lowered his finger. He had it all wrong. She had to convince him that she and Seb were innocent and the real bad guys were still out there. 'Whatever you think about the Wrenches,' she said in a quiet voice, 'Seb and I haven't done anything wrong.'

'That's right,' Seb agreed. 'We didn't have anything to do with this. Why would we want to hurt Violet?'

Smokehart glared at them. 'That's something I will no doubt discover during your interrogation, but the facts are clear: a wraithmoth was hiding in *your* room, and *your* great-grandfather was a member of the Fallen Guild.' He lowered his head till he could look Ivy straight in the eye. 'And on top of that, every instinct I have is telling me that you're up to something in Lundinor.'

Ivy looked around the room for support. Mr Littlefair shrugged. Violet was sobbing again. Valian . . .

Hang on . . . Where was Valian? Ivy looked behind her. The door was open. *Great.* He'd disappeared again. She wondered if he was going to explain himself this time . . .

Only Ethel stepped forward. 'Officer, I don't think—'

She was cut off by the sound of panting and scuttling little footsteps on the tiles behind them. Ivy turned to see a tall, dark-haired lady in a long silk dress approaching from the lounge. There was a sand-coloured dog sniffing around by her ankles. Ivy had seen them both before.

'Lady Grimes?' Smokehart exclaimed. 'What—?'

'No need to be alarmed, Officer,' Selena Grimes insisted, raising a dainty hand. 'I was just passing and wanted to see why the crowd had gathered outside. I heard them talking about a wraithmoth?'

Smokehart straightened the front of his uniform. 'Yes,' he said gravely. 'I'm afraid there is evidence of a wraithmoth attack.' He slipped a paperclip out of his

pocket and gestured towards Ivy and Seb. 'The creature was found in their room. They're the Wrench grandchildren I was telling you about.'

Selena Grimes brushed her long fishtail plait over her shoulder and looked from Seb to Ivy. 'I see.' She sounded disappointed. 'It seems I should have allowed you the freedom to question these two back then, Smokehart.' She tilted her head slightly. 'I apologize.'

Ethel's jaw dropped. As she started to protest, Ivy felt the cold, prickly arms of inevitability wrap around her.

Smokehart tossed his paperclip at Ivy; it jumped onto one of her hands. Her whispering kicked in as her wrists were pulled together by some invisible force and the paperclip fastened itself around them. When she tried to pull them apart, it felt like they'd been glued to each other.

'You are both under arrest for hiring a wraithmoth,' Smokehart growled, throwing a second paperclip at Seb's hands. 'I'll read you your rights at the station.'

Chapter Twenty-seven

Ivy winced as her head scraped under the doorframe of the underguard coach, Smokehart's bony fingers pressing into her shoulder. Once inside, she shuffled along the seat with her back to the glass and her paper-clipped hands resting on her knees.

Opposite her was another prisoner – a slim, bony man with skin the colour of coffee beans and a short fuzz of black hair on his chin. His Hobsmatch consisted of jeans and a fur-trimmed tabard embroidered with gold flowers. When Ivy caught his eye, he smiled wearily at her. There was an absent look in his turquoise gaze that made her think he wasn't entirely awake.

The coach rocked as Seb was bundled in beside her. She tried to ignore the crowd outside, but it was difficult. Murmurs of 'Fallen Guild' and 'Wrench' kept breaking into hysterical cries or angry shouts. Through the windows, Ivy picked out a few of the faces. They were seething with anger. A woman carrying a basket-ful of baby's dummies reached into the pile and grabbed one. There was a look of blind rage in her eyes.

'Seb . . .' Ivy began. 'I think that lady—'

Thud! The dummy hit the window and then . . .

Squelch! A horrible yellow mucus sprayed out. The dummy wobbled like jelly as the sound of a loud, rippling *burp!* reverberated through the carriage.

Seb growled and thumped his paperclipped hands hard against the glass. Several other uncommoners grabbed dummies from the woman's basket and started lobbing them at the coach. A wet chorus of belches sounded in Ivy's ears. She realized she'd seen that disgusting gloop before – those boys had been throwing uncommon dummies at the featherlight mailhouse yesterday.

Smokehart didn't seem annoyed or surprised by the crowd's reaction; in fact, he looked like he was enjoying it.

'What did *we* ever do to any of them?' Seb asked, grimacing as another dummy hit the glass. 'It was a mistake to think anyone down here would help us. None of them even tried to prevent our arrest.'

Ivy flinched as she heard another burp. She didn't think what Seb said was entirely fair – Ethel had made an attempt.

He bent his head. 'It sucks being related to a member of the Dirge. It's not like we can do anything to change it.'

Ivy nodded. 'I know.' She felt like they had to go around proving that they were nothing like Octavius Wrench, just so people wouldn't hate them. She'd never had to deal with anything like that before. Up to this point in her life, everyone had judged her on who she was, not who she was related to.

She rocked sideways as the coach set off. They were moving at a brisk trot, the hoofbeats as steady as a sewing machine. The crowd chased them for a while but Ivy was too involved in her own thoughts to notice them. In ten minutes or so she and Seb would be in the underguard station. Her spirits plunged as she saw herself locked up in one of those cells. There would be no chance to save her mum and dad then.

As they drove through the streets, Ivy's mind kept wandering back to the series of events that had led to this moment. There had been three dead attacks in succession now – first the grim-wolf, then the selkie, then the wraithmoth. She remembered the newspaper article's reference to the *dead uprising*. The Dirge must be getting impatient. She wondered what they were planning to do with the Great Uncommon Good object once they got hold of it.

'Mum and Dad have only got till midnight tonight,' she said, her voice cracking.

'As if I need reminding!' Seb glanced over at the

man in the corner and whispered, 'Do you think we can talk in front of him?'

Ivy shrugged. She saw that the man was staring blankly out of the window. 'We need to escape,' she said in a hushed voice. 'Leave Lundinor and go back to Bletchy Scrubb. We have to find this Great Uncommon Good object before the Dirge do. Maybe if we tell Granma, she'll have remembered something . . .'

Seb clenched his paperclipped hands. 'Good plan – but how do we get out of these? I've still got my drumsticks up my sleeve – but if I use them, I think Smokehart will hear.'

Scratch might have some ideas, Ivy thought, but before she could speak, the quiet man opposite started gesturing to his mouth with his paperclipped hands and then shaking his head.

'Uh . . .' Seb frowned in puzzlement.

Ivy tried to work out what the man was telling them. 'You . . . can't speak?' she guessed.

The stranger nodded. Ivy shuffled closer as he turned round to show her the back pocket of his jeans. Sticking out of it she saw a grey eraser – the kind she had in her pencil case at school. He tried to stretch for it with his paperclipped hands but he couldn't reach.

Ivy could. As soon as she pulled the eraser out of his pocket, she could feel that it was uncommon. 'What does it do?' she asked.

The man held up his wrists. Ivy glanced at the silver paperclip thread binding them.

She turned to Seb. 'Hold your hands up; I'm gonna try something.'

She rubbed the eraser over the thread of silver metal wrapped around his hands. The metal flaked away in seconds, leaving behind a little pile of silver filings. He pulled his hands apart. 'Give it here – I'll do yours.'

Once Ivy's paperclip was off, she rubbed out the stranger's restraints. He beamed at her before checking through the glass at the top of the coach. Smokehart and the driver were facing forward, unaware of what was going on.

The man signalled to a point in the middle of the floor. Ivy and Seb wriggled away as he rubbed his eraser across it, turning first the carpet, then the glue and wood, into dust. When he had finished, a circular piece of the floor dropped down onto the cobbles below.

Seb raised his eyebrows. 'Er – thanks.'

The man offered them both a farewell salute before dropping through the hole and rolling to the side of the road. Ivy stared nervously down at the cobbles as the coach moved away from him. 'You go first,' she told Seb.

He slid his legs through and fell onto the road with a thud. Ivy saw him getting to his feet and waving back at her.

She took one last look at Smokehart, considering how fortunate she and Seb had been to find a stranger who could help them escape. Maybe it was a bit *too* convenient . . . or maybe their luck was finally beginning to change.

Dropping through the hole, she stayed low as the coach passed overhead. When it was clear, she got to her feet, ignoring a twinge in her ankle, and dashed over to join Seb. He was standing on the corner of a road packed with little haberdashery stalls.

'Seb – you all right?'

He nodded. 'You're limping. Everything OK?'

Ivy rubbed her ankle. 'It's nothing. Let's get out of here.' She looked around, trying to get her bearings. 'Do you know where we are?'

Seb gazed along the street. All the shops appeared to sell one thing: fabric. It was displayed draped over mannequins in the windows and huge rolls were stacked on the pavements outside. Sheets of satin and bolts of silk were being inspected by curious passers-by, while hand-stitched bunting waved enthusiastically from the gables above. Ivy couldn't tell what their uncommon ability was – until she spotted a tapestry displayed in one of the windows. It depicted a storm at sea, with ships riding the waves and the sky full of clouds. As she watched, the tapestry appeared to ripple, the sky swirled and one of the great galleons crashed through the water, as if the picture had come alive.

She shook her head, trying to refocus. 'We need to move,' she said, forcing her eyes away. 'Smokehart will realize we're missing soon.'

Seb took a step forward but then rocked back on his heels. 'Wait a sec. Ivy, can you see . . . ?' His eyes widened as he stared down the street.

Ivy followed his gaze . . . Through the rippling lengths of cloth she caught glimpses of a man with neatly combed salt-and-pepper hair standing on the pavement. He was wearing a button-down shirt and brown flannel trousers.

Ivy frowned. 'Dad?'

Chapter Twenty-eight

'What is Dad *doing* here?' Ivy rubbed her eyes, making sure she wasn't seeing things. He was meant to be the Dirge's hostage but he didn't look like he'd been kidnapped at all – his shirt was pressed and his face was clean.

Seb reached for her arm. His hand was shaking. 'Is that really him?'

Their dad disappeared behind a hanging bedsheet. Ivy tensed. 'He's moving away,' she cried. 'We mustn't lose him.'

They ran past roll after roll of fabric. The air was thick with loose threads and dusty particles that caught at the back of Ivy's throat, making her cough.

'He's turning left!' Seb called.

Ivy nodded. She tried to work out if there was anything different about her dad, but she was too far away to tell. Judging by his moderate pace, he wasn't in any trouble.

She didn't understand . . .

They turned down a deserted street, where their dad came to a halt between two large stone buildings. As Ivy and Seb approached, they heard a rumble. The cobbles beneath Ivy's feet shook, as if the underguard's horses were about to come pounding down the road.

But it wasn't the underguard making the noise.

'Ivy,' Seb whispered, pointing. 'The fountain!'

They hid in a shop doorway on the opposite side of the street. A chill crept over Ivy as she watched.

Sure enough, the pale-green fountain that she and Seb had found yesterday had appeared in front of their dad. He got a hip flask out of his trouser pocket and poured something into the leaf-filled basin. Next he placed his hand deep inside it, waited a moment and then stepped back. The bricks surrounding the fountain trembled as two iron posts and a gate formed between them.

'Maybe we should go after him,' Ivy said, 'before he disappears.'

Seb frowned. 'I don't understand why he's here, let alone why he's going in—' He gave a start. 'What if the grim-wolf's still at the mansion?'

Ivy gasped. 'We need to warn him!'

They dashed straight across the street—

And into the path of someone else.

'*Valian?*' Ivy stepped back, aghast. Her face flushed

with anger, remembering his most recent disappearance. 'We were arrested!' she hissed. 'You left us!'

Valian was holding his arms out wide, trying to stop them. 'Don't go after it,' he told them, ignoring Ivy's remarks. 'Don't go into the mansion after that thing – it's dangerous.'

'After that *thing*?' Seb stretched up on tiptoe, trying to get a view of the fountain. 'That isn't a *thing*! That's our *dad*!'

Valian looked frantic. 'No it's not. It's one of the races of the dead.'

Ivy gritted her teeth as she tried to push him aside – she could see her dad disappearing through the gate!

'Please,' Valian said gently. 'You've got to trust me.'

'Trust *you*?' Ivy hesitated. The man they had followed looked *exactly* like her dad. She checked Seb. He looked just as torn as she was. 'If you want us to trust you, then you have to tell us the truth. About everything.'

'The truth.' Valian's voice was soft. He ran a hand through his long hair. 'OK, fine. If it's the only way you're gonna trust me, then I guess I have to.'

A sinking feeling swept through Ivy. Whatever the truth was, she had a hunch she wasn't going to like it.

'Go on then,' Seb said, folding his arms. 'We're waiting.'

Valian's face was grave. 'Not here. It's too dangerous.'

He led the way to a small shop with cracked green window frames and dirty glass. The sign above the door read: HOFF & WINKLE'S HOBSMATCH EMPORIUM, EST. 1847. Behind the shop was a rickety timber staircase.

As they started to ascend, Seb mumbled into Ivy's ear, 'What's he up to? Was that Dad back there or not?'

Ivy didn't know what to think. She was still confused by the shock of seeing her dad apparently alive and well. 'Valian,' she said harshly. 'If that wasn't our dad, who was it?'

'I told you,' he replied. 'A race of the dead. They're called grimps. They have the ability to shapeshift; that's why it looked like your dad.'

Ivy thought back to *Farrow's Guide* . . . She didn't remember Scratch reading about grimps in there. 'How do you know it was a grimp?'

Valian stopped in front of a plain black door at the top of the stairs. 'Because that's not the first time I've seen it. I met it when I was in the Wrench Mansion with you.'

Ivy's mouth dropped open. So *that's* what he'd been up to. 'Why didn't you tell us?'

'There's a lot I haven't told you. There's a lot I haven't told anyone.' He pointed a thumb over his shoulder. 'We'll talk inside.'

Behind the black door was a small room with threadbare curtains. A metal-framed bed sat in the corner beside a chest of drawers and a wash basin with a rusted mirror. Ivy noticed scum around the taps and crumbs on the bare floorboards. The walls were covered with posters of various rock bands, none of which she had heard of.

'You'd better sit down,' Valian told them.

'Make yourself at home,' Seb whispered into Ivy's ear as he perched on the end of the bed.

Ivy sat down slowly. Was this Valian's room? She felt uncomfortable being in there. Valian stood by the wash basin, looking at them.

'So . . . the grimp?' Seb brushed a dead fly off the bedspread.

'It was at the Wrench Mansion,' Valian repeated. 'It took a little investigation back at your gran's house before I realized that it looked exactly like your dad. After that, I started following it.'

'Wait – you went to Granma's house behind our back?' Ivy exclaimed.

Valian sighed. 'You'd understand why if you knew the whole story.' He turned and looked into the rusty mirror. 'When I found that crooked sixpence in your pocket, Ivy, I assumed you were working for the Dirge. Ethel's deal for me to be your bodyguard was the perfect excuse to stay close and find out what you were really up to. All those times I disappeared, I was off investigating on my own. Just now, in the Cabbage Moon, I went to check out your room for evidence of the wraithmoth; I managed to retrieve those for you . . .'

269

He pointed to the windowsill behind the bed.

Ivy started. Granma Sylvie's handbag was there, along with the uncommon alarm clock. She reached across and gathered them up, thankful they were safe. 'If you thought we were working for the Dirge, then why help now?' she asked.

'I know you're not working for the Dirge. After the alarm clock and the selkie attack I realized you'd been telling the truth the whole time.' He looked down and mumbled, 'I'm . . . sorry.'

Ivy shared an incredulous glance with Seb.

Valian looked up at them again. 'My name *is* Valian Kaye and I *am* a scout; that's all true.' He pointed to three framed photographs standing on the chest of drawers: two of a small girl with blonde hair, the third of a happy young couple. 'That's my family: my parents, and my little sister, Rosie.'

Ivy wondered why he was mentioning them now. 'Are they uncommoners too?'

'They *were*,' Valian corrected her. 'My parents were both scouts, like me, but . . . they're dead now.'

There was a long pause while they looked awkwardly at the floor.

Finally Ivy asked, 'What happened?'

Valian clenched his fists in their fingerless gloves. 'They were murdered by the Dirge. I've always thought the Dirge member using *Hemlock* as a code name was responsible because that was the poison found on their lips.'

Ivy gasped in horror. 'How old were you?' she asked gently.

'Nine,' Valian told her, sighing. 'That's why the underguard didn't believe me about the crooked sixpences.'

'Didn't believe you?' Seb's voice cracked. 'Why not?'

Valian looked at him. 'I found a crooked sixpence in each of my parent's glasses; that's how I know the Dirge murdered them. But the coins had disappeared by the time the underguard turned up to investigate. To this day they still think my parents died of accidental poisoning.'

Seb puffed out a sigh. 'That's . . . awful.'

Ivy's attention moved to the photos of the little blonde girl. 'Where's your sister now?'

Valian pushed himself away from the sink and slumped down on the floor. 'Good question,' he muttered. 'After our parents were killed, Rosie and I had to leave Lundinor. Social services in the common world found us a place with foster parents. We came back to say our goodbyes one last time. There was a huge crowd in the Gauntlet and I got separated from Rosie. I saw her heading off into the Dead End. She was only six; I guess she thought she might find our parents amongst the dead traders.' He sighed. 'She never came back. The underguard stopped searching for her after a week or so, but I never gave up. I never *will* give up. Half of everything I scout for now is something to help me find her. That bell I took from Ethel . . . I had a hunch it might locate Rosie, but it didn't work. It's been six years since she went missing; I still don't know what happened.'

Ivy swallowed as Valian finished. What must it feel like to lose your whole family? No wonder he acted like an outsider half the time. 'I'm so sorry,' she said weakly. She didn't know what else to say. She felt cold with regret at the things she'd thought about him.

'You must hate us,' Seb muttered, 'because of who we're related to.'

Something flickered in Valian's eyes. 'I did at first. I told you: I thought you were working for the Dirge. But I gradually realized it couldn't be true. If I'd been given the chance to save my mum and dad, I'd have acted exactly like you.'

'Why does the grimp look like our dad?' Seb asked.

Valian's face darkened. 'Grimps take the form of their host. There's a GUT law that forbids any grimp from taking an unwilling host, but like I told you earlier – the dead break the rules all the time.'

'So . . . the grimp is working for the Dirge and our dad is being used as this grimp's host?' Ivy summarized, connecting the dots. She couldn't bear to think of it. 'What does that mean?'

Valian shifted position on the floor. 'If the host is legal, then it donates hair or toenails for the grimp to feed off. Then, after a few hours, the grimp starts to resemble its host. If the host is taken illegally . . . Well, the grimp doesn't get donations. It just takes what it needs.'

Ivy was horrified. 'Are you saying that Dad is being . . . eaten?' Valian's eyes told her all she needed to know. 'Seb – *no*. We've got to do something!'

'How do we stop it?' Seb's eyes glimmered with purpose as he got to his feet.

Valian held up a hand. 'For the moment we don't. We follow it back into the Wrench Mansion. But we do it carefully. It keeps returning for something. I'd bet everything I own that your mum and dad are being held there.'

Ivy felt hot anger burning through her veins. She was more determined than ever to get them back.

'I know I've lied to you,' Valian said, 'and you've got no reason to trust me, but what you're feeling right now . . . that's exactly the way I feel about my sister. You've only got till midnight before that alarm clock rings. Let me help you. We can save them together.'

Ivy had already made up her mind, but Seb, she thought, might be more difficult to convince. 'What do you think?' she asked, looking up at her brother.

Seb was staring at the photo of Rosie. He rubbed his eyes quickly, hoping no one would notice the welling tears. 'I think we could do with a hand . . .' His gaze fell on the posters adorning Valian's walls and he frowned. 'Even if it does come from someone without a single Ripz poster in their life.'

Chapter Twenty-nine

Valian felt around in his inside pocket. 'You both remember the plan?'

Ivy nodded as she leaned forward and splashed a cupful of water into the basin of the uncommon fountain. She wiggled her fingers around under the surface and immediately felt the ground groan and tremble. As the two black gateposts emerged on either side, she wondered how the fountain worked. It had activated when Seb had put his hand in yesterday, and now with Ivy, but it had also worked for the grimp. Maybe, she guessed, it was able to read their fingerprints under the water. The grimp must have taken their dad as a host so it could use his fingerprints to gain access to the mansion.

'Remember, your parents will be behind the Ragwort or Wolfsbane doors,' Valian said.

Seb gave a nod. 'Got it.'

Ivy placed a hand in the centre of the gates. 'And

if something goes wrong, we get out any way we can and meet back at your place above Hoff and Winkle's Hobsmatch Emporium, Valian.' Her hand was trembling. The plan wasn't foolproof, but it was all they had. Maybe that was why she and Seb had left anything of value back in Valian's room. All Ivy had on her now was the uncommon yo-yo, and what remained of her dwindling confidence.

'OK.' Valian patted down his jacket pockets and gave a satisfied nod. 'Let's do this.'

Ivy didn't think it was possible for the Wrench Mansion to be any more creepy the second time round, but she was wrong. As they trudged up the hill towards the front door, dry leaves skittered across their path like rats and the wind whistled eerily. The dark sky swirled with a coming storm and the old house creaked and groaned as if warning them away.

Inside, the entrance hall was pitch black. Ivy sniffed the air. The smell of wet dog still lingered, but there was something else, something much worse. 'Ugh.' It smelled like toilets and gone-off Brussels sprouts. 'Seb, you didn't just—'

Even though he could barely see her, Seb still managed to hit her on the arm. 'No, I didn't! Even mine aren't this bad.'

Ivy heard Valian shuffling up beside her. 'I know that smell. There's only one type of creature that foul: a

Victorian sewer selkie. It must have been here recently. Be on your guard.'

Ivy shivered as she recalled the selkie that had attacked her – those empty black eyes and rows of razor-sharp teeth. She covered her nose and tried to pretend the smell wasn't there. 'There were lemon squeezers on the walls before,' she said.

Valian sighed and unzipped something, casting a silvery-blue light into the darkness. His face was eerily lit from below. 'It's from Johnny Hands...' He nodded down at the glowing object. 'Don't ask me what it does exactly. I only know that it glows sometimes.'

Ivy examined it more closely. It looked like a miniature spade with a curved steel blade and polished wooden handle. Only the metal part was glowing. '*That* was what he gave you?' she asked, recognizing the tool with a frown. 'A garden trowel?'

He scowled. 'Yeah. Compensation for giving you my yo-yo, apparently.'

Ivy smiled awkwardly.

Valian pointed across the hallway with the un-common trowel. 'Let's just find the envelope.'

They found it at the foot of the stairs. Ivy picked it up. 'Ready?' she asked. Seb grasped her shoulder and nodded; Valian laid a gloved hand on her elbow.

Ivy opened the envelope, and suddenly the world

was rotating around her. The silvery light from Valian's trowel flashed through the air, round and round and round . . .

When it stopped spinning, they were in total darkness. Valian took his hand away and stepped back, waving the trowel around. Its ghostly light revealed the brick walls of a long tunnel.

Ivy shivered. 'This isn't Octavius' study,' she pointed out. 'There should be bookcases and furniture.' *And it should smell musty and old*, she thought nervously. *This place still smells of selkie slime . . .*

Seb and Valian reached for Ivy's shoulders. She closed the envelope and then opened it up again.

Nothing happened.

'Try it again,' Valian said. She could hear the worry in his voice.

She opened the flap on the back once more, in exactly the same way. Her fingers were still tingling with warmth. 'It's definitely the same envelope. It feels uncommon. I don't get what's wrong.'

'It *feels* uncommon?' Valian raised an eyebrow.

Ivy gave a shy smile. She might as well tell him now. 'I'm a whisperer,' she said in a hushed voice.

Valian's eyes grew wide. 'You're a *what*?'

Ivy looked down, hiding her face behind her hair. It felt weird having a secret that made people see her as special. Anyway, she still didn't know how to use her gifts properly. 'Don't get excited,' she told him. 'I don't see how it's going to help us.'

'Look, we're still here,' Seb said, holding one of his drumsticks aloft. 'What's wrong with the envelope?'

Valian stared at Ivy as if he wanted to say something else, but then he pointed at the envelope. 'Give it here.' He sighed when he turned it over. Ivy looked down and read the ink stamp in the top right corner. It didn't say DIRECT MAIL any more, it said: REDIRECTED MAIL.

'*Great.* Someone's tampered with it. It must be some sort of trap.' Valian looked down the dark tunnel. 'This is our only way out now.' He screwed the envelope into a ball and threw it on the floor. Ivy shivered as she stuffed her hand back into her pocket and clasped her yo-yo.

They proceeded slowly, with Valian in front, holding out the trowel. The tunnel was around a hundred metres long, filled with cobwebs and scuttling shadows. At the very end, a small arch-shaped opening led into darkness.

As Ivy put one foot in front of the other, her dream from the previous night invaded her mind – the black hands of the uncommon alarm clock slicing away fractions of time; her mum's face disintegrating into maggots; her dad being eaten by a faceless monster.

Valian's trowel glowed brighter.

'Isn't there a dimmer switch on that thing?' Seb asked, shielding his eyes.

Valian lowered it. 'I don't think it's glowing because it's dark,' he said, peering around cautiously. 'It must be sensing something. That's why it's growing stronger.'

Ivy coughed as they made their way under the arch. The smell was getting worse, she was sure of it. It was as if the contents of every Portaloo in London had been dumped there.

Once they were through, Valian's trowel started to blaze brightly. The tunnel walls on either side of them disappeared, and in the emptiness beyond Ivy spotted a small wooden desk covered with an inch of dust. On it sat an equally dusty old typewriter and a stack of yellowed, moth-eaten papers.

'Where are we?' Seb was holding his drumsticks close to his chest. His voice echoed off whatever lay in the darkness beyond.

'This place sounds massive,' Valian said. 'Look for a light switch; the trowel won't reach far enough.'

Ivy saw that the walls were covered in moss. She felt the slimy, damp surface, searching for any change in texture.

'Over here!' Seb called, after a minute or so. 'There's some sort of handle.'

Ivy turned to see a large stainless steel lever fixed to the wall. Seb forced it down.

For a second nothing happened. Then a broken buzzing noise started above their heads; it sounded like a dying wasp. A grid of electric ceiling lights struggled into brightness and continued flickering, so that it looked as if everything below was being played in jerky slow motion.

Ivy blinked. She caught glimpses of a giant hall, as large as the main arrivals chamber in Lundinor. The ceiling was vaulted like a cathedral's, the same grey concrete as the walls and floor. Behind the small desk to Ivy's right were a dozen narrow banqueting tables that ran the entire length of the hall. Each one was topped by a long conveyor belt – the kind used in supermarket checkouts – and bordered by a row of wooden chairs. Scattered on top of the conveyor belts was a mixture of what looked like rubbish: ripped bin liners exploding with odds and ends – tissue, fabric, glass jars, brass door handles, broken china and other random household items.

Ivy searched for any sign of life, but the place appeared to be deserted. Cobwebs hung between the chairs and carpeted the conveyor belts like crocheted blankets, and dust hovered in the air. It was one of the eeriest sights Ivy had ever seen – like a ghostly recycling plant.

'What *is* this place?' Seb asked, stepping forward. 'It's like a creepy movie set.'

Ivy approached the nearest table and examined one of the chairs. There was a small iron manacle chained to the concrete floor beneath it. 'It looks like people were tied up here.' She sat down and laid her hands on the table. The chair was the perfect height for her.

Valian waved the glowing trowel in front of him. Ivy saw a look of horror in his eyes. 'I think I know what this might be,' he said. 'I've heard rumours . . . It's called a "whispering hall".' He looked at Ivy. 'They're used to harness the power of whisperers. It was barbaric. Whisperers were made to sort through rubbish all day long till they found something uncommon.' He picked up a tin can from one of the piles of junk. 'But they only existed in ancient times. This one looks as if it was built within the last fifty years.'

Ivy jumped to her feet and scrambled away from the table. 'Look at everything,' she said, suddenly understanding what this place was. 'It's all designed to fit someone my size. It's designed for—'

'Children,' Seb finished, horror glazing his eyes. 'It must have something to do with the Dirge.'

Ivy gazed around at the hundreds of chairs and pictured all the whisperers who had been imprisoned there – kids just like her – forced to move their gloveless hands through God knows what for hours and hours on end.

Valian crunched the tin can in his fist. 'I bet *this* was where all those kidnapped children came,' he spat angrily. 'They must have all been whisperers.'

Ivy remembered what Scratch had told her: whispering had been thought impossible for a child. That was probably why no one in Lundinor had figured out why the children were being taken – no one guessed they were whisperers. Only the Dirge had discovered it.

'Scratch told me that my whispering was unusually sensitive,' she said to Valian. 'Do you think that's why the Dirge hunted young whisperers – because their abilities were stronger than adults?' She thought about all those terrified children, stolen from their families and forced to work in an underground prison.

Suddenly Valian started. 'Can you hear that?'

Ivy strained her ears. There was a weird noise in the air, a kind of fluttering.

Valian's eyes widened as his trowel burned with white light. 'I think I've just realized what uncommon trowels do.' He lifted it high above his head and directed the umbrella of light between two of the long tables. It lit up a series of bulky, dim shapes approaching from the edge of the hall. 'They sense the presence of the dead.'

Ivy's eyes darted around. Figures began appearing out of the shadows, some hulking and cumbersome, others wispy and fast. Slowly she lifted her yo-yo out in front of her, trying to keep her arm steady.

Seb pointed a drumstick into the distance. 'What's in here? Selkies?'

'Others too,' Valian whispered fearfully.

They all fell silent as a thin stream of black dust snaked over the floor towards them. In places, the powdery stuff flaked away like dead skin and sprouted spiky hairs. 'What is it?' Ivy asked, coughing.

'Wraithmoth,' Valian wheezed. 'The closer it gets, the harder you'll find it to breathe.' He unzipped his jacket and rummaged around inside. 'Don't touch them. They're deadly.' He edged closer, tugging his uncommon bath plug out of his pocket and swinging it above his head like a lasso.

Seb was gasping. '*They?*'

Ivy made a panicked search into the distance. A second wraithmoth had appeared above a conveyor belt, writhing around and sending smoky tendrils into the air like an angry spider. More dark figures were just behind it, drawing closer.

She tried to think. Surely there was another way out of this place. She glanced up at the lights on the ceiling. They didn't look uncommon – there were wires running to the other end of the hall. Ivy traced them through the shadows, down a pillar and along a wall. They ended in a steel box next to a handle identical to the one Seb had pulled. Beside it she could just make out a dark rectangle – a door.

Ivy grabbed Seb and pointed. 'Do you see that?'

He nodded.

Valian was still whirling the uncommon bath plug above his head. 'What are you waiting for?!' he rasped. 'Run!'

Run. Ivy's legs jerked into action, but Seb soon overtook her. 'Ivy, quickly!' he shouted.

She followed him between two long tables but her wellies were slipping all over the place. Her arms flailed wildly as she struggled to keep her balance. 'Selkie slime!' she screamed. The floor was covered with it. She spied the second wraithmoth coming towards them.

Seb had seen it too. 'What do we do?'

The wraithmoth was blocking their path to the door, but if they turned back, they'd only meet Valian and the other creature.

With a shaking hand, Seb sliced his drumsticks once, twice through the air. A millisecond later twin shockwaves sent the creature tumbling backwards. It gave a furious hiss as fingers of black smoke wove together to repair the holes in its body.

Ivy saw the confidence drain from Seb's face. She was about to have a go with her yo-yo when she noticed a shadow creeping across the floor. The wraithmoth was shifting. With the sound of wind filling a sail, it unfolded two smoky wings over the long table on either side.

Cursing, Seb steadied himself and shouted at Ivy

without taking his eyes off the monster, 'Ivy, get to the door!'

As the wraithmoth swooped towards them, he began desperately thrashing out a beat with his drumsticks, and the wraithmoth screeched.

Ivy ducked as Seb's drumsticks sent shockwaves through the air. Riddled with holes, the wraithmoth kept rebuilding itself with ribbons of smoke. Seb concentrated on the beat, the muscles in his shoulders rippling, his eyes focused. Every sound wave he sent out acted like a bar in an invisible cage. The wraithmoth was soon trapped – but Ivy wasn't sure how long Seb would be able to keep it up.

'Just go, will you?' he yelled, through gritted teeth. 'Please, Ivy. It's the only way.'

Tears blurred Ivy's vision as she slid under the trapped wraithmoth and between the long tables. Just then, she saw a familiar sandy-haired dog trotting out from beneath one of the tables.

Selena Grimes's dog? Ivy came to a stop.

The dog yapped and then yawned and stretched its legs – but all at once its limbs elongated, and gnarled black claws burst from its paws. Its back rose up and its sandy brown hair darkened to the colour of soot. The yap deepened, and sharp black teeth emerged from its gums. It looked at Ivy with a pair of demon-red eyes, lips curling into a wicked smile.

'I know what you're going to say,' the grim-wolf announced, stalking towards her. 'My disguise is *so* much better than a grandma.'

Ivy's eyes widened. So *Selena Grimes* was Wolfsbane, the grim-wolf's mistress!

She stumbled backwards. Somewhere in the whispering hall behind her, heavy objects clattered against a conveyor belt; chairs crashed to the floor and the sound of rushing water thundered around the walls. *Selkies.* Ivy's eyes watered with their stench. But . . . she couldn't turn round to check if Valian and Seb were OK.

Squaring her shoulders, she raised her yo-yo and, through blurry eyes, tried to take aim at the grim-wolf. Flicking her wrist, she sent the yo-yo shooting down to the end of the string. As it worked its way back up towards her hand, a white cylinder of air formed on either side and broke away, heading for the grim-wolf, picking up water and selkie slime as they went.

The grim-wolf watched the cyclones approach with a smirk on its face, rearing up onto its back legs and leaping onto one of the long tables. The very edge of one cyclone caught the tip of the grim-wolf's tail, but it quickly pulled itself free and dropped back onto the floor. As it shook itself dry, Ivy's cyclones crashed into the wall behind, steaming.

'Really?' the wolf mocked. 'What are you going to

do – huff and puff and blow me down?'

Ivy glowered at it. This was definitely the same grim-wolf that had attacked them in the Wrench Mansion – it had the same obsession with nursery rhymes. She focused on the door beyond the wolf. If she could just slip past it somehow . . .

The wolf licked its lips, staring at Ivy with its demonic red eyes.

Ivy fumbled with her yo-yo again. If only she knew how to use it properly. Those last cyclones had been use-less; she needed to generate something that the grim-wolf couldn't dodge.

Suddenly she heard the scream of a selkie. Her ears burned like they'd been set on fire. She groaned and drove her hands to each side of her head, trying to block out the noise.

The grim-wolf howled and flattened its ears, lower-ing its head under its front paw.

Ivy blinked. *The wolf can hear the selkie too.* She had to use this to her advantage.

She threw her yo-yo down and dragged it back up as fast and as hard as she could. The air around her began to tremble and spin. It would be dangerous to generate such large cyclones in a confined space, but it was her only option.

Ivy unhooked her finger and hurled the yo-yo into

the air just as the grim-wolf leaped towards her. She was thrown backwards as the double vortex shot up, expanding and rotating, on a collision course with the grim-wolf.

Ivy's hair was whipped into her eyes as something hit her in the chest, knocking her backwards. She fell into a heap of rubbish, sharp objects poking her sides and wet slime seeping into her trousers. *Get up, Ivy. Get up.* The huge whirlwind had sucked in the chairs on either side, along with piles of rubbish. The grim-wolf was running on the spot at the edge of the cyclones, as if stuck on a treadmill.

Ivy looked around dazedly and saw the broken remains of a large ceramic lamp next to her – that was what had knocked her over. As she staggered to her feet, her fingers brushed something that sent a warm tingle into her skin. She turned and searched carefully till she came across the uncommon object – a leather belt with a rusty buckle.

Without stopping to think, she quickly fastened it and then lifted it above her head. Her mind racing ahead of her, she drove herself up through the air – over the whirlwinds, over the struggling grim-wolf. Landing safely on the other side, she lowered the belt to her waist and touched down.

The door in the back wall was ajar. Battling against

the pull of the maelstrom, she headed towards it and yanked it open. Her skin immediately burned with heat – the door was uncommon – but she couldn't stop: she stepped over the threshold into a small silver room bathed in green light. Directly in front of her she saw a face – a face she recognized.

'*Dad?*'

The creature that looked like Dad grinned. Its skin was see-through and its neck sagged like melted wax. 'Hello, brat.' It pointed an uncommon toilet brush at Ivy's head. 'I know you think you're smart, but if you even move a muscle' – the creature's eyes glinted – 'I'll have you.'

Chapter Thirty

Ivy stood there quaking; fear and anger bubbled inside her. She locked eyes with her dad.

Except it's not really him . . .

Her dad never looked at her like that – with an evil, malice-filled stare. Valian had explained what the creature really was: *a shapeshifter; a grimp.*

The grimp's blue eyes glittered, reflecting the flashing lights in the whispering hall behind. Ivy could still hear the ongoing battle – the clatter of rubbish and the surge of water. The grimp grumbled and, keeping its eyes and the toilet brush fixed on Ivy, edged its way round towards the uncommon door. Ivy realized that she had seen the door before – in the Hexroom. It was the same stainless steel door that the grim-wolf had emerged from; the one belonging to Wolfsbane.

'Goblin!?' the grimp shouted. A drop of saliva fell from its lips. 'Get out of there. Those selkies are back!'

Ivy heard a growl and then saw the grim-wolf

stealing towards the door. Its fur was matted, but it had obviously escaped the yo-yo tornados. It smiled as its red eyes fixed on Ivy. Once it was over the threshold, the grimp slammed the door shut with an echoing thud.

Everything around Ivy fell eerily silent, with only the memory of the selkie's scream ringing in her ears. She swallowed: if she couldn't hear Seb and Valian any more, they certainly couldn't hear her.

'Now, isn't that better?' the grimp asked, grinning as it made its way round to face her. Its voice was harsh and grating, like fingernails down a blackboard. 'Finally we can hear each other clearly.'

And see each other clearly . . .

The grimp was wearing the long grey coat and button-down shirt that Ivy's dad had been wearing when she'd waved goodbye to him three days ago. She glared at the poor imitation. Close up, it looked like a bad waxwork. The grimp had the same speckly grey hair, the blue eyes, the line of freckles on the brow, and the thin nose and flat chin. But there was something wrong with its expression.

Ivy suddenly wondered if the illusion was crumbling because it hadn't fed for a while.

'Now,' the grimp said, rubbing its hands together. Its arms hung loosely in front of it like a chimpanzee's – in marked contrast to Ivy's dad, who always stood up straight. 'Where is the object, Ivy Sparrow?' it hissed, darting its head forward. 'Where is the Great Uncommon Good?'

Ivy wished she still had her yo-yo. She'd have liked to throw it straight at the grimp's head. 'What have you done with my mum and dad?!' she shouted.

The grim-wolf – *Goblin* – sniggered. 'Uh-uh,' it tutted, shaking its furry head. 'That wasn't the correct answer.' It paced back and forth, its tail whipping through the air. 'Tell us where your grandmother hid the object. No one wants this to get messier than it needs to.'

The grimp sniggered. 'Speak for yourself, Goblin.'

Ivy grasped the leather belt and tried to inch backwards. She cast her eyes around, searching for a weapon. The room was cylindrical, with metal walls, like a huge tin can; there was only one obvious way in and out – the uncommon door through which Ivy had entered. Around the edge she saw a ring of electronic consoles with dusty switches, smashed bulbs and dark glass monitors, while in the centre stood a shaft of green light locked within a rotating metal cage. It made a strange humming noise as it spun.

'If you let us know where the object is,' Goblin purred, baring sharp teeth, 'then this can all be over.'

'I don't know!' Ivy shouted. 'I don't even know what it *is*!'

The grim-wolf tossed its head back and laughed. The

grimp took a lumbering step towards Ivy and thrust the toilet brush in her face. Blue sparks leaped into the air. Their power thrummed against her cheeks.

'Listen carefully, little girl: our mistress is a very clever woman, but not renowned for her patience. She knows the object is somewhere in the basement of the Wrench Mansion – else why would Ragwort have been down here looking for it? Have you told *him* where it is?'

Ragwort . . . Ivy shook her head, trying to decipher what the grimp meant. If their mistress, Wolfsbane, wasn't sure what Ragwort knew . . . then she couldn't have been working with him; she must be working *against* him.

Wolfsbane and Ragwort, each trying to claim one of the Great Uncommon Good for themselves. *That* was why they'd given her and Seb a deadline. It had turned into a race between them. Ivy paired her enemies up. If Goblin and the grimp were working for Selena Grimes, then the selkies, wraithmoths and others must be employed by Ragwort, or the man in grey – whoever that was.

Goblin's red eyes glowed. 'Why not tell us where the object is, Ivy? You're going to die anyway.'

'And so are your parents,' the grimp added, still grinning.

Ivy staggered backwards in shock. She wasn't going to let them kill her parents. 'Where are they?!' she yelled, but her throat was raw and it came out as a croak.

The grimp waved the toilet brush back and forth. 'It's too late for them, little girl.'

'What have you done with them?' Ivy felt tears welling and brushed them away firmly.

'Nothing . . . yet,' it said. 'I was under specific instructions to keep them alive and in one piece until midnight tonight.' It sniggered – a kind of hissing snort. 'But that was *then*. This is *now*.' It advanced towards her, lunging with the toilet brush. Ivy looked around again, but there was nowhere left to go.

She saw that the grimp's eyes were now black, like two holes in a skull. 'I'll give you one more chance to tell us where it is. And then it's goodbye.'

Ivy shook her head furiously. 'I don't *know*!' she repeated.

The grimp shrugged. 'Oh well. I'll try asking your brother. Maybe he can be . . . persuaded with other methods.'

Goblin growled, teeth bared.

Burning rage spread through Ivy. 'You leave my brother alone!' She leaped towards the grimp, the belt lashing out behind her like a whip.

The grimp simply disappeared like a ghost, and she went crashing headfirst into a dark computer screen.

When she clambered to her feet, the grimp was in front of her again. She could hear Goblin snorting with laughter. The grimp looked at her with a cruel, amused expression. 'Maybe I won't kill you just yet; maybe I'll just toss you in the ghoul hole; then I can take my time later.'

Ghoul hole . . . The name tugged at the edges of Ivy's memory.

The grimp licked its lips. 'Don't worry. You'll have company.' It thrust the toilet brush towards Ivy's heart.

Ivy groaned as the brush made impact, her body shaking violently. Pain ripped through her chest. She was aware of the grimp dragging her somewhere: she heard the creak of metal bars and saw a flash of green light as she was pushed over. Then she was falling. There was a loud crack before a wave of cold spread through her body and everything stopped.

Chapter Thirty-one

Acid-green light pierced Ivy's eyes as she tried to lift
her head. The first thing she felt was pain . . . *everywhere*. Her head was sore, her ribs felt bruised and her
eyes stung.

The floor felt smooth and icy, like metal. Using both
hands, she pushed herself up against the curved wall
behind her, forcing her eyes open. She appeared to be
at the bottom of a cylindrical steel shaft around two
metres in diameter. Above, she could see only darkness.
On the floor beside her lay the uncommon belt and two
crumpled bodies. *Mum and Dad.*

As fast as she could, Ivy shuffled towards them, using
the wall to support her. Her mum was lying face up with
her eyes closed, strands of hair clinging to a film of
sweat on her forehead. She was wearing her blue nurse's
uniform and only one shoe. Ivy's dad lay curled on his
side next to her. The sleeves of his white shirt were
rolled up and his hands were bloodied and swollen. Ivy
flinched as she saw that some of his fingernails were

missing and his neat grey hair had been shorn off in patches. When Ivy was close enough, she reached out with a trembling hand and touched his arm. His skin was cold.

'Dad?' Her throat was dry and crackly. 'Can you hear me? It's Ivy.'

Her dad whimpered and moved his head slightly. His eyelids fluttered. 'Ivy?'

Tears poured down Ivy's cheeks. She squeezed her dad's arm, avoiding his damaged hand. 'Don't worry,' she said softly. 'I'll get you out of here.' Then, 'I love you, Dad; you're going to be OK, I promise. I love you.'

She wriggled over to her mum and pushed the hair off her face. Her mum's skin was warmer than her dad's, but there was a nasty lump on her head and she didn't open her eyes. 'Mum?' Ivy sniffed. 'Mum? It's going to be all right. We're gonna get out of here.'

Ivy quickly scanned her surroundings, looking for some fissure in the steel that she could use as a foothold.

Please, please . . .

But the walls were as smooth as liquid silver. She felt around in her jeans pocket, remembering the button Violet had given her yesterday. Her hands pulsed with heat as they brushed against it. She held the ivory disc in her palm. It wasn't going to get them out of there, but Violet had told her that the button restored health, so it might help her parents. She counted the holes in the button's centre: three. That meant it could be used at least once on each of them.

Carefully Ivy placed the button in the top pocket of her mum's tunic. To her relief, her mum stirred almost immediately. Her blue eyes fluttered open, but she seemed unable to speak. Patting her mum on the cheek, Ivy removed the button and put it in her dad's shirt pocket. She noticed her mum watching, a glazed expression on her face. Ivy's vision started to blur. She shook her head, but it only made it worse. Her mind felt cloudy, like things were slowing down. Her thoughts wandered out of control, as if she was falling asleep. Slowly – or was it quickly? – the events of the past two days seemed to drift away . . . until all she knew was the cold, dark oblivion of a hole at the end of everything . . .

'Ivy?'

Ivy. I like that name.

'Ivy? Can you hear me?'

There it is again.

'Oh, blast. Maybe this thing hasn't worked. Ivy, it's Mum. Wake up; come back to me.'

It sounds familiar . . .

'Ivy, listen to me!' the voice said sternly. It sounded clearer. 'Ivy, open your eyes!'

Ivy blinked. Everything went green. A fuzzy face hovered in front of her: large watery eyes, mousy brown hair, and a mouth that crinkled. 'Ivy? Sweetie?'

Ivy knew that the face was important; it meant something to her. She clenched her teeth against the pressure in her head. Somehow she had to remember who this was. She *had* to.

Then . . .

'Mum?'

'Ivy!' her mum croaked, louder. She was struggling to push herself upright. There was a pinch of colour in her cheeks, but her shoulders were trembling.

Ivy's mind was suddenly washed with clarity, as if she'd just bobbed up onto the surface of the ocean and was heaving in fresh air, the darkness gone.

The ghoul hole . . .

The grimp had pushed her into a ghoul hole. Now she remembered why the name was familiar. She had seen a ghoul hole in the underguard station. Scratch had told her about them – they use them for muckers because they disorientate captives and make them lose their memories of their time inside, so that when they leave, it feels like no time has passed at all.

Ivy had to stop herself forgetting. She looked at her mum and then at her dad, who was stirring. She tried to picture the faces of Seb and Granma Sylvie; of all her friends at school, her favourite teachers. She reminded herself of Valian, of the selkies, the wraith-moth, and the grim-wolf. Shakily she reached for her mum's hand and tried to help her sit up. They were both trembling and Ivy wasn't sure she had any strength left.

'Mum!' She reached over and hugged her. Tears spilled out and soaked into the lapel of her mum's tunic. She sniffed and pushed her mum back, awash with relief. 'Mum, I need you to trust me and do what I say. Do you think you can hold this and not let go?'

She held the uncommon trouser belt out towards her mum.

The deep worry-lines on her mum's forehead crinkled, but she did as she was told.

Ivy smiled as best she could and wriggled over to

check on her dad. There was more colour in his cheeks now. She reached for the button in his shirt pocket.

'It's not there,' her mum croaked.

Ivy turned back to face her. 'What?'

'The button. I saw what you did with it for your father, and when you didn't come round, I put it in *your* pocket, hoping it would help.'

Ivy reached into her own pocket and, sure enough, felt the little button resting inside. As the warmth of her whispering spread through her, the stinging in her eyes disappeared and the pain in her head began to dull. Her legs were feeling strong again. Maybe she could even stand up. The button was working. 'We're gonna have to hold Dad between us,' she told her mum. 'The belt will do the rest. It'll work – just don't let go.'

Ivy's mum looked at Ivy. Her eyes were bloodshot and ringed with dark circles, but they were trusting. She nodded, then reached for the belt.

Ivy shifted over to her dad and, with her mum's help, pulled him upright.

'Ivy?' he murmured as they put their arms round him. Ivy clamped her other arm round her mum's waist. They stank of selkie slime, but Ivy didn't care. They were her parents. And they were alive.

'Now raise your arms, Mum, if you can.' She remembered how the belt simply carried you. *She should be able to do this, no matter how weak she is.*

They floated up steadily, cold air blowing through their hair. As they approached the top of the shaft, Ivy saw the rotating cage – a whirring haze of grey through the green light. She wondered who or *what* might be waiting for them behind the bars.

Suddenly the cage screeched to a halt. A shadow moved behind the bars. Ivy tried to wriggle away from it. 'Mum, Dad, hang on!'

A hand shot through one of the gaps and grabbed Ivy by the neck, sucking all the air from her lungs. She recognized the black gloves – the knuckles encrusted with steel studs. A severe but polished face hovered at the other end of them: smooth, pale skin; long straight nose, dark glasses; thin white lips . . .

Officer Smokehart.

Emerging from the ghoul hole, Ivy collapsed onto the cold steel floor, her mum and dad falling beside her. Around her were the silvery walls of the tin-can room – the one with all the old monitors and switch-boards – only this time, everything looked blurry and distorted. Officer Smokehart's face floated in front of her eyes. She could hear his voice, but his words were out of sync with his lips.

'. . . no one else here. The boy must have had warning we were coming and got out.' He was talking to another underguard – the squat, red-faced constable who had arrested Ivy and Seb earlier. 'Get some transport ready for the adults and prepare two uncommon whistles for use. They will need to have their memories stripped before we take them back to the station.'

Memories stripped . . . ? Ivy didn't even want to imagine what that involved. She couldn't let that happen – this was her mum and dad! Her head was swimming as she searched the room for Seb or Valian. She couldn't see either of them.

'Sir,' she heard the constable say, long before she saw the word form on his lips, 'do you want me to send a featherlight back to the station? Get some help down here to search the rest of the mansion?'

Smokehart stiffened. 'No, I'll do it myself. I don't want any stone left unturned.'

Ivy tried to swallow, but her mouth was too dry. She croaked out two words. 'What . . . happened . . . ?'

Smokehart approached almost in slow motion, his dark glasses fixed on her face. 'You can hear me?' He sounded surprised. Ivy managed a nod.

'In that case,' he hissed, 'let me enlighten you.' He crouched down till he was level with her and curled his lip into a snarl. 'After you and your brother escaped from the coach, I suspected you might meet up with Valian Kaye again, so I tracked him down. I found the three of you by that fountain. I had a hunch you'd lead me somewhere interesting, but when you opened the gates to the Wrench Mansion, I couldn't quite believe it. I snuck in behind you and, once you were up the hill and out of sight, I opened the gate again to let my constable through.'

Ivy frowned, even though it hurt. She wondered *how* Smokehart had come through behind them. She hadn't seen anything.

He must have read her expression because he smiled and slowly lowered his dark glasses.

Ivy recoiled.

Smokehart's eye sockets were empty – or, no; not quite. There was a swirling cone of black dust in each of them, drilling back into his skull. Looking at them, Ivy felt cold despair. 'I'm dead,' Smokehart said matter-of-factly. 'One of the Eyre Folk, to be specific. We make excellent underguards. Strong, fast and, like many of the dead, we can disappear. So you wouldn't have seen me strolling *through* the gate behind you and waiting in the darkness.'

A chill slid down Ivy's spine. She should have guessed.

'In the mansion a trail of animal tracks led us to a door in the basement,' Smokehart continued. 'We realized it was uncommon when it opened into a different room every time. This place was the first that held any interest.'

Ivy wondered if Seb and Valian had survived the

fight with the wraithmoths and selkies in the whispering hall. Smokehart couldn't have found it yet.

She turned to her parents. Her mum was slumped against the wall, her head tilted to one side. Ivy wasn't sure if she was unconscious, but her eyes were closed and her body was still. Her dad was moving feebly, trying to sit up.

'My parents,' Ivy wheezed, in a small voice. 'Are you going to help them?'

Officer Smokehart drew closer: Ivy could feel his cold, dead breath against her cheek. He shot a glance at the constable, checking he was otherwise occupied. 'Oh, don't worry about your parents, Ivy Wrench. I intend to keep them nice and snug back at the underguard station. And as soon as you and your brother are locked away beside them, I might even consider releasing your mucker mother. If you try and escape again, though . . . Well, let's just say I don't think your parents will fare too well against some of our more . . . interesting inmates.'

'What?' Ivy realized that there was no point in trying to explain about the uncommon alarm clock.

'Constable?' Officer Smokehart called. 'Are you ready with the transport?'

The constable was busy pulling two pieces of folded grey plastic out of his tool belt. 'Almost there, sir.'

Smokehart turned towards the uncommon door, which was propped open with a bucket. Through it, Ivy caught a glimpse of some dark room in the Wrench Mansion.

He sighed with pleasure. 'That house has been out of my reach for over forty years, but not any longer. Everything that happened to the Wrenches on Twelfth Night 1969 will soon become clear: how they disappeared, where they ended up, what their real motives and identities were. No more mystery. No more lies. The truth will be revealed, order will be restored and the law will finally be upheld.'

Ivy turned away. Smokehart had no idea of the real truth . . .

Something glittered at the corner of Ivy's eye. She turned to find a feather bobbing in the air, scrawling a message in front of the constable. 'Uh, sir, Lady Selena Grimes is asking what we found down here. She wants to know if there's anything to report and whether she should be concerned for traders' safety?' He looked at Ivy and her parents nervously.

'Tell her we have found one of the runaways in very incriminating circumstances and we are taking her and her parents back to the station immediately. Everything is under control.'

The constable nodded enthusiastically and began writing a reply.

Ivy gritted her teeth, wishing she could tell Smokehart the truth. *Selena Grimes is Wolfsbane. She is a member of the Dirge!*

Ivy remembered the respectful way Smokehart had acted around Selena Grimes – bowing to her orders, scared of contradicting her. She had fooled him, just like she had fooled everyone else. As Quartermaster of the Dead End, Selena Grimes had the whole of Lundinor wrapped around her little finger. Ivy wondered, with a shiver, if any of the other Dirge members had taken important positions.

Officer Smokehart grabbed her arm with his gloved hand, tightening his fingers. 'No paperclip for you this time. I'll keep hold of you; that way I can be certain you won't escape.' With his other hand, he pointed to Ivy's parents. 'Get them bagged up now!'

Ivy reached for her dad, who was trying to sit up beside her. '*Dad!*' she screamed. 'Dad!'

'Ivy?' he murmured. 'Is that you?'

The constable stepped forward; he was holding a large brass whistle on a gold chain. He bent down next to Ivy's dad and quickly blew the thing in his ear. It made no sound at all, but Ivy's dad went very still. His eyes began to glaze over.

'Leave him alone!' Ivy croaked frantically. She tried to pull herself free, but Smokehart yanked back so hard she thought her arm might be ripped out of its socket.

'Make sure you erase everything from the last two days,' Officer Smokehart ordered. 'I don't want a single memory escaping, even from the uncommon father. It is our duty to protect all uncommon secrets.'

After counting for a moment, the constable hurried round to Ivy's dad's other ear and repeated the procedure. Ivy's dad slowly closed his eyes, as if drifting off into a pleasant sleep. The officer used the whistle in exactly the same way on Ivy's mum, before unfolding two pieces of grey plastic sheeting. There was a zip down the middle of each and the words BODY BAG printed on the side. He dragged Ivy's mum onto the first.

Ivy watched in horror: her mum's body was quite limp. Maybe she should have left Violet's button in her mum's pocket for longer; the healing effects seemed to be wearing off.

Once the constable had zipped the bag over Ivy's mum's head, the material went flat as her body disappeared. While he started to move Ivy's dad, Smokehart pointed at the uncommon door.

'Make sure you keep that propped open,' he reminded his constable. 'I don't want to spend another five hours trying to get back here.'

Ivy's head felt fuzzy again. *Five hours? Wait* . . . 'What time is it?' she asked. She pictured the hands of the uncommon alarm clock counting down to midnight, when her parents were going to die. She could see the words of the Dirge, written by that black feather: *The clock is ticking.*

'Just past eleven,' Smokehart said curtly. 'So by my calculations you've got a little under an hour in the cell till midnight and then' – he grinned – '*Happy New Year.*'

Ivy started. 'New Year . . . ?'

A smile creased Smokehart's lips. 'Oh, don't tell me you haven't realized.' He looked around the room, over at the ghoul hole and then back to Ivy. 'You've been stuck in that ghoul hole for over four hours.'

Chapter Thirty-two

No . . .

No, this can't be happening.

Ivy stumbled along at Smokehart's side as he dragged her through the gates. He was holding both her wrists together with just one of his strong hands. Now that she knew he was dead, she was no longer surprised that he seemed like a robot.

She heard the gates clang shut behind her as she stumbled out into a shadowy street in some other part of Lundinor. The place was bustling with underguards. Several constables were scraping samples of cement from the brick wall. One sergeant had bagged up a handful of leaves from the fountain basin, while another was experimentally prodding the metal surround.

Ivy tried to ignore the pain – though her body hurt all over. *It's almost midnight*, she reminded herself, her stomach turning over. *There's no time left.*

Ragwort and Selena Grimes were still out there, and in under an hour Ivy's parents would be dead if she didn't do something. She couldn't assume that Seb or Valian had escaped. It was up to her now.

Smokehart tugged her into the street. Getting away from him was the only way to save everyone.

He must have a weakness, Ivy thought. *Everyone has a weakness.*

A few underguards spoke to Smokehart as they passed by.

'Congratulations, sir,' one of them said, straightening. 'I can't wait to read your report on Twelfth Night.'

Smokehart paused to reply, still holding Ivy in his crushing grasp.

'As I have said all along, the key to the whole mystery is what happened in the mansion that night – that's the evidence we've been lacking all these years.'

Smokehart's words triggered a thought in Ivy's head.

What happened in the house on Twelfth Night . . .

Ivy knew some of that already. Violet Eyelet had been there that evening, dropping off the objects she'd scouted for the Wrenches. Ivy wondered if there were any clues hiding in the details of Violet's story; clues she'd previously missed.

All at once a deafening siren went off. Ivy couldn't tell where the noise was coming from, but it was almost as loud as a selkie.

'Not now,' Smokehart groaned.

'Sir!' one of the underguards cried. 'That's Mr Punch's alarm. We need to go to the Market Cross immediately. It's the law – even for underguards.'

'I know, I know,' he grumbled. He raised his voice as he turned to the other underguards. 'Make sure you leave everything where it is. I don't want any evidence tampered with.' He glared at Ivy. 'You stay with me. Remember: I have your parents.'

In a matter of seconds the pavement was heaving with uncommoners. Smokehart shouted at them to let him through and, on the whole, they obeyed. Still, Ivy knew that this was her best chance to break away. She just needed to get away from Smokehart's iron grip.

The crowd gathered at a T-junction as everyone turned onto the Gauntlet. Smokehart was jostled, and his fingers tensed around Ivy's wrist. She noticed tiny crimson spots spreading over the pale skin of his neck. It had happened several times before, but Ivy had no idea what it meant. *Farrow's Guide* had mentioned something about Smokehart's race, the Eyre Folk. If only she could remember . . .

There was a clatter of hoofs behind them. Smokehart stepped aside, pulling Ivy with him, and turned to see an underguard coach. The red-faced constable was driving it.

'What are you doing here?' Smokehart spluttered. 'You're meant to be in the mansion. You've got to let us all back in!' The red spots on his neck began creeping up to his face.

'But I heard the alarm!' the constable argued, one hand securing his hat. 'It's the law. We have to go, *don't we?*'

Ivy's head spun as the information came to her: *Farrow's Guide* had said that Eyre Folk 'spook' when they're emotional – that's what the 'sweating blood' thing was called. And it was *uncontrollable* – Smokehart couldn't stop it. If she was going to escape, now was the time.

She thought for a second. Smokehart was keeping her parents at the station and she had no doubt that his threats were real. If she ran away, it might put them both in more danger . . .

But then, the Dirge's threats were real too, and they were infinitely more dangerous. After seeing the whispering hall, Ivy understood what they were capable of. It wasn't just her parents' lives at stake – it was the safety of everyone in Lundinor and beyond.

The decision was made. She had to go.

'Constable!' Smokehart roared. Ivy could see blood bubbling everywhere through his skin. 'What have you done?'

The constable slid lower in his seat. '*Sir?*'

Ivy's wrists and hands were slippery. She could see the scarlet fluid running down her arm from

Smokehart's fingers; as he grew angrier, so his grip was loosening. Suddenly, with all her might, she yanked her wrists free. She dived into the crowd, pushing and squeezing until she reached the other side of the street. She could hear Smokehart's cold voice rising out of the throng behind her.

'Your parents, Ivy Wrench! I have your parents!'

Tears poured down her cheeks as she ran. She didn't care where she was heading, as long as it was away from Smokehart. Once the crowd was far behind her, she stopped in the doorway of an empty shop to get her breath back.

She pictured the uncommon alarm clock ticking away in Valian's room. There was only one sure-fire way to save her parents in time: stop the Dirge. If they got their hands on one of the Great Uncommon Good, who knew what kind of evil they'd unleash on Lundinor and on the rest of the world. She had to reach it first. Granma Sylvie *must* have left Lundinor with it on Twelfth Night. Now Ivy had a little under an hour to find out where she'd hidden it.

'Violet was in the mansion that night,' she whispered to herself as she ran through the clues. Something told her that she needed to go back and talk to Violet. She'd probably be in the Market Cross now, along with everyone else. It would be risky to go back there, though; that's where Smokehart would be.

If only Seb and Valian were still here, Ivy thought. At least then she could get a second opinion. She wondered if she had enough time to check the room above Hoff & Winkle's Hobsmatch Emporium to see whether they'd made it. She weighed up the risks . . .

There wasn't a moment to lose.

Chapter Thirty-three

There was a tension in the air at the Market Cross. Uncommoners stood around muttering to each other.

Flinching from the noise of the siren, Ivy pushed her way through chain mail, lace cuffs and crinoline petticoats. The crowd had gathered in a circle around the middle of the square. Stopping a few rows back, Ivy spotted a couple of familiar faces on the opposite side, but no Violet. Ethel and Mr Littlefair were standing behind a family dressed in karate gis; Johnny Hands was beside a group of traders wearing sombreros; and Albert Merribus, whose white hair was sticking out as if he'd had an electric shock, was waiting by some under-guards: these ones had silver-braided epaulets and the letters SB on their lapels. *Special Branch*, Ivy realized. She noticed with a sinking feeling that Selena Grimes was nowhere to be seen.

In the centre of the square a huge oyster shell had been placed on a wooden table. Once the crowd had hushed, the shell closed, swallowing the throbbing siren with it.

Ivy stood on tiptoe to see an exceedingly tall man in a ringmaster's red tailcoat and black top hat take centre stage. A name ran in whispers through the crowd . . .

'Mr Punch . . .'

'It's Mr Punch . . .'

'. . . *the Guardian of Lundinor.*'

Ivy inspected him curiously. She recognized his name. He was the man who had beaten Octavius Wrench to the position of Quartermaster of the Great Cavern in that election on Twelfth Night 1969.

Except . . .

He didn't look old enough. This Mr Punch was fresh-faced, young and lean, with broad shoulders and a straight ginger beard. Beneath the hat, a pair of brilliant aquamarine eyes sparkled with intelligence. That colour gave Ivy an odd feeling of déjà-vu . . .

Mr Punch held a conch shell to his lips. 'My thanks to all of you for gathering here so quickly. I'm afraid I have worrying news.' His voice was so deep and sonorous, it sent vibrations through Ivy's chest. 'Yesterday, as most of you know, a trader was attacked by a wraithmoth – a creature of the dead we have not seen for many years. A few hours ago I received reports of shadows gathering outside the Great Gates.' Mr Punch coughed and turned to address another section of the crowd. As he did so, his face seemed to change – his beard grew curly, his skin darker, and his hat disappeared. 'Our investigations revealed evidence that selkies and wraithmoths had been in the arrivals chambers, sabotaging the air filters.'

The crowd started to mutter. Ivy frowned. *Ragwort* – the man in grey – was the one controlling the selkies and wraithmoths. He was behind this. She wondered what his motives were.

'Our engineers are doing their utmost to restore the uncommon technology,' Mr Punch continued, 'but until they succeed, I'm afraid I have to insist that all living uncommoners remain in Lundinor. The air outside the Great Gates is toxic, and until the filters can be repaired it is too dangerous for you to go out.'

Ivy shuddered. *Ragwort wants everyone trapped inside* . . .

'As you know, GUT law prevents bag travel to the common world from inside the Great Gates, so we will all have to remain here until the situation can be resolved.' Mr Punch shifted round again, and this time his whole face appeared to change – the shape of his nose, lips and forehead. Ivy rubbed her eyes. She must still be suffering from the effects of being in the ghoul hole. Maybe it gave you hallucinations.

He cleared his throat. 'I am confident that the underguard will find these saboteurs very soon. They have informed me that they will be responding to featherlight twenty-four hours a day. If you do see anything suspicious, I want you to report it immediately. Mr Merribus has generously offered free featherlights for the next few days.' Ivy spotted Merribus nodding.

'It is an uncertain time in the streets,' Mr Punch went on – one minute he was the ringmaster; the next, an older man in a grey flannel suit. 'I want you all to be extra vigilant and look out for each other. We have faced threats before, and we have overcome them. We are stronger when we work together and trust in each other. I would ask you all to remember that.' His words hung in the air for a moment, before he nodded and turned away.

As Ivy watched him disappear back into the crowd, she couldn't help wondering what he was really thinking. If he really *was* the Guardian of Lundinor, surely he suspected that the Dirge were at work again. Had he looked into Ivy and Seb's arrest after the wraithmoth attack yesterday? And what did he plan to do about it, if anything?

The crowd began shuffling away, discussing Mr Punch's news. Ivy craned her neck, trying to find a safe route out. Suddenly she spied a puff of fluffy white hair beneath a bobbing bonnet.

Violet.

'Violet, over h—!' Ivy stopped, remembering not to attract attention. She squeezed through the crowd.

Violet Eyelet turned as Ivy reached her. She was wearing two pairs of spectacles – one broken, the other fogged up. She looked more awake than she had after the wraithmoth attack, but her face was badly scratched.

'*Ivy?*' she whispered. 'I thought you'd been arrested.'

'I was,' Ivy said. 'Look, I need to ask you something.'

Violet glanced around warily. 'Best not talk here; the underguard will be looking for you.'

She led Ivy out of the crowd, behind a row of empty kiosks. 'I'm very sorry about yesterday,' she said. 'We all are. We shouldn't have let Smokehart take the pair of you like that; it was monstrous of us.' She pushed her broken spectacles further up her nose. 'I was just so shaken up by that—' She couldn't say *wraithmoth*.

'Don't worry about that now,' Ivy told her. 'I need to ask you about Twelfth Night 1969. It's important.'

Violet squinted. 'All right, but I doubt it'll help. I told the underguard everything before.'

Ivy hoped that there was something they'd missed.

She'd been to the mansion now; she knew all about the fountain entrance and the layout inside. Maybe that would help her. 'Can you tell me what happened when you went into the Wrench Mansion? *Exactly* what you saw?'

Violet removed her glasses and frowned. 'Sylvie took me up the hill and into the house. Octavius wasn't there because he was waiting for the election results at the Market Cross, so – for the first time ever – I gave my scouted objects to Helena Wrench, his wife. Helena was a sweet lady. I remember she offered me a drink of Nelson's Tipple when I got there – fancy stuff; the kind they drink in the West End. I'd never tried it before.' She smiled. 'Nor have I since.'

Ivy tried to picture it: Helena Wrench – with those sad blue eyes – greeting Violet. The image of Helena's face was one of the first memories to return to Granma Sylvie. Ivy wondered if there was more significance to it than she had previously thought.

Violet's voice lowered to a whisper. 'Helena led me into this huge dining room – candelabras along the table, chandeliers suspended from the ceiling, creepy oil paintings hanging on the walls; but she still made me feel at ease – unlike Octavius. He always looked down his nose at me. He absolutely hated me using an old sack as my collection bag; thought it was unsightly. Helena was fine with it. She . . .' Violet paused and blinked. 'Helena . . . That night she had a funny turn, I remember. I gave her my sack of objects and she let go of it right away, as if I'd handed her a hot potato. I thought I'd done something wrong because she asked me to leave immediately; virtually pushed me through the door. I didn't even have time to pick up my sack.' She frowned, struggling for the details. 'Sylvie didn't know what had come over her mother. After she'd shown me out the gates, she went back inside to see if her mother was OK. That was the last time I saw her.'

Ivy had gone very still. She stared into the middle distance as realization gripped her. *A hot potato* . . . She knew exactly what that felt like.

'Did anyone else see you?' she asked urgently. 'Was there anyone else in the mansion?'

Violet frowned. 'One of Sylvie's brothers was there, I think; he was setting the table. Blond hair, portly.'

Ivy's mind raced back to the family portrait in the Wrench Mansion. She had to steady herself against Violet's arm as the truth became clear . . .

Him. It had been him all along.

Chapter Thirty-four

The lights were on behind the dirty windows of Hoff & Winkle's Hobsmatch Emporium when Ivy finally got there. She'd had to risk asking several street bells along the way to make sure she was heading in the right direction. She scurried round the back, slipped up the stairs and stood outside the door to Valian's room. There was no sound coming from within.

Ivy closed her eyes. If Seb wasn't there, she mustn't get upset – there wasn't time. Anyway, it didn't mean he wasn't alive; it just meant he hadn't made it back. She had to go on and save their mum and dad without him, no matter what.

She opened her eyes and knocked lightly.

Nothing at first.

Silence.

Then . . .

'Ivy?'

It was Valian.

Ivy's heart pounded. The door opened inwards, and

behind Valian's scrawny figure she glimpsed the outline of another person.

'Seb?' she whispered, daring to hope – though she had seen enough in the last two days to know that shadows could trick you.

'*Ivy?*' Seb's voice sounded hoarse. He got up from the bed and stepped into the light. His face was covered in angry red scratches and his hair had dried in matted dreads. As Ivy ran towards him, she heard Scratch shouting excitedly from the bed. She gave her brother a thankful hug.

'You're alive!' he sobbed. 'We didn't know what'd happened.'

Ivy allowed herself a few long breaths of relief. *He's OK* . . . She felt Seb wince as she squeezed harder, so she let go. 'Are you all right?' She turned to Valian. 'What about you?'

Valian's eyes were serious. 'We barely got away with our lives. We held them off as long as we could. I thought it was all over.'

'Me too,' Seb added. 'But then the underguard alarm sounded in the mansion, and the dead just . . . disappeared. It was like they were spooked.' He smiled glumly. 'Oh, the irony.'

Ivy thought back to what Smokehart had told her about searching the mansion. They must have used the alarm then.

'You should be proud of your brother,' Valian said. 'He was awesome with those drumsticks. It was like he'd been using them all his life. I wouldn't have survived without him.'

Seb slapped Valian on the shoulder. 'Neither of us would have survived without the other. We did OK back there – we were a team.'

Ivy smiled. It was nice to know that she and Seb had someone on their side.

'Ivy,' Seb said, 'we don't have much time left. Mum and Dad—'

'Smokehart has them at the underguard station,' Ivy told him. 'I found them after I went through that door in the whispering hall.' She reached for the un-common alarm clock, which was lying next to Scratch on Valian's bed. The ticking spread through her body and her heart began to quicken. The black hands were hovering dangerously close to midnight; they only had half an hour left.

'I think I know how to save them,' Ivy announced, her mind racing. 'Come on – I'll explain on the way.'

They hurried through the back streets of Lundinor. The Market Cross was still busy, but further out the roads were empty: no doubt people had retreated indoors after Mr Punch's announcement. The streets were murky; mist rolled around their feet and there was a strange, musty smell in the air.

'*Selena Grimes!*' Valian exclaimed, after hearing what had happened to Ivy in the whispering hall. 'It's common knowledge that she's a ghoul, but *Wolfsbane?*' He rubbed his chin. 'I should've seen it earlier. She was Quartermaster when Rosie went missing. She's fooled everyone.' His face flushed. 'No one will believe us, though. Lady Grimes a member of the Dirge? Trust me, you need evidence before going to the underguard with that bombshell.'

Ivy knew that he was speaking from experience. 'At least *we* know who she really is.'

Seb slipped his drumsticks out of his sleeves. 'So, they were competing to see who could find the Great Uncommon Good first . . . How did you find out who the man in grey – Ragwort – was?'

'Violet said something about Helena Wrench that reminded me of myself; of how I reacted once when I touched something uncommon. Scratch told me that whispering runs in the family, so it made sense that our great-grandmother, Helena, was a whisperer, just like me.' Ivy turned a corner, leading Seb and Valian out onto a wide street. 'That night, Twelfth Night 1969, Violet brought something incredible to Helena; something so powerful that when Helena touched it, she dropped it. It must have frightened her. Violet wouldn't have had a clue what it was, of course – she was only interested in buttons.'

Seb stopped in his tracks as he realized. 'One of the Great Uncommon Good – that's what she'd found?'

Valian looked dazed. 'You're kidding.'

Ivy shook her head gravely. 'Helena knew how powerful it was and what it could do in the wrong hands; in the hands of her husband, for example. She must have known or suspected that he was a member of the Dirge.'

Seb set off again. 'She must have been scared of him,' he pointed out. 'If she was a whisperer, she probably had to keep it secret because the Dirge ran those whispering halls.'

'Exactly,' Ivy agreed. 'Helena knew she couldn't let him find the object. Maybe she tried to destroy it; I don't know. But it didn't work. She had no option but to send the object away; to hide it where no one would find it.'

Seb's eyes grew wide. 'She gave it to Granma,' he realized. 'She gave it to her that very night and told her to disappear.' He slowed down as he worked it out. 'That's why Granma left! That's why she put on that bracelet; she *had* to hide herself away, she *had* to forget.'

That's right. Ivy's throat tightened. It was a bittersweet feeling – of sadness, but also of immense pride. Granma Sylvie had done the bravest, most selfless thing Ivy could imagine. She had voluntarily given up the memory of her whole life in order to keep the location of the Great Uncommon Good a secret.

'And there was only one person who saw all this,' Ivy said as they slowed down to enter a small courtyard; 'one person who was there when Violet dropped off the object and when Helena gave it to Sylvie and told her to leave.' She turned to Seb. 'You remember that portrait in the Wrench Mansion? The one that showed the whole family? There was only one member – other than Sylvie – with blond hair.' Ivy recalled a chubby face with small dark eyes and pale hair: the second-youngest of the family, Cartimore.

'So Cartimore Wrench saw the Great Uncommon Good object,' Valian summarized, 'and he's been searching for it all this time. He must have told Selena Grimes about it years ago, when he first joined the Dirge.'

Seb's eyes flashed. 'And when Granma's bracelet was cut off and she appeared again, they both restarted their campaigns to retrieve it.'

'But Granma's forgotten where it is,' Ivy said. 'That's why Cartimore sent the selkie to read my mind and planted the wraithmoth in our room at the Cabbage Moon to spy on us. This whole time Cartimore and Selena thought we knew where it was. The grimp and the grim-wolf were both in the mansion; I think Selena suspected it was hidden there.'

'So where is Cartimore now?' Seb asked. 'If he's been keeping an eye on us, he must be close by in Lundinor.'

Ivy nodded grimly. She'd been thinking about that. 'Who's the one person who knew all along the things that only Cartimore Wrench would know?' she asked, leading them round the final corner. 'Someone who gave us that clue about going north to the Wrench Mansion; someone who's been able to read all the communications across Lundinor for years.' She turned to Valian as she came to a stop. 'You told me yourself that he turned up forty years ago, right when the Wrench Family went into hiding.'

She pointed, and they all looked up at the spindly tower standing in the middle of the square in front of them: the featherlight mailhouse.

Chapter Thirty-five

Albert Merribus or Cartimore Wrench or Ragwort or the man in grey – *whoever he really was* – was nowhere to be seen. The mailhouse was empty.

Ivy, Seb and Valian found themselves in a circular room. Desks and bookshelves were covered in dirty teacups, leather-bound books, jars of different-coloured feathers and old cheese rinds. On one side, a stained porcelain wash basin was fixed to the wall, and hanging between the eaves of the pointed roof was a ratty canvas hammock. Ivy sniffed, smelling old socks, dust and bird poo. She guessed that Cartimore had been living here alone all these years, his anger and obsession festering.

She heard a scratching noise and turned round to find Valian clambering out from beneath one of the desks. 'There's an uncommon map down here with the name Sylvie Wrench on it,' he said. 'That's what Cartimore's been using to track your gran. It shows that she's in the hospital right now.'

Ivy's eyes fixed on an upturned garden hoe propped against the wall. A wrinkled grey trench coat and wide-brimmed hat were hanging from it – the clothes of the man in grey.

'Guys,' Seb said, his voice unsteady. 'There's another door here.' Ivy hadn't seen it at first because it was exactly the same colour as the walls, like tea-stained paper. She recognized it as Seb rubbed the dust off. 'It's the Ragwort door from the Hexroom.' He tried opening it, but it wouldn't budge. 'Well, I guess this means we're definitely right: Merribus *is* Ragwort. What do we do now?'

Ivy racked her brains. All the evidence was there now. Surely Smokehart would have to believe them.

Valian got to his feet. 'I'm going after them,' he said in a tight voice. 'Wolfsbane *and* Ragwort. They might know where Rosie is.'

Ivy opened her mouth, but she could see there was no point in trying to stop him. His jaw was set. She nudged open the door they'd come in through. She didn't want to split up again – they'd only just got back together – but the clock was ticking. She could almost feel it, slicing away precious seconds while they were standing there deciding what to do. 'I think the only way to do this is to split up,' she said.

Valian checked his uncommon trowel. It wasn't glowing . . . yet. 'Agreed. I'll go to the Dead End. My guess is that Selena will be prowling around there; it's her territory, after all.'

Seb's face was serious. 'Ivy, one of us has to go to the underguard station. Mum and Dad are still in there. Whatever's coming for them, we've got to stop it.'

Ivy retrieved the uncommon alarm clock from her pocket, flinching as her whispering started up. The hands were still black. The clock face shimmered, but she looked away before the image of her mum's face appeared.

'We *have* to protect them,' she said firmly.

'I'll go,' Seb offered. 'We don't have time to argue.'

Ivy gave a shaky nod. She didn't fancy Seb's chances against one or more of the Dirge's dead cronies, but they didn't have time to come up with a better plan. 'All right then. I'll go to the House of Bells and find Ethel and then Violet. With their help, we might be able to convince Smokehart of the truth about Granma Sylvie, and maybe he can stop the Dirge before it's too late.'

She looked back down into the deadly face of the alarm clock. The spindly black hands were approaching midnight.

Ivy gazed up at the shop. Like its neighbours, the House of Bells looked dark and empty. The blind was drawn over the main window, and through the glass door Ivy could see only the rough outline of the front room, sketched in shadows in the darkness.

A thought struck her: *What if Ethel hasn't made it back yet?*

She climbed the steps to the front door and opened it quietly. Voices greeted her as she stepped over the threshold, but they weren't Ethel's.

'Really, Cartimore,' a dry voice chided. 'Disabling the air filters was a clumsy plan. Everyone suspects something – the underguard have been swarming all over the place. If all you needed to do was to empty this building, there are easier ways. Your methods are always so crude. Do you want people to uncover your identity?'

Ivy went very still as the door clicked shut behind her. Had she heard that name correctly . . . *Cartimore*?

She tiptoed towards a thin sliver of light coming from the door to the storeroom, staring open-mouthed at the walls. Every single bell had been covered in some sort of thick slime which, she guessed from the eye-watering smell in the air, was probably of selkie origin. Even the desk bell – as large and powerful as it was – had been silenced behind a membrane of green jelly, prevented from moving even a centimetre to release a squeak of alarm.

'It wouldn't be such a bad thing,' a coarse voice replied. 'I'd love to see the faces of the half-wits around here when they realize who I really am. Just for a moment I'd like to see their eyes – to see their fear again.' He sniggered. Ivy could hear the cantankerous tones of Albert Merribus mixed with something more intelligent.

There came a crunch and a hiss from the storeroom. Cartimore cursed. 'It must be here somewhere; it must be. Those runts of Sylvie's have been in here every day since they arrived in Lundinor, and Ethel Dread was Sylvie's friend when we were younger. The children have given it to her for safekeeping, I know they have.'

There was a sigh. 'I have no patience for your guess-work,' the other voice said, and Ivy suddenly recognized it: *Selena Grimes.* 'Need I remind you that when you joined the Dirge you made a binding deal, Cartimore? If your sister ever came out of hiding, you would tell us how to find the object and we would do everything in our power to help you get it back from her. Now, we have fulfilled our end of the bargain. Where is the object?'

Cartimore growled. 'Don't pretend you're doing this for the Dirge. I know you've been hunting for it behind my back, hoping to use it for yourself. Do you think I didn't notice that grimp of yours sneaking into the mansion after me?'

'Look at my hands,' Selena snapped. 'They bear the mark of loyalty, the same as yours. Everything I have done has been in the service of the Dirge. Our brothers and sisters of the Fallen Guild are closer than ever before to finding the other four Great Uncommon Good. Very soon the six of us will be unrivalled in our power. But first we need the object you promised us when you joined. Now, if it's not here and it's not in the mansion, then where, oh where, dear Cartimore, is it? Or do I have to consider the possibility that you were lying all along?'

Ivy had a bad feeling in the pit of her stomach, listening to the Dirge's plans. Whatever they intended to use the Great Uncommon Good for, it couldn't be good.

'What do you think, Goblin, my sweet?' Selena called gently. 'Maybe you can help refresh Cartimore's memory . . .'

Ivy heard the padding of heavy paws. 'As you wish, mistress,' a voice growled. The jelly surrounding the desk bell quivered. *Goblin.* The last time Ivy had seen the grim-wolf was just before the grimp threw her in the ghoul hole. Her chest tightened.

'Now, Selena, there's . . . no need for that.' Cartimore's voice wobbled. 'You must believe me. I saw it in my sister's hands when I was a boy – an old sack, easy to miss. My mother told her it was one of the Great Five. It must have power beyond imagining.'

Ivy tried to think. *An old sack . . . That* was what they were after? It must have been Violet's bag – the one she carried her scouted objects in.

In front of her, the desk bell started to shake, murmuring something. Ivy couldn't understand what it was saying.

Goblin howled in warning. 'There's someone outside, mistress!'

A cold shiver ran down the nape of Ivy's neck. She had to get out of there.

Too late, she turned to make a dash for it, but the grim-wolf had already heard her. It came tearing through the storeroom door, slamming it open with a *bang!* Ivy froze. The wolf's eyes were fixed on her face. She scrambled backwards.

And then fell . . .

She landed with a thud behind the counter. Pain shot up her spine as the wolf made an about-turn, lightning quick, and sprang towards her. She was faintly aware of the desk bell trying to speak from within its gelatinous prison, but before she had time to think about it, Selena Grimes came slinking *through* the back wall and stopped right at Ivy's feet. Cartimore followed behind her, limping through the open doorway.

'Well, well, Goblin' – Selena smiled at her grim-wolf – 'what have you found here?' She had taken off her gloves, and Ivy saw that her hands were squirming with maggots, the skin flaking off around blackened fingernails.

Ivy's body pulsed with terror. She was trapped. There was nowhere to go. Even if she could get out, the grim-wolf would chase her. Somewhere in the back of her mind she noted the fact that Selena Grimes was dead – a ghoul, if she had to guess. Selena was tall and her feet were once again covered by an ankle-length dress.

'Why, if it isn't the grand-niece herself, dropping by for a visit!' Selena clapped her rotting hands together. 'How delightful, Cartimore.' She bent down towards Ivy, her smile revealing needle-sharp teeth. 'I think she's come alone.'

Ivy stared at her great-uncle in horror. He looked nothing like his portrait. There, he was painted with a full head of golden-blond hair and appeared over-fed. Now he was gaunt and bony. His frayed clothes were stained and he moved around awkwardly like a man twice his age. 'The runt is no grand-niece of mine,' he growled, his lips curling back into a snarl. 'Step aside, Selena; I'll deal with her myself.' He approached Ivy, limping. She tried to retreat. 'You should never have been born in the first place,' he spat. His eyes were the same amber colour as Granma Sylvie's, but all the warmth had been sucked out of them. 'Sylvie dishonoured the family by marrying a commoner. You and the rest of her offspring have brought shame upon the Wrench name. And *she* was the person who forced me into hiding. Forty years I've lived in that grubby little hole. Forty years listening, waiting, *hunting* for her. She deserves to pay for this – for what she made me!'

'Cartimore, please.' Selena Grimes's voice sliced through his rant. 'There isn't time for this. You've already set the alarm clock. Your puppets will see to it that the parents die at midnight. You can finish your little reunion later; the girl isn't going anywhere. Right now, we need to establish whether the object is here or not.'

Cartimore quaked with fury. 'But I must eliminate her now, Selena, don't you see? She is like the rotten part of the apple. She needs to be cut out.' He fished around in his pocket and withdrew a metal corkscrew. The device gave an angry snake-like hiss – Ivy could have sworn she saw a forked tongue protruding from the end.

Selena rolled her eyes. 'Fine, if you must. But be quick about it and don't make a mess.'

Cartimore beamed as he extended his hand towards Ivy. The corkscrew shimmered and flashed with white light. It was coming to life, twitching and shivering. 'Where is it, runt? Where did you put it?'

Ivy stared at the corkscrew. Fear overwhelmed her senses. She was going to die *right now*. Her mind drifted to Seb, her mum, her dad and Granma Sylvie. She pictured the faces of her friends at school and of the traders she'd met in Lundinor. She thought of Scratch.

'*Elsells*,' murmured a soft voice. '*Els ells*.'

Ivy blinked.

'*Els bells,*' the voice said again urgently. 'Hell's bells, Ivy! *Hell's bells!*'

Ivy snapped back to reality. She'd inched away from the corkscrew and now had her back against the corner of the desk. Her hand was resting on the slime-covered base of the desk bell. And it felt oddly warm; splinters of heat were shooting up her arm.

'*Hell's bells!*' the voice shouted again – Ivy realized it was just in her head. 'Ivy Sparrow! Can you hear me?'

It was the desk bell. Ivy glanced at it. It was her whispering that was doing this. She could feel it.

'Hell's bells, Ivy. Hell's bells.'

Ivy had seen that phrase before; she looked for the glass case behind Ethel's desk. It was covered in slime, but the bells within it were . . . *free.*

'Unless you tell me, runt, this is going to sting a little.' Cartimore cackled, lunging towards Ivy's throat with the corkscrew. It had now completed its transformation into a metal snake the size of a longsword. Its scales were silvery black like the night sky, its eyes two soulless slashes of pitch. As the snake opened its mouth, its fangs glittered, and at the back of its throat Ivy saw the darkness light up with flame.

She dived to her left and, in one swift movement, smashed the ebony-framed glass case with her knuckles. Ivy ignored the pain and grabbed the rope at the bottom of each bell, shaking them violently.

A shrill voice coughed. '*Cerberus!*' the bell on the left called.

'*Erebus!*' the right bell added.

Then together: '*WAAAALLLLKIES!*'

Ivy slumped back against the wall as the ground shook. A sound like an approaching train filled the room. Cartimore scrambled away, trying to control the snake, which was squirming in his hands, desperate to escape. His face paled, and as Ivy watched in horror, the blood vessels in his eyes burst.

'Selena! What's happening . . . ? *Argh!*' he screamed as the serpent finally broke free and slithered off across the floor and under the front door. 'You idiot girl!' he shouted, and dived towards Ivy, lashing out with his gloved hand. She gritted her teeth as his knuckles met her cheek.

The grim-wolf howled. Selena swept up her skirt into one hand, revealing air between her and the floor. She turned towards the wall, aiming for a quick exit. 'Cartimore, there isn't time! Go! Get out of here! The beasts will be—'

But before she could finish her warning, the dogs arrived. Now Ivy realized why the bells were called hell's bells: they had summoned the *hounds of hell*. Two dogs, each the size of a horse, smashed through the back wall. They steamed with heat, and around their feet the wooden floor was smoking. The air filled with the noxious smells of sulphur and charcoal. Shards of wood pierced the gunge that had imprisoned the bells, which immediately started screaming, 'ETHEL!' 'GUARDS!' 'HELP!'

Ivy looked down. The hellhounds had missed her by inches, but Cartimore was lying in a heap, covered in slime. Goblin took one look at the hounds, gave a whine, and disappeared into the folds of Selena's black skirt.

'S-Selena!' Cartimore shouted, his voice wobbling. 'H-help me!'

Selena glanced at the hounds and glided half-way through the wall. Only her head and shoulders remained in the room.

Cartimore didn't seem surprised by her betrayal. He simply stuck his hand inside his coat and pulled out what looked like a glossy celebrity magazine.

'Don't look at it, Ivy,' a voice urged. 'Uncommon magazines stun people. He's trying to paralyse the hounds.'

Ivy turned. The desk bell was talking to her again, though this time not in her head – the slime that had encased the bells was dissolving now that the hell-hounds had arrived.

'It won't work,' the bell insisted. 'The hounds are impervious to uncommon objects. Only the bells can order them back to hell.'

The hellhounds assessed the room with their fire-pit eyes. At the sight of Cartimore their growling intensified. They sniffed the air and opened their mouths, forked black tongues rolling out over their colossal teeth. Ivy was fairly certain that they wanted to eat Cartimore and then destroy the entire place before running out onto the streets of Lundinor. *Just a nice little walkies; sure.* She looked over her shoulder. The two hell's bells were still swinging slightly on their hooks.

The desk bell spoke. 'Ring them again.'

Ivy heard angry knocking. She looked over the top of the counter to see Selena disappearing through the wall. *Damn.* Ivy couldn't believe she'd escaped. She turned, and through the front door saw Officer Smokehart, Ethel and Valian.

She was so relieved, she almost forgot to ring the bells. Then the hellhounds barked. The glass in the front door and window shattered, sending the visitors tumbling backwards. Ivy came to her senses, grabbed the cord beneath each bell and shook them frantically.

'*Cerberus!*' the first bell yelled. '*Erebus!*' the second followed.

'*HOME TIME!*'

The hellhounds groaned and stamped their feet, sending a shower of flames around the room. Ivy started coughing. It was growing difficult to breathe.

Tendrils of black smoke crept up through the floor-boards and wrapped themselves around each hound. The floor opened up, the wooden boards splitting apart, revealing only darkness and flames beneath. The hounds barked loudly before leaping into the pit.

The shop was left sizzling and stinking of sulphur. The bells shook off slime to douse the small fires, and through the thick smoke Ivy saw the unmistakable out-line of her brother.

In the centre of the room, Cartimore groaned as a tall figure in black loomed over him.

'Cartimore Edward Wrench,' Officer Smokehart announced, 'I arrest you in the name of the four quartermasters of Lundinor. You have the right to remain silent, but anything you do say can be used against you in an uncommon court of trade.' He bent down and used a paperclip to fasten Cartimore's hands together.

Seb reached to help Ivy up. 'Seb – the alarm clock,' she whispered. 'We have to check it.'

She got it out of her pocket. The glass was still dirty and the bells rusted, but the hands were no longer black. They had turned white now, and had moved past mid-night. Ivy saw her reflection in the glass. Her face was black with soot and splattered with slime, and her hair plastered to her forehead. But she wasn't dying, and the rotting faces of her parents were no longer visible. The countdown to their death had stopped. The Dirge had failed.

Ivy threw her arms around Seb. *It's over*, she thought. *It's really over.*

She spied Officer Smokehart looking right at her. 'Charges relating to you and the wraithmoth attack are dropped,' he said. His voice sounded detached, although there was the hint of a smile on his lips. She noticed the other underguards, gaping at the man Smokehart had just called Cartimore Wrench.

For the first time ever, Ivy thought, Smokehart actually looked happy. He had solved part of the Twelfth Night mystery, after all.

Chapter Thirty-six

Ivy stood gazing up at a pointy-roofed, two-storey building with leaded windows and fig-purple walls. Around her, uncommoners were emerging from shops and taverns into the morning hush. There was a buzz of conversation – as there had been every morning since the arrest of Cartimore Wrench. Ivy spotted a skinny boy on a flying rug zipping around the chimney tops, throwing newspapers down onto the doorsteps below. She wondered if yesterday's trial would be on the front pages . . .

She stretched contentedly. Last night, which she had spent in her own bed at home, had been untroubled by dreams of the uncommon alarm clock. Her body was healing, even though she'd probably still have the bruises when she went back to school next week. She wondered if her friends would ask her what she'd done for New Year's Eve.

She'd have to lie, if they did. The truth was a secret only she, Seb and Granma Sylvie could share.

Ivy climbed the steps to the front door of Mr Punch's Curiosity Shop. The leaded windows sparkled; behind them, seashells, mirrors, teacups and other trinkets danced around at the end of silver chains. Above the door was a large wooden sign showing a black top hat – like the one Mr Punch had worn to deliver his emergency announcement. She paused as she wondered again why he had sent a featherlight to invite her here today. He was the most important man in Lundinor, after all, and she was a nobody.

The hanging objects jangled as Ivy pushed the front door open and stepped inside. Immediately she sensed that there was something different about this shop. Huge apricot-coloured ceiling lamps filled the room with warm light, and the air was perfumed with incense, which made her nose tingle. Bizarrely the floor was covered in sand, which crunched underfoot. The room was full of glass cabinets and metal trunks; the counters were crammed with the widest selection of *stuff* Ivy had ever seen in one place.

She carefully made her way forward, gaping at the objects on display. She could see why it was called a *curiosity* shop. She wondered what abilities each of the items possessed. Perhaps uncommon fountain pens were mightier than swords and uncommon pocket watches could turn back time. She doubted you wore uncommon ice-skates on your feet.

One object in particular caught Ivy's eye. Next to a white-lace parasol was a fur-trimmed tabard. She picked it up and saw that it was embroidered with gold flowers.

She frowned. She'd seen it before – on that bony man who had helped her escape from the underguard coach.

Next to the tabard lay a wooden sign. One edge was splintered, but she could tell that it wasn't uncommon. She read the words painted on the front:

INVISIBILITY CANDLES: 8 GRADE

Wait a sec . . .

Ivy was puzzled. The candle trader had been holding this sign, the morning she first arrived in Lundinor. Why on earth would it be here, in Mr Punch's curiosity shop?

Her mind buzzing, she jerked as a voice broke the silence.

'Hello there.'

Ivy turned round, the tabard flapping in her hand. She squinted into the shadows at the back of the shop. 'Hello?' she called uncertainly. 'Uh, my name's—'

'I know who you are.' It was a voice Ivy had never heard before: well-spoken but warm, like that of your favourite teacher.

She coughed and slowly slid the tabard back onto the shelf. 'Um, Mr Punch asked me to stop by—'

'Indeed he did,' the voice agreed, a little louder. Slowly a face appeared out of the darkness. Ivy inhaled with surprise. A middle-aged man with spectacles and a wiry white beard stepped forward. He was wearing a smart blue shirt with a black waistcoat and matching trousers. It was the kind of thing Ivy's dad might wear; definitely *not* the Hobsmatch of someone who traded in Lundinor. She looked at the man carefully. She didn't recognize him. Maybe he was Mr Punch's assistant.

'Happy New Year, Ivy Sparrow,' he said, smiling. 'I didn't get a chance to tell you yesterday, when I met you in court.'

Ivy frowned. She could swear she'd never seen this man before. 'Uh – are you sure we met yesterday? I don't—'

Just then, she saw his face change. His white beard shortened, his spectacles disappeared and his skin turned the colour of milky tea.

'Oh yes, I'm sure. I'm the one who thanked you, remember? For saving the citizens of Lundinor? For unmasking one of the members of the Dirge? It was a clever and brave thing that you and your brother did – and under so much pressure from that uncommon alarm clock.'

Ivy narrowed her eyes. It was Mr Punch who had said all those things to her yesterday . . .

She thought back to Cartimore's trial. It had been their evidence – hers and Seb's, along with the incriminating map and door that Smokehart had found in the featherlight mailhouse – that had helped convict Cartimore of organizing the wraithmoth attack and paying the selkies to sabotage the air filters. However, Cartimore had refused to answer any of the underguard's questions about his motives, so everyone in Lundinor was none the wiser about the Great Uncommon Good and the true reason for Granma Sylvie's disappearance.

At the end of Ivy's statement Smokehart had asked her if there was anything she wished to add, but she had shaken her head. Nobody would have believed her about Selena Grimes, least of all Smokehart. Ethel had agreed that she and Seb should keep the information secret until they could all find proper evidence. Still, Ivy couldn't help feeling that somewhere out there, Selena and the three remaining members of the Dirge were plotting to find the other four Great Uncommon Good.

The bearded man tilted his head. 'Do you wish things had turned out differently?'

Ivy frowned. She didn't want to consider the *what ifs*; it would only make her frustrated and bitter – like Cartimore had become after all those years. The truth was, Selena Grimes couldn't hide any more. Wherever and whenever she and the Dirge made their next move,

Ivy, Seb, Valian and the others would be there, waiting for them. For all the death threats and danger, it seemed like everything had happened for a reason. Granma Sylvie now knew the truth about her past – which meant that Ivy and Seb had discovered their heritage as uncommoners, as part of Lundinor. Ivy wouldn't change that for the world.

'No,' she answered finally. 'Cartimore's gone now, that's what counts.' *Gone to a ghoul hole for life*, she reminded herself.

The man smiled. 'Good. Now I have a gift for you.' He turned round and retrieved something from the counter behind him, then beckoned her over.

Ivy stepped forward nervously. She wasn't sure why he would be giving her anything – no one gave anything for free in Lundinor.

He handed her a pair of small white gloves.

'These are for *me*?' On an impulse, she put them on. They were made of soft cotton with tucks over the knuckles, like smart dress gloves. A brown paper tag had been tied to one of the fingers. When Ivy held it up she discovered neat handwriting on the back:

Awarded to Miss Ivy Sparrow in gratitude for her highly commendable efforts in the fight against the Dirge.

Ivy smiled. She could feel the uncommon nature of the gloves – a gentle warmth – soaking through her fingertips and igniting her whispering. 'But . . . these are uncommon,' she said. 'Does this mean that I can *take the glove*?'

The man chuckled and looked at the gloves approvingly. 'It means you have just taken it.'

Ivy stared down at her hands. The gloves were whispering in a way no other object had before. Her skin tingled and even her feet grew warm, as if she was standing in a hot bath. In her ears she could hear singing – not just one voice, but a whole choir, haunting and beautiful. She felt like she was being welcomed home.

Her eyes gleamed. 'Thank you.' She watched the man curiously as his face changed again. His beard disappeared and a sprinkling of freckles spread across his forehead. 'Um – are you . . . Mr Punch?' she asked.

'Most know me by that name, yes.' His blue-green eyes twinkled. Ivy now knew why they seemed so familiar.

'I've met you before . . . You gave me that invisibility candle in the arrivals chamber . . . and helped us escape from the underguard coach. That was you both times, wasn't it?' There had indeed been something a bit too convenient about their lucky escape. 'Why do you look different every time I see you?'

Mr Punch leaned back against the counter. 'I'm a hob, Ivy,' he said. 'One of the rarest races of the dead.

Hobs are made from more than one soul, and our appearance can change.' His face blurred and shifted – first he was Mr Punch, then the shop assistant, the bony man and the old candle trader. 'Not everyone is able to see us changing, however. Only whisperers.'

Ivy blushed, realizing that Mr Punch must know her secret. 'You've been helping me all along,' she said. 'Why?'

His turquoise eyes looked at her kindly. 'I've been watching over you and your family for a long time, Ivy Sparrow. Your granma came to me on Twelfth Night 1969 asking for help; asking for something to keep her and the Great Uncommon Good safe. I had been fighting the Dirge for years; I was aware that if they got hold of the object, the consequences would be unthinkable. It was I who gave your granma the uncommon bracelet. I understood that if she ever reappeared, it meant that the bracelet had come off.'

Ivy realized then why people called Mr Punch the Guardian of Lundinor. She wondered in how many other ways he had protected people from the Dirge. 'Do you know where my granma hid the Great Uncommon Good? Did she tell you?'

Mr Punch's face changed once more. His nose got bigger, his skin blanched and his hair grew ginger and curly. A black top hat appeared on his head. 'Your granma made sure that only she knew where the object was hidden. That way, it was only her memory that had to be erased.'

Ivy couldn't imagine how Granma Sylvie had made such a decision. She wondered where she'd have hidden something as dangerous as one of the Great Uncommon Good. Her granma must have felt so much pressure to get it right. She might even have been heading for the hiding place when she had her car accident.

Ivy shivered. *The accident in the snow.* Granma Sylvie had never meant for that to happen; it wasn't part of the plan. It must have been caused by her memory loss – maybe it all started while she was driving, throwing her off course . . .

Which meant she wouldn't have had time to hide the Great Uncommon Good.

Which meant she must have kept it with her all this time, not knowing what it was . . .

Ivy remembered Cartimore telling Selena that the object was an old sack, easy to miss.

Oh . . . my . . .

Ivy went very still.

Mr Punch's white beard returned. He nodded towards the door. 'It is time to leave now, I think.'

Ivy wandered over to the door in a trance. *It had been there the whole time . . . The whole time!*

'I'll see you again next trading season,' Mr Punch

said as he held the door open for her. 'You'll enjoy Lundinor in the spring. It's very . . . different.'

Ivy skidded to a halt in front of the Great Gates. Valian and Seb were waiting for her beneath the stone feet of Sir Clement.

'Well?' Seb asked. 'What did Mr Punch want?'

Ivy shook her head, too out of breath to speak. Still panting, she held up her newly gloved hands.

'You took the glove?' Seb realized. 'Cool. Do you think they'll let me do that? Next time, maybe.'

Ivy was glad that he wanted to visit Lundinor again, like she did.

Valian nudged her shoulder. 'Well done, kid. Welcome to the family. And look – they've made it official.' He slid a copy of the *Barrow Post* in front of her. 'This was printed this morning.'

Ivy scanned the headlines:

NEW YEAR'S EVE CLOSES WITH A BANG!
SON OF OCTAVIUS WRENCH DISCOVERED POSING AS MAILMASTER FOR OVER FORTY YEARS

She followed Valian's finger down to the small paragraph at the bottom of the page.

Lundinor welcomes to the Trade the great-grandchildren of Octavius Wrench, fourteen-year-old Sebastian and eleven-year-old Ivy Sparrow, who have lived their whole lives as commoners. Their bloodline will be of some concern to many traders in Lundinor and around the world, especially in light of the dramatic revelations of New Year's Eve. Mr Punch himself, however, has vouched for their innocence; it seems they knew nothing of the Trade. It has been revealed that their grandmother, Sylvie Sparrow (formerly Wrench), has been living the past four decades as a victim of an uncommon memory-loss bracelet. The International Uncommon Council has decreed that all former charges against her be dropped, following her cooperation and assistance in the arrest of her brother, Cartimore. Ms Sparrow arrives in Lundinor with a considerable uncommon inheritance, as the sole owner of the Wrench estate. Underguards of the First Cohort have confirmed that her two grandchildren were in fact arrested for engineering a wraithmoth attack on 31 December, but have since been cleared. Officer Smokehart, who made the arrest, was unavailable for comment. After solving part of the Twelfth Night mystery, he will no doubt be in line for promotion in time for the reopening of Lundinor in the spring.

Ivy felt Seb's hand on her shoulder. 'Uh, Ivy, when you've finished reading that, do you wanna tell me why you made me get this dirty old thing from Granma Sylvie's back garden? I didn't really understand your featherlight.'

Ivy looked up from the newspaper. 'Did you bring it?'

Seb eyed her strangely and passed across the tattered old hessian sack that Granma Sylvie grew potatoes in. Ivy removed her gloves and held out her hands. As soon as her fingers brushed the rough material, fire shot through them, into her hand and then along her forearm. She heard a voice mumbling incoherently. Ivy's stomach turned over, and she dropped the sack immediately.

'Ivy?' Seb asked. 'What's wrong?'

She blinked back tears of pain as her body returned to normal. She straightened up again. 'I remember tripping over this before,' she croaked. 'Only I didn't touch it. Actually I've *never* touched it.'

Seb nodded. 'Yeah, so what . . . ?' His voice died in his throat.

Valian stared down at the bag in shock. 'No. Way.'

Ivy put her gloves back on, reached down and picked up the bag. 'It's the most powerful uncommon bag in existence,' she said simply. 'One of the Great Uncommon Good. Who knows where it could transport you?'

Valian gawped at it, while Seb peered around, checking that there was no one close by.

Ivy looked at Valian. She thought of his tiny room and wondered what his life was like in the common world. His sole concern was finding Rosie – Ivy knew that. She imagined what it would be like to lose Seb.

'I'm giving it to you,' she told Valian decisively. 'I don't want it.' She had no desire to use one of the Great Uncommon Good. Why did she need that much power? And anyway, the bag might be able to help Valian find his sister.

Very slowly he took the bag and said, 'You know, my deal with Ethel is over. I don't have to be your bodyguard any more.'

Ivy smiled sadly and nodded. She would miss him. She'd fought alongside him; he'd put everything on the line to help save her and Seb and their parents. They were now friends for life.

'I've been looking for Rosie on my own for ever,' Valian added. 'I thought that working with other people would slow me down, but over the last few days I've realized that I could use a whisperer and an uncommon drummer.'

Ivy smiled. 'We could use a scout too.'

'I can't promise it won't be dangerous,' Valian warned.

Seb shrugged. 'Danger isn't my issue. I'm more

concerned about this . . .' He fished around in the pocket of his hoodie and brought out a USB stick. 'No decent drummer would be seen dead with someone who doesn't listen to The Ripz. This has their first two albums on it.' He handed the memory stick over to Valian. 'It's my only condition.'

'If you insist.' Valian smiled. 'Actually that reminds me: Ethel told me to give you this, Ivy.' He pulled a familiar tarnished silver bell out of his pocket and handed it over.

'Scratch!' Ivy cried, taking him gratefully.

Scratch whirred. 'Ivy! Asked Scratch Ethel if staying with you and didn't Ethel no say.'

Ivy saw that there was a note attached and turned him over to read it:

Just remember: he's on loan. If you want to pay for him, he's four and a half grade. Non-negotiable.

She laughed. Valian cocked his head, reading the note over her shoulder. 'Typical. She never bargains.'

The street bell swayed. '*The departure caverns are located on the other side of the main arrivals chamber,*' it said in a stiff voice. '*Third tunnel on the left.*'

Ivy let go of the clanger. 'This way home,' she told Seb.

Together they plodded across the chamber. The last time Ivy had been there it had been throbbing with noise and activity, but now it was strangely empty. Abandoned trunks and suitcases lined the walls and the stalactites loomed overhead, casting spiky fingers of shadow across the floor.

In the distance Ivy spied a figure with a large bag emerging from one of the tunnels.

Seb nudged her shoulder. 'Is that who I think it is?'

She squinted into the distance. The traveller had a head of long pale hair that appeared to glow in the yellow light. '*Granma Sylvie . . . ?*'

Ivy dashed towards her, but Seb, as always, got there first.

'Granma!' he called, his arms wide as he reached her side. Ivy laughed as Granma Sylvie's face turned crimson.

'Nice to see you too,' she said, her voice muffled by Seb's embrace. She pushed him away and straightened up. 'You look older,' she told him. 'And stronger. I heard you managed to keep up your drum practice while you were away . . .'

Seb shrugged, smiling. 'Needs must, Granma.'

'What are you doing here?' Ivy asked, her arms round Granma Sylvie. 'Mum said you wouldn't be discharged from hospital till tomorrow.'

Her granma smiled mischievously. 'The doctors

let me out early. Your parents have invited me up to London for a few days to rest. I think they want to look after me, poor things. Of course, I only accepted so that I could spend some time with you two. You're meant to be at the shops right now, according to them.'

Ivy's mouth opened and closed as she stepped back. They'd had to tell a little white lie in order to return to Lundinor.

'Don't worry – I covered for you,' Granma Sylvie reassured them. 'But dinner will be on the table in thirty minutes, so we'd better get out of here.'

Ivy wondered how Granma Sylvie felt about being back in Lundinor after all this time. The events of the past few days . . . it wasn't the kind of thing you could get over quickly. It was going to take a long time. There were still lots of questions, and not all of them would be answered.

'How are you?' Ivy asked. 'I mean, *really*.'

Granma Sylvie ran a hand through Ivy's thick curls. 'All the better for seeing you,' she admitted. 'I just can't believe who was behind all this.'

Ivy shivered. *Cartimore* . . . She wondered what her granma thought about him being imprisoned in a ghoul hole.

'I know he's my brother,' Granma Sylvie said, 'but it doesn't feel like it. I have no memories of us growing up together and we certainly don't share the same values now.'

'What's that thing people say about the black sheep of the family?' Seb asked. 'There's always one?'

'In the case of my family, it appears there was *more* than one. Still, Cartimore's gone now; he can't hurt any of us again.' Granma Sylvie smiled. 'And anyway, I've gained more than I've lost. Ethel never gave up on me all these years; our friendship is a gift I'm going to treasure.'

Ivy held Granma Sylvie's hand as they set off. 'Does any of it seem familiar yet?' she asked. She'd been dying to discuss it all – to tell her granma about all the amazing things she'd seen, and see if Granma Sylvie remembered any of them.

Granma Sylvie's eyes grew misty as she looked at the Great Gates in the distance. 'It's strange, but all I really remember is the smell of this place: like leather and boot polish and hot chestnuts. It smells like . . . home.' Her voice cracked as she finished. 'I've spoken to Mr Punch. He gave me these . . .'

She reached into her coat pocket and pulled out a long glove. It was made of old yellowed silk, with an elasticated frilled cuff. 'When I put them on, it's like wearing a uniform. I can feel that they're special, only I can't remember the job I'm meant to do with them.' She sighed. 'It might be a long time before my memory recovers, if it ever does.'

'Well then,' Seb said cheerily, patting her on the shoulder, 'you'll just have to learn about everything with us.'

Ivy squeezed Granma Sylvie's hand. 'That's right. We'll do it together.'

As they made their way back to the departures chamber, Ivy's thoughts turned to home, to London. 'Do you think Mum and Dad are going to be all right?' she asked. 'Do you think they'll get over it?'

'Get over the flu, you mean?' Seb reminded her. After the underguards had wiped their parents' memories with uncommon whistles, false memories had been implanted of contracting a virus and being bedridden for the whole of New Year. Ivy would have to be careful not to slip up and reveal the truth.

'I think they'll be OK,' Granma Sylvie said. 'Let's just keep an eye on them.'

'*OK?*' Seb retorted. 'Dad looks better than ever after those buttons Violet used on him! Have you *seen* his hair? And Mum looks about ten years younger as well – she thinks it's that face cream I got her for Christmas.'

Ivy couldn't help laughing.

'So did you really meet Mr Punch, then?' Seb asked her.

'Oh yes. I'll explain it all when we're home.'

'Ivy,' he said, looking at her new gloves. 'We are gonna come back here, right? Valian said it opens again in the spring.'

Ivy shrugged. 'I think we have to. Someone's got to stop Selena.'

Seb nodded gravely. 'Yeah.' His mouth twitched into a smile. 'But also, I was thinking earlier about all the cool stuff we might've missed this time round. Like, I know my uncommon drumsticks are awesome, but there must be something better than that. And then it came to me . . .'

'What did?' Granma Sylvie asked.

'Cars, you guys! I can't believe I've only just thought of it now! Uncommoners must drive amazing cars. I wonder if they trade spare parts – uncommon tyres and stuff.'

Ivy shook her head. 'Is that what you've been thinking about? Driving an uncommon car?'

'What's wrong with that? I'll be able to take lessons in a couple of years. Anyway, what've *you* been thinking about?'

Ivy laughed. She and Seb had faced death; they'd fought monsters and talking wolves, discovered a whole new branch of their family and used everyday objects to bend the laws of science. 'I've been thinking how everything feels different now,' she admitted. 'We're not muckers any more; we're uncommoners. Haven't you thought about how our lives will change?'

'I dunno about that,' Seb replied. 'But one thing's for sure: I'm never going to look at a toilet brush in the same way again.'

Acknowledgements

My gratitude goes to Sarah Davies and the teams at the Greenhouse Literary Agency and Rights People, for all the hard work they've done and continue to do on my behalf.

I'd like to send lots of love to everyone I worked with closely at Foyles Bookshop on Charing Cross Road: Neil, Cleaver, Kate, BXL, Mac, Rupert and Sean – you made that place feel like home and were a constant source of inspiration. Sam and Jo – this book wouldn't have happened had I not had the incredible fortune to work with both of you for so long. Thanks for teaching me how to be a good children's bookseller; I know it's helped me to become a better children's writer. Thanks also to all the publishing sales representatives who were full of encouragement: Andy Penguin, Foy, the gorgeous Heidi, lovely Lucy Cornwell, Tobes, Glen, Birchy and my bestie, Peter Fry. I miss you all.

A very special thank you to Ginny Garramone who valiantly read several early drafts, and to Gemma Cooper and Robin Stevens for showing real kindness and making me feel like part of the family. Jim Dean, thanks for the twitter advice – sorry I'm such a social-media failure. Dawn Kurtagich, I apologize now for shaking my fists at the sky during our skype calls; you've been a ray of sunshine after some pretty bad storms.

Maintaining my sanity throughout the process is due, in part, to the brilliant and beautiful Sarah Bryars, who has coached me out of many a panic, and the truly lovely George Hanratty – a conversation with you can work wonders. Thank you both for being there.

Sarwat 'the guru' Chadda, you are a complete legend. I wouldn't have written a decent draft without your guidance, or found Greenhouse. I owe you one . . . thousand.

Tamara Macfarlane, thank you for taking me under your wing and inviting me into your wonderland at Tales On Moon Lane. Kath, Leah, Julia and especially Tereze, you've been so patient and I am utterly grateful.

Thank you to everyone in the Blue Bar book group who has supported me, in particular Frann Preston-Gannon, Lesley Preston and Robert Croma for reading an early draft, and Roy Butlin, who pretended to hate it. It's funny how only a few words from you gave me the confidence to write a lot more.

To my agent Polly Nolan, it has been an utter privilege getting to know you and working with you. You are the most graceful tough cookie I've ever met and I still can't believe someone as talented as you has decided to be my champion. If you were an uncommon object you'd be a grade ten, no question.

To my long serving friends: Natalia, you not only gave me the inspiration for Ivy's incredible hair, but also the most loving support throughout the whole process. Nichol, this all started with that copy of *Eragon* – who knows what I'd have ended up doing without it. Thank you for pointing me in the right direction, and for being there every step of the way.

Tara. What can I say? It's so comforting to have a best friend who's a writer too. Your belief in me has been unflinching and you were the first person who answered that phone call. Thanks for being there during the meltdowns and always managing to make me feel better.

Finally, I wouldn't have written a story about a girl who has to save her family, if I didn't have an incredible one of my own: Mum and Beth – I hope you know that. You're my lucky stars.

About the Author

Londoner Jennifer Bell began working in children's books as a specialist bookseller at Foyles – one of the world's most famous bookshops – in Charing Cross Road. There she looked after the shop's five not-so-deadly piranha fish as well as recommending children's books to celebrities, royalty and even astronauts. After having the privilege of listening to children talk about their favourite books for many years, she started writing one of her own. Jennifer came up for the idea of *The Crooked Sixpence* while packing for a holiday and wishing she could just disappear inside her suitcase and be there already. The world of Lundinor is inspired by sayings from traditional English nursery rhymes as well as the stories Jennifer grew up with about the cockney markets her grandparents used to visit.

About the Illustrator

Illustrator Karl James Mountford was born in Germany and brought up around the UK. He now lives in Wales where his sketchbooks rarely get a day off. Karl works in both traditional and digital mediums to create his illustrative work. He graduated with a masters degree in illustration and visual communication from Swansea College of Art.

Ivy Sparrow's thrilling adventures
in Lundinor continue in

CONNECT WITH JENNIFER BELL:

@jenrosebell

#TheCrookedSixpence

Learn more about the magical world of

and find out about upcoming events:

WWW.JENNIFER-BELL-AUTHOR.COM